With his arms wrapped around my waist, Derrick held me close to his torso as he sang "Let's Chill," by a hot R&B group named GUY.

I started to cry because I loved it when my baby sang to me. I really loved him and wanted to spend the rest of my life with him. I more than loved him... I worshipped him. No one could make me feel the way that he made me feel. It was the SINFUL sex I tell you.

Following my serenade, we kissed ever so slowly as he slid his hands down the small of my back and over the rest of my voluptuous body. Derrick instantly became erect and slowly started to take off my prom dress.

Yes, I had a prom dress on that night! It magnified the curves of my voluptuous frame while Derrick wore a tux that made you say damn! We just never made it to the prom. When my dress hit the floor, I saw his jaw drop. I was wearing a white corset with matching white thigh high stockings and garter belts. The kind you wear under a wedding dress.

"Damn baby! You look sexy as hell. You're the sexiest Bitch I know," he said with a Kool-Aid smile on his face.

"Thanks baby," I would respond giggling.

With my 36DD breast, my 27" waist and my 38" hips, I knew that I looked the bomb. One look into Derrick's eyes left no doubt as to what he wanted to do to me, as he stared at my large stiff nipples that poked through my corset. Derrick in a flash got out of his tuxedo.

ZONIE FELDER

JANUARY JACKSON AND FRIENDS

THE PREMIERE

iUniverse, Inc.
Bloomington

January Jackson and Friends
The Premiere

Copyright © 2012 Zonie Felder

iUniverse books may be ordered through booksellers or by contacting:

iUniverse
1663 Liberty Drive
Bloomington, IN 47403
www.iuniverse.com
1-800-Authors (1-800-288-4677)

ISBN: 978-1-4620-8355-8 (sc)
ISBN: 978-1-4620-8354-1 (hc)
ISBN: 978-1-4620-8353-4 (e)

Library of Congress Control Number: 2011962921

Printed in the United States of America

iUniverse rev. date: 2/1/2012

THE DEDICATION: To my family and friends; whom I love very much, thanks for all of your support and words of encouragement. I am incredibly blessed to have all of you guys in my life. I, especially, want to thank God for my mother for instilling within me that I was beautiful, smart, and that I can be whatever I set my mind to be. She is truly the wind beneath my wings. She has always made me feel loved and cherished.

Dear Reader,

This is my debut erotic novel and like January Jackson I'm so excited. January Jackson and her childhood friends Monica, Terry, Charlene and Jasmine discover how hard it is to keep their promise to maintain their friendships in light of recent happenings. These childhood friends discover that memories are not just the only thing that they share. Behold lust and passion clouding judgment and choices that forever changes their friendships with unspeakable betrayals. See just how ugly these beautiful women become when their secrets are revealed and hidden truths are un-surfaced.

January, an established restaurant owner, has come upon a recipe for disaster that has all of the following ingredients: feuding friends, breathless liaisons, and tainted relationships. Very, very erotic this book will take you on an emotional roller coaster ride and leave you longing for more.

Reaching a new level of success, January invites her best friends to celebrate with her when a surprise the likes of which no one has ever expected turns her celebration into something else, entirely. January is forced to choose sides as lines are drawn in the sand.

Be sure to let me know what you think. Visit my face book page at Zonie Felder.

With love,

Zonie Felder

CHAPTER 1

The Promise (Introduction)

Wow! I can't believe how time flies. One minute, it's the year 1992... It's summertime in "Chill Town," Jersey City, N.J. and we've just graduated from Saint Mary's High School. "End of the Road" by the R&B group Boys II Men is playing on heavy rotation on all of the radio stations. Michael Jackson psyched us out by putting actor/comedian Eddie Murphy, as a pharaoh, and a world's famous super model from Africa named Iman, as his queen, in his "Remember the Time" video from his Dangerous album. We're mesmerized by the many moves of Michael Jordan, a sexy basketball player from the Chicago Bulls who leads his team to a second NBA Championship defeating the Portland Trailblazers. Full of spit and vinegar Charlene, Terry, Jasmine, Monica, and I felt the world was our oyster. No one could stop us for we were a force to be reckoned with.

Head over heels in love with Derrick, Charlene got pregnant. She didn't let her unexpected pregnancy change her plans to accept a scholarship to attend Jersey City State College. She knew that her destiny was best placed in her hands and not in Derricks. An arrogant Derrick skipped college and went straight to California to play professional basketball for the Los Angeles Clippers. Astute, Terry always wanted to be a lawyer. She chose to attend NYU on scholarship where she met her attentive fiancé Dexter. Having mad skills, Jasmine continued to do hair in her grandmother's house while she attended the Natural Motion institute for cosmetology. Pussy driven Eddie, who had been dating Jasmine on and off again since they were in grammar school, moved in with Jasmine and her grandmother to supposedly save money for their dream wedding. While attending Hudson County Community College to obtain an associate degree in business, Eddie held a part-time job at his

1

uncle's garage and at an after hour joint on Myrtle Avenue as a bouncer. An adventurous Monica after reading an article about the money to be made in Atlanta, Georgia moved to the ATL to pursue a career in real estate. An admirer **of** food, I doubled majored in business and culinary arts at Johnson and Wales University which is world famous for the culinary arts, in Rhode Island. Determined to excel nothing was going to stop us from achieving our goals.

Then boom! It's the year 2009… Far beyond our wildest dreams, we get our first African-American president; Barack Obama inaugurated on January 20, 2009. "Blame It" by actor/comedian/R&B singer Jamie Foxx featuring T-Pain becomes an overnight hit. With its' catchy hook…"Blame it on the goose (goose) Got you feeling loose (loose) Blame it on the Patron (patron) Got you in a zone (zone)," the hit song had everyone in America blaming it on the alcohol. Including Eddie who was often seen creeping with women other than Jasmine. On June 25, 2009 the world lost two American Icons. Actress Farrah Fawcett, the "Charlie's Angels" star dies at the age of sixty-two and the king of pop, Michael Jackson dies at fifty-one.

After surviving eight years under a Bush regime that left our country in the middle of an economic recession, America is desperate for change. No longer is America willing to accept a slap on the wrist to greedy business men and politicians, who trampled upon the hopes and dreams of many Americans with their unethical business practices. To overcome, America must learn from the mistakes of the past and dare herself to rewrite her future. History has shown that it will get worse before it can get better and only the strong will survive.

We're now in our mid-thirties and we're feeling the weight of the world as we get ready to embark on the big 35. We get ready to fulfill our destiny. Seventeen years ago we declared it and now we have claimed it. We made a promise that we were all going to stay friends and be successful by the age of thirty-five. Some more so than others but we all did it.

After some turbulent years, Jasmine Wright and Eddie Montgomery are still holding it down with three adorable children. Up until two years ago they lived with Jasmine's grandmother the endearing Mrs. Mary Wright. Widowed, Mrs. Wright single handedly raised her granddaughter ever since her beloved daughter Jackie died of AIDS when Jasmine was only ten years old. Mrs. Wright had a heart attack and died in the house at the young age of seventy-five. Jasmine couldn't stand to stay in her grandmother's house after her sudden death so she sold the house and moved her family to Avenel, New Jersey. With the money from the sale of the house and her grandmother's insurance policy, Jasmine purchased her dream house.

I just adore Jasmine's house. A 3500sqt., 4 bedroom, 2 and a half bath,

2 car garage house that featured: a large living room and dining room, a contemporary kitchen, a family room with hardwood floors and a fireplace, a first floor laundry room, a master bedroom with bath, a basement recreation room, office and gym, a deck pool, and a large backyard. Jasmine's grandmother would've been proud of her selection.

To financially maintain this dream house, Jasmine opened her own beauty parlor while Eddie opened a successful detailing shop/garage. Eddie drives a black and gold tricked out (2007) GM Yukon Denali with a suede black and gold interior while Jasmine drives a cinnamon metallic (2008) Ford Edge with black leather interior. (Everyone knows that Jasmine actually moved her family from Jersey City to Avenel to put some distance between Eddie and his many admirers.)

Terry and Dexter Delgado are still happily married with no children. They got married straight after graduating from the NYU School of Law in Greenwich Village, N.Y. Married for nine years, in total Terry and Dexter have been together for seventeen years. They are both corporate attorneys. Recently Terry made partnership at her law firm while Dexter reluctantly took a pay cut instead of voluntarily resigning, due to the costly loss of the sexual harassment lawsuit placed against his law firm. They live in Brooklyn Heights a posh upper middle class neighborhood in Brooklyn, N.Y. They totally gutted out and renovated a prewar townhouse that they purchased in the year 2000 from a widow who refused to give her house to her only son after her husband's death. To further add insult to injury, she sold the house 20% lower than the market value. Now Terry, who originally wanted to purchase a condo in Manhattan, saw the blood in the water and like a true shark went in for the kill.

Their awesome 2500sqt.townhouse presently has an elevator, 3 massive size bedrooms with walk-in closets, 2 baths, hard wood floors, voice intercom, a full size laundry room, a fitness room, a library/study/office room, a large living and dining room, a separate media room with a fireplace, and a showroom quality kitchen that featured: granite counters, stainless steel appliances, and cherry wood cabinets with nickel pulls. Terry truly out did herself.

Dexter drives a black (2008) Cadillac Escalade EXT with a cream leather interior while Terry, like the true diva she is, has been provided with a driver courtesy of her firm.

Terry never knew why that old lady was so upset with her son, until a month ago when she got an unexpected visit from the ladies son Jason. He wanted to show his new lover Rupert the neighborhood that he grew up in and the infamous house that was stolen from him.

With his left hand on his hip and right hand waving in the air, Jason tried to plead his case. "My father promised this old house to me on his death bed, but my mother chose to disregard my father's dying wishes and sold it to you. That old biddy had no right to do that! She just couldn't stand my openly gay lifestyle. Can you believe that bitch! She didn't mind that I was gay… it was the fact that I was o-p-e-n-l-y gay. We were all getting along just fine until I came out a couple of years ago. My mother had a fit and made my father change his will. You see, my father was gay and deep down my mother knew that he was and didn't mind it at all. Well, at least as long as he kept it in the closet. Unlike my father I'm a proud gay man and I refuse to hide in shame!" Jason barked, ending his story with a finger snap and neck roll.

Perturbed at having to hear his story, Terry asked, "If what you're saying is true then why didn't you pursue litigation?"

"My father specified within his will that if I contested it that I would automatically forfeit my inheritance. I wasn't about to let that go down!"

As Terry rudely began closing her door in their faces, she sighed, "Oh well, what was your loss was definitely my gain." (How cold? How cruel? How…Terry that was.)

A zealous Monica, who is currently single and openly bi-sexual, had great success over the years as a real estate agent in the ATL before the real estate market took a mean hit from the economy. Monica managed to stay afloat by re-inventing herself as an interior decorator. About four months ago I believe March 12th to be precise, Monica came back to Jersey to celebrate Eddie's 35th birthday and just never went back. Shocked that her old room was given to a foster child, Monica with her own money renovated her parents' basement. See, Monica normally stays at Charlene's house when she comes to Jersey. Her parents felt, since her room wasn't being used, they should give a foster teenager a home. In exchange, they would have someone to look after them.

Being an interior decorator, Monica took the project of remodeling her parents' basement personal. Paying attention to detail, she elaborately designed and decorated the spacious one bedroom apartment to her liking. Taking no short cuts, Monica installed expensive Italian ceramic tile throughout the apartment. These floors literally made you think that you were in Italy, they were beautiful! This apartment featured: recessed lighting, 2 walk-in closets, an open island kitchen that had white cabinets featuring glass doors, and modern top of the line stainless steel appliances. The sheet rocked walls were painted cinnamon while the high ceilings and crown moldings were painted white. To add the final touch of luxury to her master piece, Monica then installed a fancy chandelier. Since the basement already had a full bathroom and laundry room, Monica was all set.

Monica drives a silver (2007) Mercedes-Benz CLK350 convertible with black leather interior. Monica believes to be successful one must drive a vehicle that exudes success.

I know what you're asking yourself. If Monica could afford to ride a 2007 Mercedes-Benz and renovate her parents' basement, then why won't she just get her own shit? Simple, she thinks that she's getting over. She only decided to invest in her parents' house because she's their only child. Standing to get everything if something were to happen to them, Monica would rather wait them out and live with someone for free be it a sugar daddy, a sugar mama or whoever than spend her precious money.

Charlene Jones is now a blissful Charlene Wiggins. A newlywed of three months, Charlene eloped to Las Vegas, Nevada with her newly retired Marine sergeant named Godfrey Wiggins aka "POPPA BEAR" that she had only met six months ago while vacationing in Miami, Florida. The charming Godfrey, who was ten years her senior, was attending an event for Breast Cancer when he met Charlene. He knew from the moment that he saw her that she was the one. Never before married Godfrey had finally found what he had been searching for. Godfrey moved to Jersey City to live with Charlene and her daughter Destiny who is presently seventeen years old.

Charlene lives at Liberty Heights in Jersey City, N.J. She owns a pristine 2400sqt.two- level townhouse that Destiny's father Derrick purchased for her fifteen years ago. This 3 bedroom townhouse has wide open living and entertaining space on the main social level as well as lots of natural light streaming in. Entertaining becomes effortless with the living room, dining room, family/media room, gourmet kitchen with breakfast bar, and guest powder room all on the main floor. On the second level the luxurious master bedroom has a walk-in closet and a bathroom while the other two bedrooms also large in size only have the walk-in closets. By having the laundry room on the second level, it becomes no fuss to do your laundry. Adding the final touch of splendor to the second level is the lavish full size spa-like marble bath with dual vanities, extra deep soaking tub and separate frameless glass shower. The complex offers security, two assigned parking spots per townhouse, a professional style fitness center, an outdoor pool with an on-duty lifeguard, tennis courts, basketball courts, and fenced in dog runs. (Watch out New York City because Jersey City got it going on!)

Also purchased by Derrick, Charlene drives a red (2007) Jaguar X-TYPE with a cream leather interior and a sun roof.

Derrick provided everything for Charlene and Destiny. Charlene never had to pay a bill unless she wanted too. He was even paying Charlene $10,000 a month for child support. Charlene felt that was more than fair considering Derrick paid for all of her monthly expenses. Always planning for the future, Derrick set up a multimillion dollar trust fund for Destiny. The age for access to this trust fund was originally twenty-one years old, until Charlene and Derrick decided to secretly change it to twenty-five years old. Times are rough and there are too many predators out there waiting to take advantage of a trusting young woman.

Shortly after Derrick got married in 2004, Charlene launched a Hip Hop clothing line called "2TRUE." Inspired by Destiny, Charlene decided to make Destiny the face of her clothing line and its' spokesperson. Charlene wanted to be able to support herself, should Derrick suddenly decide to cut her off financially. I don't blame her. You know how men tend to change when they hook up with other women that are not their children's mother. And to put the cherry on top of the sundae, Charlene opened her very own "2TRUE" store in the historic downtown district of Jersey City. I'm so proud of her.

Filthy rich, Derrick "The Truth" Johnson splits his time between the glitzy LA lifestyle of a celebrity and the more quiet personal existence he enjoys with his darling seventeen year old daughter Destiny in Saddle River, New Jersey.

Recently retired from professional basketball, he has proven to be a resourceful business man. With the success from his string of sports bars and sushi restaurants, Derrick is presently in negotiations with a major network to take on a sports casting position. Derrick, understanding how fortunate he is constantly gives back to his community. He funds a New Jersey based organization that pays for after school care and summer camp for many of the families suffering hard times as a result of the economy. Often hosting charity events and speaking to the youth about the importance of an education, Derrick "The Truth" Johnson is dedicated to the development of the youth in the urban community.

On the down side, Derrick is in the middle of a nasty divorce with his wife of five years Mei-Li. The exquisite Mei-Li occupies their super fabulous condo in Los Angeles, California while Derrick is currently residing at his Saddle River, New Jersey mansion.

Derrick's dreamy Saddle River estate is approximately 50 acres. This breathe taking 25,000sqt.mansion features: 5 luxurious master bedrooms-each equipped with a 50" flat screen television, a mini bar, a walk-in closet, a spa-like marble bath with dual vanities, an extra deep soaking tub and separate frameless glass shower, 10 guest bedrooms, 10 additional full baths, 5 Jacuzzis, a large living room, a large dining room, a large state of the art kitchen, a library, an office, a deluxe laundry room, a professional style fitness room, an elevator, 2 billiard rooms, a movie theater that seats 25 people, a recording studio, a nightclub with a private VIP room, an indoor pool, an outdoor pool, a pool house, a professional size basketball and tennis court, an enormous barbecue pit, an ice cream parlor style bar, a dog kennel, a pond, a helipad for his helicopter, 22 golf carts- used to travel across the estate, and a garage that holds his bountiful amount of vehicles.

Just to name a few of his vehicles, Derrick owns: a black (2007) Cadillac stretch limousine, a red (2007) Cadillac Escalade EXT with cream leather interior, a silver (2008) Cadillac Escalade ESV with black leather interior, a black on black (2009) Maybach, a yellow (2008) Lamborghini with a black and yellow bumble bee leather interior, and a silver (2009) AMG kitted 600 Mercedes-Benz with black leather interior.

Does this brother have it going on or what?

Charlene wants us to believe that the only reason she deals with Derrick is because of Destiny. Bullshit if I ever heard of any. You can't tell me that she's not giving up some of those goodies to ensure that he stays "generous." I know that I would, if I was her. I believe Charlene suddenly got married to Godfrey to get Derrick's attention. She heard that he was in the middle of getting a divorce and decided to stick it to him, to make him come after her. Frankly, I don't think that it worked but … who asked me anyway???

And who am I?

The original big momma!

My name is January Jackson, born and raised in "Chill Town," Jersey City, New Jersey. HOLLA! I also live at Liberty Heights a couple of houses away from Charlene. Our 2-level, 3 bedroom townhouses are identical except that I have a corner townhouse which is slightly bigger at 2600sqt. I have sliding doors from my kitchen that leads to my oversized balcony where I sit drinking raspberry herbal tea while enjoying the awesome view of the pier and the Hudson River. Every day, I climb up my winding stairs to go to my luxurious master retreat room and jump into my, oh so comfy, king size bed. Trying to unwind from a hard day at work, I soak in my Jacuzzi while I drink Moscato and eat chocolate covered strawberries. Waiting to be awakened from my beautiful dream, I pinch myself sometimes because I can't believe that I live in such a chi- chi house. Meaning, the house that I shared with my parents was half the size of the house that I live in now by myself. I fell in love with Charlene's place fifteen years ago. So five years ago, when Charlene told me that there was an amazing townhouse available for rent down the street from her… I jumped on it. Now to some of you this may seem like dick riding but I don't care. I love my home!

I have published two award winning cookbooks and own a successful Caribbean-Soul food Restaurant & Lounge named JANUARYS located in downtown Brooklyn, New York. Living life beyond my wildest dreams, I humbly accepted an offer to have my very own cooking show with a major cable network. Feeling validated by my peers, I relished in the opportunity to be able to strut my stuff in front of my family and friends on national television. Having completed taping the pilot episode of my show, a clip from the episode will be previewed at the premiere party, I'm gassed up.

To reward myself for a job well done, I traded in my sporty navy blue 2001 Cherokee Jeep for a luxurious black on black leather (2009) Lexus SUV. Hey, I was helping to boost the economy. I mean car dealerships were practically giving away vehicles. Why not capitalize on this and treat myself at the same time, I cleverly thought to myself.

Newly engaged to sexy ass Chad Delgado, Dexter's first cousin; whom I've been dating on and off again for the past nine years, I was pleasantly surprised three months ago when he gave me a 3 karat diamond ring while we were in Las Vegas to witness Charlene's and Godfrey's wedding. I was so thrown back by Chad's sudden proposal that I actually thought about declining it. Everything seemed to be going my way lately and I was waiting for the ceiling to suddenly drop.

Chad owns a 2100sqt.loft in Loft City a luxury building located in Brooklyn, New York. Chad has a typical bachelor pad for a mujeriego, a womanizer. Equipped with an open island kitchen, a bathroom with a deep whirl pool tub, hardwood floors, and plenty of natural light streaming in, Chad's place is contemporary. His loft has a king size bed, (2) mini bars, (2) 42" flat screen televisions, a super loud stereo system, a stripper pole, and a condom tree with an assortment of flavored condoms. Now, does the description of Chad's place sound like a man who's ready to get married? Hmm, exactly what I'm thinking.

His building with elegant hallways has a fitness center, a club room, a lobby with full time concierge, a garage, a courtyard, and a full size laundry room. Chad took over his father's bodega and owns a barbershop and two doobie shops. Chad, who accompanied me when I bought my new SUV, also got himself a new vehicle. He gave his tricked out 2004 Honda Accord to a family member and bought a black on black leather (2009) BMW M3 convertible. He paid for it in cash!!

"I don't believe in owing the man money. What the man doesn't know won't hurt him. I would rather feel the pinch now and be chilling later with no worry of a car note." Chad said, as I looked at him, while he handed over the briefcase full of money to the car dealer.

Ever since he took over his father's bodega four years ago, Chad has been paying for everything in cash. Citing to me some bull that he must have seen on Sunday's Meet the Press, Chad said. "I don't trust banks and credit card companies anymore. You saw how the government had to bail them out, with our tax money. Those lucky bastards don't even have to pay the government back yet they continue to justify turning people down for loans and charging people high interest rates."

I don't know who Chad thought he was fooling with his little skit but you got to give it to the guy though, for sounding like he really gave a damn about the economy. I've come to the conclusion that it is best not to ask questions when you are not ready to hear the answers. Believing and knowing the truth is two different things. Knowing the truth requires action while believing in his truth allows me to bust a couple of nuts.

See, Chad is like the military with the "Don't ask, Don't tell" policy which forced gays to keep their sexual orientation secret in order to serve in the military. Everyone knows that there are gay soldiers in the military but out loud, they don't want to admit it. I would like to believe that Chad is getting all of his money from his many business investments. Being the daughter of a cop I know otherwise but out loud, you will never hear me admit it. I just love my engagement ring!

The cable network is throwing a premiere party in the ballroom at The J Décor Hotel located in mid-town Manhattan to showcase their new fall line- up this season. Sunday July 5, 2009 is going to be a treasured highlight in my life. Exactly a month before my 35th birthday, this LEO is souped up. Since I was given only ten tickets which included Chad and I, I invited Terry, Dexter, Jasmine, Eddie, Charlene, Godfrey, Derrick, and Monica.

I decided to leave Monica's ticket at the front desk because no one had seen or heard from her in months. Checking for Monica, I kept going to her parents' house to no avail.

All her parents would say, "You know Monica, she's like the wind. You can never catch her."

Already this weekend was shaping up unusually but none of us was prepared for how it all turned out.

All I kept thinking to myself…, did I do something to upset Monica? Unless she's on vacation, I normally speak to her twice a week. Maybe it's the announcement of my engagement to Chad? The last we spoke, we were joking about how we were both going to end up being spinsters. Hmm, I wonder?

CHAPTER 2

CLIQUE: N. PARTY; A COTERIE; A SET.

SOME FORM BY INTERESTS, SOME FORM BY BLOOD, AND SOME FORM BY LIES THAT BIND YOU.

It feels like Charlene, Monica, Jasmine, Terry, and I were destined to be lifelong friends. We've known each other since our kindergarten days at Saint Mary's. Located downtown, Saint Mary's Grammar and High School stood side by side; therefore it was only natural that we all went to and graduated from Saint Mary's High School. Jasmine, Monica, and I originally met because we were neighbors. Living near our school in a little community that consisted of one and two family houses, located on a dead end street, we felt safe and isolated from the rest of the world.

Charlene and her father lived all the way in the heights with her Aunt Bird, who owned a two family house. Terry lived in Lincoln Projects, near route 440, in building seven on the 12th floor. Lincoln Projects consisted of seven enormous twelve story buildings that were notorious for being dangerous. From a large and well known family, Terry felt just as safe and isolated from the rest of the world as we felt about our little dead end street.

All of us, each different and unique, gravitated towards each other like bees to honey. We clicked like pieces to a puzzle, creating a beautiful mosaic. United, we became one big masterpiece... a clique. Naturally a clique within a clique developed. Charlene, Jasmine, and Monica at times hung tight, while Terry and I at times hung tight. See, girlfriends don't always want to admit it, but there is always a set within a set. There is always a friendly dose of jealousy and competition mixed within any group of girlfriends. Someone has to be the leader, someone has to be the follower, and someone has to be the neutral/indifferent friend.

Charlene, Jasmine, and Monica formed the jock & party set. Tantalizing and alluring to the eye, their pure beauty and charming personalities would hypnotize guys. Their ideology was to be like the Ancient Romans- to love thy body is to love thy self. They dated and hung around people that were involved in sports and all the current events. Being cheerleaders, they often organized the schools pep rallies and after school parties.

Terry and I formed the scholar and political set. Poised and extremely driven, we thrived on scholastic competition and little on acquiring the attention of the fellas at school. We were on the Model United Nations Debate Team, writers for the schools newspaper review, and in the nature club. We were more concerned with and involved with anything that had to do with obtaining a scholarship.

Jasmine would go back and forth between the two sets when she felt the pressure of trying to keep up with the in crowd was too much for her.

It was natural for Charlene and Monica because they lived and craved for the attention that they received from being popular. Charlene had to sink or swim when it came to living in the limelight because of her relationship with Derrick while Monica was willing to do whatever it took to get in Charlene's spot.

The five of us together formed the ultimate clique. We would all party together and help each other with our studies. We had the best of both worlds and never felt like outsiders. Both sets respected each other therefore we wouldn't let anyone at school disrespect anyone in our clique.

Terry's ideology was that other minorities had a greater chance at achieving success because they had a buddy system mentality. They would help pull up each other when the other one was falling. When one made it, they all made it. Terry felt that we as people (African Americans) don't stick together enough. We owed it to one another first as human beings, apart of the human race, to help each other. Greater, as African Americans to ensure that we continue to exist; we must lift one another up. Before we can point our finger at others, we must first check ourselves. So, as you can see there was an obvious split in views. As a clique, we tried to mesh the two ideologies together for the greater good to be well rounded… to be our sisters' keeper. When one fought, we all fought.

One chilling September day, in our junior year in high school, the loyalty of our clique was tested. Terry got jumped by some girls in Mahogany Projects. Mahogany Projects consisted of seven, twelve story buildings like Lincoln Projects. Also like Lincoln Projects, Mahogany Projects had a reputation of being rough. Terry never feared travelling to other projects.

A tutor for hire, Terry alone went to Mahogany Projects that faithful day to tutor one of her many clients. As soon as Terry got off the bus, she observed

11

two girls from her building bum rush an old man to get off of the bus. Terry abruptly made a left turn. They abruptly made a left turn. Terry stopped. They stopped. A puzzled Terry then decided to turn around. "What's up?"

Before they could answer, Terry realized that she was now surrounded by five girls. It became obviously clear what was up. It was time to knuckle up or get fucked up!

Shocked and horrified, the clique quickly ran to see how Terry was doing. Terry was tough but against five girls? Well let's say you could see how the story unfolded all across Terry's swollen face.

Allegedly, a hustler named Big Rob from Mahogany Projects accused Terry of stealing approximately $5,000 in cash and a substantial amount of cocaine worth about another. Without a doubt I knew that the words Terry, stealing, and drugs did not belong in the same sentence. Everything about that story didn't ring right with me.

Since Terry knew two of the girls lived in her building, she agonized about how her building was going to respond to this blatant act of betrayal.

I guess fearful of retaliation the two girls from Terry's building only held Terry down while the other girls kept stomping and punching on Terry as they yelled, "Die bitch!"

Before Terry went into unconsciousness, she heard one of the girls mention something about green contacts. When Terry came to in the hospital, she wouldn't tell the police or her parents what she knew about her assailants. At first Terry didn't even want to tell us anything. "Guys, I understand your concerns but I'm still trying to put everything together. It all happened so fast, everything is still a blur."

Understanding how traumatized Terry was, we decided to give her some space. We were just happy that she was alive and didn't suffer from any life threatening injuries. Terry cheated death. She would've been killed if it wasn't for this little old lady, on the 2nd floor, who threw a pot of hot water onto the assailants. "It wasn't a fair fight! Someone had to help even the odds." The little old lady told the police, as she couldn't describe or identify the assailants because she didn't have on her glasses.

Charlene, Jasmine, and I struggling to keep it together wanted to seek out the two girls that Terry knew and give them a beat down. Monica, feeling uneasy about the whole situation, wanted us to continue to put pressure on Terry to tell the police everything that she knew. Terry's lips were sealed. She wouldn't even cooperate with her brothers, who were on the streets trying to find out who jumped their beloved sister. Upset that the individuals who were involved hadn't been caught, the Parent Teacher Association at our school placed a small reward for any information that would lead to an arrest. Still, no one was talking. That was strange because someone knew what was the real? Jersey City is entirely too small for nobody not to know. It's like this, either by acquaintance or by relation, living in Jersey City everybody knows everybody.

Terry missed two weeks from school. Visiting her every day, we would give her all her missed assignments and get well cards.

My father took this incident personal. Random or deliberate this could've easily happened to me and he was furious. "Terry, you got to trust me. Just tell me something…anything that will help us catch the monsters that are responsible for this mess. It's like looking for a needle in a haystack without your assistance."

Terry hugged my father and affectionately said, "Aww, thanks pops… I love you too."

When Terry came back to school she didn't talk much. Withdrawn Terry would just look at you as if she could see right through you, right through to your soul. With her face still jacked up Terry diligently prepared for an up and coming Model United Nations debate in January.

As if she knew more than what she was letting on, Monica appeared to be extremely nervous and jumpy since Terry came back to school. Everyone in the clique picked up on that especially Terry.

One day Jasmine feeling a little silly made a joke. "Monica what's wrong girlfriend? Lately, you've been jumpier than a crack head on crack."

Everyone started laughing except Monica and Terry.

"Now, I know why I'm not laughing but Monica why aren't you laughing?" Terry sighed, as she stood directly in Monica's path.

"No reason other than the fact that I don't see what was so funny." Monica said, as she tried to get around Terry.

Suddenly, it became silent. Terry stared at Monica as if she wanted to choke the shit out of her. Monica caught the drift and looked away, as if she didn't see that Terry was seizing her up.

I pulled Terry to the side. "What's the real? What's up with you and Monica?"

Vexed, Terry responded, "You will see…, all will be revealed in due time."

Well, I don't know about the others but I felt that something heavy was about to take place between Monica and Terry. They were giving off bad vibes.

It was a cold, eerie Halloween and the school gave us a half a day due to all the mischief that was happening around the city.

"I'm having a meeting at my house at 5pm to deal with some unfinished business. My peep's is going to help us straighten this all out. Bitches are going to learn that they fucked with the wrong one. Wear a black hoodie, a black pair of pants, some black sneakers, and don't be late!" Terry ordered, like a drill sergeant, before she got on the Bergen avenue bus.

Everyone showed up on time, except Monica. When we arrived at Terry's house she introduced us to her twenty-five year old cousin named Nicole from Philly. She's the type of cousin you called on when you're having beef, major beef. Nicole with her hair going back in cornrows had a two inch scar diagonally going across her right cheek. Elaborating to us how she had gotten her scar when she did a bid in Los Angeles, she was cinnamon brown in complexion. About 6'1" and weighing 350 pounds, Nicole clearly intimidated everyone in the room except Terry. That was one big bitch!

"I know you'll are anxious to know what's up? Well, thanks to Nicole, I finally found out why I was jumped and who stole Big Rob's stash. I also know the identities of the other three bitches that jumped me and where they live."

"Word," we all shouted.

Holding a bottle of hair remover in each hand, Terry continued. "Now is the time for payback. If we do it now, on Halloween night, no one will think to blame us for what is about to go down. They will think it was a Halloween prank that went horribly wrong."

After an hour of Terry telling us the details of her plan for revenge, surprisingly Monica without her trademark green contacts showed up.

"Why Monica, where are your beautiful green contacts?" Terry asked smiling. "Could it be that you thought that I also invited Big Rob so that we could all take a trip down memory lane?"

With teary eyes, Monica exclaimed. "I'm sorry Terry! I didn't know that they were going to jump you. I wasn't thinking!"

Shocked, all our jaws dropped except Terry's and Nicole's. They were looking at Monica with pure disgust and outrage.

"It all started when I met this dude named Big Rob at a house party in Clinton Woods. He was flashing a lot of loot so I starting kicking it with him. He lived and hustled out of Mahogany Projects. He told me that he was the man around Mahogany Projects for coke and dope. He asked me for my name and before I realized what I had said... it was too late. I had told him that I was Terry from Lincoln Projects. I thought that would give me some street cred, so no one would bother me when I would go in and out of Mahogany Projects to see him. It worked for about a month until one day all hell broke loose. The mutha fucka got slick and accused me of stealing his stash while he was asleep."

Unable to maintain eye contact with anyone, Monica further exclaimed, "I really didn't take his shit! He set me up! Big Rob took it and blamed it all on me. I didn't know that he was hustling for someone else and spending all their doe on me. I would've kicked it with that guy and forgot about Big Rob. He was just the middle man and I don't do middle men."

In total disbelief, I smacked the taste out of Monica's mouth. "You silly bitch, all this time you knew the real and you didn't say a word! Terry could've been killed behind your foolishness. You have some gall calling yourself our sister, you stupid…stupid bitch!"

Charlene then yoked up Monica. "Bitch, you're going to make this shit right!"

A highly emotional Jasmine started crying. "How could you do this to Terry…how could you?"

"I was set up!" Monica exclaimed, as she broke free from Charlene's grip.

For a moment, it looked as if Monica started to get enraged as if she was really about to take on Charlene and I for hitting her. Hmm, I wish she would've.

"Silence," Terry yelled, as she walked straight up to Monica and looked her dead into her eyes.

"Bitch, I know what I heard and I know you. You took that stash, alright. If I spoke the truth about your part in my jumping, shit your ass would've been dead man walking. You would've been dealt with by either Big Rob or someone in my family. Like Charlene said earlier, you're going to make this shit right! After we handle our business tonight this incident is to never be spoken about again, by anybody. We could all go to jail if we get caught and I don't do jail. Do you understand me?"

Agreeing, we all nodded our heads.

A fidgeting Monica with a guilty voice said, "Well, what's the plan?"

"We're only going to fuck up the three girls that I originally didn't know so that way we won't be recognized. It has been brought to my attention that they live in Newark. So much shit happens in Newark these days that it will be next to impossible to trace this back to us. Especially, sense nothing happened to those two skanks; who lived in my very own building. It wouldn't make much sense to anybody that it was me. Nicole has been scoping those Newark girls for a couple of weeks. She found out that they hustled out of Greenwood Projects in Newark, on the corner of Lexington and Wade. Their crew is throwing a Halloween costume party tonight at this local bar called Hoodwinks. Well, that's where we're going to go this evening wearing these face masks that I took from my brothers. We're all going to go over to Newark to make things right in the universe, to be our sisters' keeper."

In unison we all chanted, except Monica, "When one fights, we all fight."

15

"Guys, don't worry. I got everything covered. I stole a van for transportation and brought the heat just in case shit gets out of hand." Nicole assured us.

"WHAT THE FUCK TERRY! YOU AND YOUR COUSIN ARE TAKING THIS THING A LITTLE TOO FAR. DO YOU REALIZE WHAT YOU'RE SAYING? THIS IS REAL LIFE… THIS IS NOT THE MOVIES!" Monica hysterically exclaimed.

"DO YOU REALIZE BITCH THAT YOU STARTED THIS SHIT AND THAT YOU'RE GOING TO HELP FINISH THIS IT? THEY'RE GOING TO REGRET EVER PLACING THEIR HANDS ON A TUCKER!" Nicole shouted at Monica, as if she was going to bust a cap in her ass if she said another word.

"Listen, I wouldn't jeopardize my future aspirations to become a lawyer on a foolish plan. My cousin and I have planned for every possible outcome. Our plan is tight. To disguise what's the real, we're going to beat those bitches up and use this hair removal cream to make them b-a-l-d like a baby's bottom."

With the exception of Monica, we burst into laughter as she looked on in horror realizing that Terry and Nicole were very, very serious about their plan.

In solidarity this time we all declared, "To be our sisters' keeper when one fights, we all fight."

By the time Big Rob realized that he had gotten the wrong person jumped; Man Man, the person he was hustling for pistol whipped him. He didn't believe his bullshit story that some mysterious little girl took his cash and bundles of coke. To make matters worse, Man Man heard through the grape vine that he better handle Big Rob or he was going to be handled.

Now as for Monica she got that shit off. Other than that short lived stint with dating Big Rob, Monica didn't live or hang around Mahogany Projects therefore no one knew her true identity.

Whatever happened to those two girls from Terry's building, you ask? Allegedly, in fear that their fate would be the same as the girls in Newark, they moved somewhere down south. Sounds too perfect? I agree. Knowing Terry and how she holds on to grudges something just didn't sound right about that story. It sounds too much like a Terry ending.

As for me, I wanted to know what the fuck Monica did with all of that coke? Enquiring minds would like to know.

(Sagittarius) Terry Tucker was born December 15, 1974 to Floyd and Rebecca Tucker. A take charge type of person it was only fitting that Terry was the eldest of six children. Always pitching in to help her parents with her younger siblings Terry was a born leader. Her father worked full-time for the sanitation department and part-time as a security guard, while her mother was a stay at home mom who earned extra money by babysitting the neighborhood children. Terry having a rich caramel complexion would often go to the doobie shop to maintain her ebony shoulder length hair. Trying not to be a financial burden on her parents, she would do odd jobs and tutor people for money during the school year. Power driven, Terry always knew that she was going to be a rich and successful lawyer. About 5'8" and weighing 160 pounds Terry was fit as well as smart as a whip.

(Leo) I was born August 5, 1974 to Jesse and Francine Jackson. It wasn't easy being the only child of a cop and a seamstress. When I wasn't hanging outside with my friends I could be found up under my parents. Over protective, my parents made it their business to know my whereabouts and all of my activities. Creative and talented, my mother would either be whipping up something good to eat or with her sewing machine humming turning out one of her many master pieces. While using only a photo from a magazine, she could re-create anything. An intuitive problem solver by nature with a strong sense of justice, my father was destined to be a cop. Perhaps the ugly things he saw everyday on the job led him to believe that I was too friendly and trusting however I disagree. I'm just a people person. Both hard workers my parents instilled in me that I could be whatever I wanted to be. I would like to think that I am the embodiment of my parents' greatest qualities. Despite my faults I strive every day to exceed my parents' expectations. Having a mocha complexion and off black shoulder length hair, I wore my hair in a bob throughout the year, except in the summer when I wore box braids. The largest in the clique I was 5'8" and weighed 245 pounds. I guess you can see why my mom made most of my clothes. LOL!

(AQUARIUS) Charlene was born January 20, 1974 to Willie and Julia Jones in France, on an U.S. military base. While stationed overseas her African American father, who was in The United States Marines, met and married her French mother, who was a jazz singer in a popular nightclub. Being the only child Charlene was pampered as her father loved to lavish gifts upon her. She was truly the apple of her father's eye a bond that only grew stronger after her mother's untimely death. Broken, Marine Sgt. Jones and his three year old baby girl returned to Jersey City, New Jersey, to live with his sister Bird Jones when his wife of five years died of breast cancer. Charlene's father gave into his depression and was only able to hold it together with the assistance of his family.

Identical to her French mother, Charlene had grey colored eyes and was fair-skinned in complexion. Besides the thick lips and hips inherited from her father's side, you could barely tell that Charlene was indeed an African American woman. She didn't look anything like her father, who was coal black in complexion. He would often have to go through great lengths to prove to people that Charlene was indeed his daughter. Looking like night and day, you couldn't tell that Charlene and her father had a lot in common. They were hopeless romantics, extremely sentimental and loved being consumed by love. They idolized their lovers and would go through great depths to make them happy. Always the optimist Charlene believed in fairytale endings. Charlene had long, wavy, golden brown hair that she would use water and mousse to maintain its wavy look. She was 5'7" and weighed roughly 160 pounds. A trend setter, Charlene would set the tone for what was in and what was out in fashion. All the girls envied her while all the boys wanted to taste her goods. Many times I wondered if Charlene let Monica taste her goodies. I mean, sometimes Charlene and Monica argued like they were an old married couple. I cleaned that up pretty well. LOL!

(LIBRA) Monica was born October 12, 1972 to Victoria Bell and father was unknown. Adopted by Bill and Janet Freeman when she was six years old, Monica was actually a year older than the rest of us. She was placed a grade behind because her birth mother never enrolled her in school. The Freemans were in their late thirties and had been trying for years to have a baby. They wanted a new born but settled on Monica, because the agency told them that due to the high demand for newborns the likely-hood of them getting a new born was slim to none. Well to do, the Freemans owned three beauty supply stores.

Smooth and even, Monica had beautiful chestnut skin. The first to rock green contacts in school, Monica gave Charlene a run for her money. She was 5'5" and weighed 130 pounds. Slim and petite, Monica wore whatever she wanted and looked mesmerizing in it. Always styling her hair in the latest styles, Monica would change her hair color as often as most people would change their underwear. Black, brown, blonde, purple, and blue she had them all. Monica was always the dare devil of the group. She would do anything once and twice if she liked it. Free spirited, Monica always lived on the edge and would pressure Charlene and Jasmine to follow her in her escapades. If you ask me, I feel Monica needs to see a therapist. It's one thing to be adventurous and it's another thing to be psycho!

(CANCER) Jasmine was born July 18, 1974 to Bill Edwards and Jackie Wright. She was only five years old when her father skipped out on her and her mother. Shortly after her mother would discover that the only man that she ever had sex with and the father of her beautiful daughter gave her HIV. When her mother died of AIDS, Jasmine, at the age of ten years old, had to learn early on that life wasn't fair. Like the many other grandmothers in the African American community forced to raise their grandchildren due to family crisis, Mrs. Wright stepped up to the occasion.

I believe the circumstances of her mother's death made Jasmine extremely emotional and needy. Being the nurturing type, she was forever trying to keep the peace in the clique. Loyal as hell, Jasmine would throw down quick and in a hurry if she thought anybody was messing with anyone of us. She would especially find herself in the middle of fights hanging around with Charlene and Monica. The girls at school had a love/ hate type of relationship with them. They loved to hate them and envied them for being so beautiful and popular.

Having a cinnamon brown complexion, looking like a Native American, Jasmine rocked her jet black hair exaggeratedly long and straight like Pocahontas. About 5'3" and weighing 140 pounds, Jasmine was a little cutie for sure. Men would gape and stare at her as if she was a tall glass of ice cold lemonade on a flaming hot summer day. They wanted her to quench their thirst.

Childhood sweethearts ever since grammar school, Jasmine's and Eddie's devotion would constantly be tested for the rest of their lives. I believe that they committed too young. They didn't give themselves enough time to grow-up. How can one ever know how to be a man or woman if you don't get a chance to learn from trial and error? To me, Jasmine and Eddie needed to date other people.

Jasmine would always proclaim, "I don't need to date around. I found my king. Eddie is the only man that I've ever been with and he's the only man that I will ever need."

Well, I can't say that I totally believe that. I mean, I was always told that birds of a feather flock together. Jasmine hung too close for comfort with Charlene and Monica. When Jasmine would get drunk as a skunk, she would get loose as a goose. She would either tongue kiss Monica or take off her clothes. If Jasmine is telling the truth, I have a goose that lays golden eggs to show you.

Eddie sleeps around with anything on two legs. He has given her crabs, chlamydia and lord knows what else. She might as well have slept around considering all the sexually transmitted diseases that he has given her over the years. Who can forget the first time Eddie gave Jasmine crabs? She refused to believe that Eddie gave them to her instead placing blame on a public toilet, even Eddie had to shake his head in disbelief.

As you can see why Charlene, Monica, and Jasmine got along so well they thought they were Charlie's Angels. I knew about the interests that made them so close but I often wondered about the lies that bounded them together. Now, by no means am I an angel. Terry and I share some secrets that the others don't know about. I've come to believe that if it's for the greater good than it is okay to keep some secrets away from the rest of the clique.

The physically fit, Derrick Johnson and Eddie Montgomery were best friends. They originally became close because they were the only two freshmen who started on the varsity squad. Derrick eventually became the captain while Eddie was just happy to not have been cut off the team. Derrick always felt people were sweating him because of his famous father, but with Eddie it was different. Instantly, he found himself bonding with Eddie as if he had known him his entire life. Derrick admired the close relationship Eddie had with his father and brothers. They would often stay over each other's houses when you saw one you would most likely see the other.

(CANCER) Derrick was born June 25, 1974 to Darrell and Angela Johnson. As the only child of famous parents greatness was expected of him. His mother had suffered four miscarriages before she gave birth to him. All the miscarriages were in their last trimester and all were to be named Darrell. Derrick was a miracle therefore his mother decided to name him after the doctor who delivered him.

Derrick's father was a professional basketball player. When his career ended in the states, he played overseas. Mr. Johnson and his family returned to America so that Derrick could play basketball at Saint Mary's High School. Mr. Johnson's ex-teammate from his pro-basketball years in the states was named head coach of the basketball team.

Derrick could speak fluent Spanish, Mandarin, and Italian. Smart and witty, he was a hit with ladies. Standing 6'5" at 230 pounds of pure muscle, he looked like a gladiator. Having a chestnut complexion, dreamy brown eyes, and a freshly cut fade; he was a very intense person. People just gravitated towards him: the teachers, the students, the females, the males, the young, and the old.

Charlene and Monica both laid eyes on him for the first time during freshman orientation. Charlene called "dibbs" first which meant hands off. Monica felt it should've been left up to him to decide but that went against the rules. Derrick spoke to both of them that day but only asked Charlene for her number. Monica was s-a-l-t-y. Every chance she could, Monica would flirt with Derrick. Charlene and Derrick dated "exclusively" from freshman year to the infamous prom night. Now, if you believe that I have some pirate treasure for sale.

(PISCES) Eddie was born March 12, 1974 to Edward and Joanne Montgomery. The eldest of five sons, Eddie was put to work at an early age. He worked with his father in his uncle's garage and delivered The Jersey Journal before school. A registered nurse, his mother left his father and brothers when he was only fifteen years old. She was tired of her husband's drinking and constant womanizing. She didn't try to take her sons because she knew that her husband wouldn't give them up without a fight. Beaten down, she was just tired of the constant fighting. Mr. Montgomery at times would be abusive to his wife when he was drunk. Once sober he would forget about his drunken escapades and carry on as if they never happened.

Having inherited his father's womanizing ways, Eddie was definitely a ladies man. His smooth and deep dark complexion made you think of a chocolate bar. Accompanied by his deep sexy voice, Eddie was plain and simply sexy chocolate… if I must say so myself. Being 5'9" and weighing 230 pounds, a stocky and cocky, Eddie had a style all of his own. A hard working Eddie always managed to keep some paper in his pockets, a drink in his hand, and was usually the best dressed man in the room.

Jasmine and Eddie have always been that's all that I can say. No matter what Eddie did to Jasmine she refused let him go. She was joined at the hip with Eddie and was determined to make him her baby daddy. Don't get it twisted, Eddie wanted to be kept. I mean, who was he going to find that would turn a blind eye to all his cheating? Jasmine truly believed that he wasn't out there, even after contracting sexually transmitted diseases. I guess we know who fell asleep during health class.

During our senior year, in high school, I overheard Eddie tell one of his teammates that he and Derrick were running trains on girls at Derrick's house. And I don't mean that they were playing with toy choo choo trains either. I just froze. I didn't know what to do or say. Should I curse Eddie out or should I tell Jasmine? I decided to tell Terry. She would surely know what to do, I thought to myself.

"January, you better keep your big mouth shut. Don't say anything to anybody and I mean anybody. Some people like to stay in the dark and don't want to know the truth. Charlene and Jasmine are that type. They are fairytale subscribers. They like to keep their heads up in the clouds. Jasmine won't take heed to the message. She will only want to kill the messenger…you!"

You can see why Derrick and Eddie got along so well. They thought that they were god's gift to women. They have the same interests and share lies that will forever bind them.

The children of Dominican twin brothers, Chad, Venus, and Dexter Delgado are first cousins- born and raised in Crown Heights, Brooklyn.

(SCORPIO) Fraternal twins, Chad and Venus were born November 19, 1974 to Hector and Carmen Delgado. The Delgado family owned and operated a bodega. At an early age, Chad and Venus would help their parents with the store especially since their mother spoke very little English. Mrs. Delgado and her daughter Venus would prepare family recipes daily for the store while the Delgado men oversaw the rest of the business. Mr. Delgado who spoke fluent English emphasized to his children the need to master the English language.

He also stressed the importance of family above all else. "Money comes and goes but your family will always be your family."

Chad was very arrogant and cocky. He liked being a boss. He made it his business to know any and everybody playing the game on his level. He had mad street cred. With a deep caramel complexion, Chad sported a black curly brook. He was 5'10" and weighed a whopping 215 pounds of pure sexiness. Chad dressed preppy and would smell devilishly good. His scent would linger in the air long after he left the room. He wore a single, thick gold chain with a medallion that said "Brooklyn" and a flashy diamond studded watch. Chad was very close to his sister. Often forgetting she was a girl, he used to rough house with her. He didn't want anybody to be able to get one off on her in a fight. Vowing never to leave Brooklyn, Chad had his money invested in his neighborhood.

Venus, out of the closet for years, was poised and strong willed. She accomplished anything that she had set her mind to. Mr. Delgado noticed early on that Venus fancied females. He would often try to set her up on dates with men. To Mr. Delgado, Venus was his adorable and misunderstood little princess. Venus was 5'10" and weighed 200 pounds. Having a deep caramel complexion, she wore her jet black hair in a curly fade. Very athletic, she played girls basketball and volleyball in high school. Venus had a passion for cooking, so she enrolled herself into a culinary institute. Graduating in the top ten percent of her class, Venus took her craft seriously and was eager to prove herself.

(LEO) Dexter was born July 23, 1974 to Victor and Elizabeth Delgado. The Delgados owned two adjoining commercial storefront buildings with eight apartments in each building. Victor Delgado worked long hours maintaining the buildings while his wife worked long hours as a legal secretary in a prominent law firm.

Dexter was an only child and tried to satisfy his need for siblings with his first cousins, Chad and Venus. Studious, Dexter could always be found reading a book and debating with his mother the validity of what he just read. An almond complected Dexter took great pride in his shortly cropped hair sporting enough waves to make you get sea sick. His perfectly trimmed black goatee framed a pair of lips that I know Terry thanked the lord for every night. Dexter, a heartthrob, was 6'1" and weighed 230 pounds. His manliness and deep voice alone could make you melt, especially when you heard your name roll off his tongue. Wearing glasses that hid his dreamy hazel eyes, he was definitely a man of splendor.

Chad was overprotective of his cousin Dexter and sister Venus. He felt

Dexter was too soft and that it was his duty to toughen him up. Ignoring their twin status, Chad always saw Venus as his little sister and tried to treat her as such.

Interests and blood bind the Delgado family and only time will reveal if lies can unbind them.

CHAPTER 3

LOVE CHILD-(Charlene)

Ever since my mother died of cancer, my father has never been the same. As early as I can remember, all I would hear my father talk about was my mother. I remember when Julia would do this and I remember when Julia use to do that my father would say smiling. My mother was the love of his life. I'm constantly reminded that I look identical to my mother. So, you know in my father's eyes that I was *Julia* and not *Charlene*. Never to marry again, my father made me the center of his universe. I took it in stride though. I just vowed to myself that if I was ever blessed to have any children, I wouldn't place such a burden on them. If it wasn't for my Aunt Bird, my father's sister, and my girlfriends Jasmine, Monica, January, and Terry, I would've forgotten that my name was indeed Charlene. They have kept me sane.

My father and I moved into my Aunt Bird's house in the Heights when we returned to the states. Old fashioned my aunt felt that children were best to be seen and not heard. My father and my aunt often would get into it over me being a little too out spoken. A bit of a prude, my aunt's idea of being outspoken was if you addressed her before she was ready to address you. My aunt taught me how to cook and sew. I would often help her design the church choir robes. If it wasn't for her, I would've never gotten bit by the fashion bug. Always designing her church dresses, it became natural for me to create patterns and make original designs.

My Aunt Bird enrolled me into dance school and girl scouts in exchange for me singing in her church's choir. Little did Aunt Bird know; she didn't have to bribe me. I love to sing. My Aunt Bird eventually convinced all of my girlfriend's parents to enroll them into girl scouts and into her church's choir. We had so much fun. Every Sunday after church my aunt use to cook a feast fit for a king. We all stayed in the church's choir, until our sophomore year in high school. We all quit because my Aunt Bird didn't want Monica to stay in the choir anymore.

"Monica's heart is definitely not into the lord. It clearly comes across in the way she sings and gyrates' her body. We're singing for the lord, not trying out for Showtime at the Apollo!" My Aunt Bird exclaimed, as she clutched her Bible.

My aunt even went as far as to meet with Monica's parents to talk to them about some of her observations. Concerned, my aunt thought that it was the only Christian thing to do.

My aunt even spoke to my father. I never told the clique but my father actually wanted me to stop hanging with Monica. He agreed with whatever my aunt said and forbid me to congregate with her. Aunt Bird clearly crossed the line. She should've either spoken to Monica or she could've discussed her concerns with me and maybe I would've passed them along to Monica. My aunt caused me to have to deceive my father. My hand was forced. I had to pretend to not speak to Monica anymore. My father and my Aunt Bird believe to this day that my affiliation with Monica is the reason that everything went south for me at the end of my senior year in high school.

Freshman year my run as daddy's little girl ended and so began my whirlwind romance with Derrick Johnson. I never understood the true depth of my father's love for my mother until I met Derrick. I use to think that my father was a little off…, you know touched. The notion that there could be love at first sight was unbelievable until it happened to me.

Even my father recognized it when he saw us together. "You two remind me of when I first met your mother. We were so zealous and full of life." As my father continued to share with us his memories of love and laughter, he also issued a warning to us. "Many people would kill for what you two have… True love. True love has been known to make people jealous. And jealousy can kill *True love* if you let it. True love is beautiful and rare. It's very fragile. One must be delicate when handling *True love*. If not cherished and handled with care it will lose its' value, its' luster, and will never be the same or even worse…go away."

I have often wondered to myself if I had only taken my father's warnings seriously, how different my life would have turned out to be?

I use to sing, dance, and do some modeling from time to time. I was pretty good at it too. I just didn't pursue it because I didn't want to add any more fuel to the fire. Resembling my mother, an established jazz singer and dancer, my father tended to call me by her name. He finally started calling me *Charlene* once I started dating Derrick and I didn't want him to revert back to his old ways.

My father really liked Derrick for me and was excited for us. He often invited Derrick over for dinner and tried his best to make him feel as if he was at home. I adored the Johnsons and I believe that the feelings were mutual. They always made me feel welcomed. Now, you know my Aunt Bird must have liked Derrick and his parents if she invited them over for Thanksgiving and Christmas dinner. My Aunt Bird is a tough cookie. If she didn't like you, she felt it was the only Christian thing to do to let you know why.

It was in my senior year in high school when I finally found out what my Aunt Bird was talking about when she said Monica's heart wasn't in the choir. Monica was creeping around with some of the men and young boys of the male choir. See, Monica never wore panties or stockings. Growing up, it was considered unladylike to go to church without wearing panties or stockings, especially if you were wearing a skirt or a dress.

Monica would charge ten dollars for three pumps! This scandalous bitch was charging for pumps. This is how she got it off. She would pretend to bend down for something while making sure that someone was watching her. Once that person saw her goodies and that she indeed wasn't wearing any panties or stockings, she would then disappear with that person. All she had to do was lift up her dress for easy access.

She was making a killing from the men because she knew that they would want more than three pumps. You would be surprised to know how all those young men of the church were robbing their dear old grandmothers and stunned mothers just so that they could get at a little taste of Monica. She was even charging three dollars to purchase a condom. So, in total one would need thirteen dollars for three pumps from Monica.

How fucking disgusting!

Do you want to know how I found out? Well, I missed singing in the choir so solo I decided to return to the church's choir. Someone propositioned me! They were hoping that I got down like Monica. In shock, I slapped the shit out of the person and told my Aunt Bird. When I told my Aunt Bird, I confirmed her suspicions.

My Aunt Bird went in front of the church the following Sunday. "I call for everyone to pray with me for the sinners to the left of them and for the sinners to the right. We have people, beside and amongst us, who prey on the flesh of the young. Let us pray for these people so that they will have a change of heart and ask for repentance. I know who you are! In the name of my savior Jesus Christ, I say GET THEE BEHIND ME SATIN!"

Then everyone started chanting "pray…pray…pray!"

I started to cry, for I was hurt that my friend came to my aunt's church and caused so much pain…so much pain. I never returned to that church again. My aunt tried to warn me about Monica and her wicked ways but I didn't take heed. I never looked at Monica the same after that incident. First the jumping of Terry and now this…I was truly hurt. Nothing, no longer surprised me when it came to Monica and what she was capable of doing.

My senior year in high school forever changed my life. Derrick was the star and I was his sun. Derrick was the artist and I was his brush. I just loved myself some Derrick. An experienced lover, Derrick was my first and best lover that I had ever had. He was very, very talented. He could fuck. I don't think you understood me. He could FUCK! Always with condoms we had SINFUL sex. We were only sixteen years old when we started, yet he sexed me as if he was a thirty year old man. He wouldn't stop until he came at least three times which took him at least three hours or until I came at least four times.

Prom night was the best we ever did it. It was really special. We skipped the prom and the limo driver whisked us away to Atlantic City, New Jersey where his father reserved a fancy suite in a five star hotel and casino. It was so romantic. Derrick had rose petals thrown everywhere in the suite. With the fully stocked mini bar, a stereo playing all of our favorite songs, and an intimate dinner set for two; I was blown away.

Derrick had everything EXCEPT the damn condoms!

Yes, this would be the first time that we did it without any protection. I was scared like a mother fucker. I think he did it on purpose because his father always stocked him up with condoms.

Always smiling, as he tried not to stare at my breasts, Mr. Johnson would often talk to me about sex and the use of birth control. "Charlene, you're a beautiful young lady and I really like you for my son. To be frank, I'm not ready to be called grandpa. Darling, have you considered taking birth control pills?"

"I would love to be on the pill, Mr. Johnson. It's Derrick that doesn't want me to be on the pill. He is afraid that the pill might change my appetite for him. He said he has seen firsthand how the hormones in the pills have affected some of the girls that he used to date. He wants us to continue using condoms." Blushing the entire time, I would try to ignore the obvious hard on Mr. Johnson would get when he talked to me about sex.

Derrick has been sexually active since he was twelve years old. Because of his height and his build, he looked older than what he really was. Looking at Derrick is a very gratifying experience when you first meet him. He has a captivating grandeur that will find you not taking your eyes off him. He just exudes sexiness. You instantly feel weak and lose control for you want him to have his way with you. There is no shame in your game. You want to fuck him!

With his arms wrapped around my waist, Derrick held me close to his torso as he sang "Let's Chill," by a hot R&B group named GUY. I started to cry because I loved it when my baby sang to me. I really loved him and wanted to spend the rest of my life with him. I more than loved him… I worshipped him. No one could make me feel the way that he made me feel. It was the SINFUL sex I tell you.

Following my serenade, we kissed ever so slowly as he slid his hands down the small of my back and over the rest of my voluptuous body. Derrick instantly became erect and slowly started to take off my prom dress.

Yes, I had a prom dress on that night! It magnified the curves of my voluptuous frame while Derrick wore a tux that made you say damn! We just never made it to the prom. When my dress hit the floor I saw his jaw drop. I was wearing a white corset with matching white thigh high stockings and garter belts. The kind you wear under a wedding dress.

"Damn baby! You look sexy as hell. You're the sexiest Bitch I know," he said with a Kool-Aid smile on his face.

"Thanks baby," I would respond giggling.

With my 36DD breast, my 27" waist and my 38" hips, I knew that I looked the bomb. One look into Derrick's eyes left no doubt to what he wanted to do to me, as he stared at my large stiff nipples that poked through my corset. Derrick in a flash got out of his tuxedo.

Once naked, my baby pulled me close and began nibbling down my neck. Feeling his hot breath along my neck all I could do was surrender. My weakness is my neck. Instinctively, Derrick began sucking it ever so gently. I moaned with desire for it felt like he was devouring my clit. He then unfastened my corset and started licking my large succulent nipples with his long fat tongue. Derrick smashed my breast together as his strong yet gentle tongue tantalized my nipples. I started to quiver as the ripples of pleasure went straight to my clit.

"Ahhhhh…, ahhhhh…, oooooh," I moaned, as his masterful tongue felt so delicious.

The tingly sensations made my knees get weak and I started to collapse but Derrick picked me up and placed me in the center of the king size bed. Every touch…every kiss…every lick…made me feel like I was going to explode. The sexual chemistry we shared was bananas!

"AH! AH! AH!" I sighed. "OH, MY GOD! …TAKE ME DERRICK… PLEASE BABY …I BEG YOU…I CAN'T TAKE NO MORE TORTURE! PLEASE BABY… FUCK ME! I NEED TO FEEL YOU INSIDE OF ME!" I yelled in ecstasy.

"In due time baby girl, in due time, we have all night long." He said as he softly planted kisses all over my body. Kissing along my belly, he slowly worked his way south of the border. Tenderly kissing my outer thighs his soft lips ignited sparks of electric ecstasy as he headed towards my inner thighs.

"Ooh, ooh, ooh." I moaned with desire, as my va-jay-jay in anticipation was getting impatient. Once he arrived at her doorstep, he parted her lips with his fingers and lavished her with tender kisses. Then he started to French kiss her. "UMMMMMMM," I moaned. "OH MY," I sighed as he then took the tip of his tongue and started thrashing it across the bulb of my clit. "OH MY," I babbled again as flutters of pure ecstasy were taking over me. Steadily, I felt the flutters turn into massive waves and then like an earth quake…, vibrations. Becoming stronger and more intense, as he repeatedly beat my clit faster and faster, the vibrations were getting the best of me. I was about to…"OH! OH BABY! OOOH BABY," I yelled, as I couldn't keep it in much longer.

Jerking side to side, shaking, and quivering while Derrick ravished my swollen clit, I started squirting globs of hot cum into his mouth. "UMMMMM…," he moaned, as he swallowed every drop of my essence while he continued to roll his fat tongue up and down my throbbing clit.

"AHHHHHHHH, AHHHHHHH, AHHHHHHH!" I roared, as I was having an intense orgasm. I thought I was having a heart attack. Clutching my chest, I screamed "STOP…STOP BABY…I CAN'T TAKE NO MORE!"

Taking his cue, Derrick immediately got on top of me and inserted his massive dick inside of my pulsating va-jay-jay. "AHH, AHHH, AHHHH," he moaned, as he started fucking me with deep hard thrusts. "THIS PUSSY IS ALWAYS GOING TO BE MINE. NOBODY IS EVER GOING TO MAKE LOVE TO YOU THE WAY THAT I DO. I'M KING OF THIS PUSSY!" He proclaimed. With his tongue hanging out of his mouth, Derrick stroked my va-jay-jay, in and out, side to side, to the left, and then to the right. "OH YEAH… YEAH! YEAH! GOOD PUSSY…UMMMMM! GOOD PUSSY! YEAH! SAY THIS IS MY PUSSY! SAY IT!"

"It's…it's…OOOH! …IT'S YOUR PUSSY!" I exclaimed, for the pleasure was too overwhelming. "OH BABY! OH BABY!" I wailed as I swerved my hips throwing all I had into this rhythmic ride. Sweating profusely, he pounded me into audible submission. Grabbing for the towel that he had placed earlier by the side of the bed I wiped the sweat from his face. In and out, in and out; he just wouldn't stop hammering my va-jay-jay.

"Yeah…, yeah…, yeah, that's what I'm talking about… umm… umm… GOOD PUSSY… GOOD PUSSY! I've been waiting years to do this to you, UGHHHHHHHHHHH…" He yelled as he was coming inside of me.

I can't believe it! Derrick just came inside of me. But wait… he is still pumping, I said to myself. "Oh! Oh! Oh my," I further exclaimed, as he started fucking me faster, as if he was under a magical spell.

"Yeah… yeah, I'm not done with you yet baby girl!"

He wasn't lying either as he turned me into a whimpering, stuttering pile of flesh.

"Yeah, baby girl… fuck your man! FUCK ME! FUCK ME! OH! OH! OH…," then he grabbed my hips and lifted me up.

The next thing I knew, I was straddling him. I started riding him for all I was worth, trying my best now to turn him out. "Yeah, now I'm in control." I sighed, as Derrick took my words to heart and began fucking me back.

"YEAH, BABY GIRL… TAKE THAT DICK… TAKE THAT DICK!"

My pussy was getting even wetter as I watched his eyes roll to the back of his head. He was putting in work and loved every bit of it!

"OOOOOOH… I'M CUMMING AGAIN… AHHHHHHHHH!" He exclaimed as he continued to pump inside of me.

Licking my nipples, Derrick now made my eyes roll behind my head. The combined sensations I got from his licking and fucking made me feel punch drunk. I thought I had died and went to heaven. I was moving in and out of consciousness. "OOOOOOOOOOOH," I moaned in ecstasy, as flutters of pleasure went surging through my body. Then he flipped me over and really took charge, stroking me like a musical instrument. Shaking and trembling, I sighed. "OH! OH! OH MY! What are you trying to do to me?"

"UHHHHHHHHH!" he roared, while he came inside of me again. Drained, he collapsed on top of me nearly lifeless.

"Derrick, you're heavy!" I said, pushing him off of me.

"Sorry babe, I couldn't help it. Do you want something to drink?" He asked, in a tender voice.

"No thank you baby," I answered, as I tried to collect my thoughts. I looked at the clock. "Wow, we've been fucking for hours. I guess we're finished," I said, in a playful voice as I started to giggle.

"No, I'm not finished yet with your sexy ass," he said as he smiled like a Cheshire cat.

"Oh, yes you are! We're not using condoms, Derrick. What are you trying to do?"

"What, do you think I'm trying to do?"

"I don't know?"

"Well I don't know either." Derrick said, as he sat next to me on the bed.

I was still laying down when he started playing with the tip of my clit with his two fingers. Then he placed the back of his thumb in my va-jay-jay and started pressing…and pressing. I think he was thumb fucking me. "Ooooooooooh," I moaned. I didn't know what the hell he was doing but it felt wonderful. Like I told you before we have SINFUL sex. I wanted to suck his beautifully circumcised dick but he wouldn't let me.

Derrick smacked my butt and gave me an order, in a deep sexy voice, "Bend over."

"Oh goody" I playfully muttered, for I love how my baby fucked me doggy style.

On a mission, Derrick rubbed my clit from behind as he hit it. Gently, he stroked me as I started to tremble uncontrollably. My knees gave way, leaving me flat on the bed as Derrick drove his dick deeper inside of me. Maintaining a slow steady pace Derrick professed, "I love you Charlene, please say that you will stay with me forever."

At that point, it was becoming clear that something besides love was happening here. "WHAT THE FUCK IS GOING ON!" I said, as I attempted to get him off of me.

As he pulled out with a puzzled look on his face, he countered, "What do you mean?"

"I mean what the fuck is going on, Derrick?" I repeated, this time in a calmer voice.

"Well … I was going to tell you in the morning."

"Tell me what?"

"I'm not going to college. Last week, I signed with the Los Angeles Clippers and I'm going to California straight after graduation."

"Great we're going to Ca-li-forn-ia!"

"No baby, I'm going to California… alone."

"Didn't you just say that you wanted us to stay together, forever?"

"Yeah, I want you to wait for me. I want to go to Cali by myself so that I can stay focused on the game. Hopefully you can stay here with our son or daughter until I'm ready to send for you two."

"WHAT! WHAT THE FUCK ARE YOU SAYING, DERRICK? If I'm pregnant…then we're pregnant. And if we're pregnant…then we're getting married and we're both going to California as a family."

"No baby, I will make more progress and money if I appear to be available. My agent says……"

"Fuck what your agent says." I cut him off mid- sentence. "Did your agent just nut in me three times, Derrick?"

"Well, no baby… I actually came in you five times. Two of them were quick little nuts. I surprised myself tonight. I'm gooood." He bragged.

"I can't believe you, Derrick. I never knew that you were so selfish. We could've gotten engaged and both went to California. You could've played ball while I attended the local college. But noooo, instead, you want to go to Los Angeles and leave me here in Jersey City, alone to raise our baby. You didn't have to try to get me pregnant for me to stay with you. I love you. I'm here for the long haul."

With confidence, he sighed. "Oh, you're pregnant. I keep track of your cycle. One of those five nuts made my LOVE CHILD."

Crying, I ran into the bathroom and locked myself in there until the morning. Derrick had to piss in an empty beer bottle because I wouldn't let him in to use the bathroom. I felt so stupid. We should've used condoms.

I waited three weeks before I took a pregnancy test. I was pregnant alright. I asked Monica, Jasmine and January to go with me to the clinic. I didn't want to ask Terry because I didn't need a lecture about how our black sisters are killing our future. Always preaching, Terry can be a little too much at times. There are times when you just want someone to stand by you, right or wrong without judging your decisions or every movement. This right here was one of those times.

I broke up with Derrick and told him that I wasn't pregnant. I didn't want him to find out because he would've pressured me to have our baby. Jasmine and January pleaded with me to tell Derrick and to discuss my decision to have an abortion with him.

Monica disagreed. "Fuck Derrick, he put you in this predicament in the first place. He knows about the birds and the bees."

"I blame myself for this mess because I should've made him go and buy some condoms from the shop that was located in the hotel lobby. We should've used condoms, period! We'd always used them before."

"This is not about who is to blame…this is about the baby!" Jasmine said, as she started to cry as usual.

A part of me wants to have my baby because I do love Derrick and the other part of me wants to have the abortion to secretly get back at Derrick. Like I told you before the type of sex Derrick and I had … was SINFUL. If I would've been on the pill or used condoms, I wouldn't have to be wearing these big Hollywood styled shades while going into this abortion clinic. I should've valued my body, my temple enough to have used some protection. I knew better and when you know better you do better.

Once at to the clinic, Jasmine and January chickened out. They decided to wait for us inside the car.

January sighed. "Charlene, I really think that you're going to regret this especially since you didn't even tell Derrick."

"I agree with January. If not with Derrick at least talk it over with your father. I know if I got pregnant by my Eddie, I would tell my grandmother. It's not too late to change your mind." Jasmine motioned as she reopened the car door.

Monica, in disgust, sucked her teeth and rolled her eyes at Jasmine and

January. Then she tightly grabbed my hand as she opened the door to the clinic. "I always knew that they would punk out without their precious Terry leading them. Forget them, let's go in."

Instantly, I knew that if Monica wouldn't have gone in with me I would've turned back around. Jasmine and January were right. I needed to talk to the two most important men in my life before making such a decision. As Monica and I looked around, we both were in a state of shock. Holy cow! We knew about ten of the girls that were in here.

Then Terry popped up inside my mind. "What the fuck are we doing to ourselves? Young vibrant sisters alone going to the clinic without our mates who helped us create these situations. It takes two. It takes two."

The thought of Terry opened up the floodgates. All kinds of thoughts just kept popping up inside my mind. What the fuck should I do? Then it happened, I thought about my mom. Breast Cancer robbed me of the years that I could've spent with her. Now, I'm about to kill my unborn baby, her grandbaby. I felt a sharp pain in my heart. I realized that like Derrick, I was being selfish. I was depriving my unborn baby the opportunity to be loved and wanted by his or her parents. I know that Derrick and I would love and cherish our baby. I guess I'm mad at the fact that I got caught playing house. If I wanted to do adult things like having sex then I needed to be responsible at all times by using some sort of protection.

Then to put the icing on top of the cake, Mrs. Ford from health class popped up inside my head. "It's reckless, in this day and time, to have unprotected sex. It is best to practice abstinence. Other than abstinence the proper use of condoms are your best alternative to "help prevent" an unplanned pregnancy and contraction of the HIV virus."

"That's it! Let's leave Monica. The whole time that I was oohing and aahing, with Derrick, I knew what made babies. I knew that we weren't using any protection. In a nut shell, if Derrick would've proposed to me and took me to California, I would've had our baby. So because he doesn't want me the way that I want him is that any reason to abort our baby that was created out of love and not out of lust? I love Derrick and I love my baby. This is not just Derrick's love child! This baby is also my love child!"

"Are you sure?"

"Yes, I'm sure. I'm sure that it was my destiny to get pregnant and that it is my destiny to have my LOVE CHILD." Smiling, I thought to myself… wouldn't it be wonderful if I had a girl so that I could name her Destiny.

Don't get me wrong, I am pro-choice. I just chose to take responsibility for my actions. I knew Derrick wasn't strapped and I gladly let him ooze inside of me. After I have my baby… my freaky ass is going to get on the pill and make sure that I always keep my own stash of condoms. It's never too late to practice abstinence but like I told you before the type of sex Derrick and I had was sinful. It would take a miracle to make me give that up.

Once my father got over the initial shock of it all, he was very supportive. "I know your mother would've loved seeing you and Derrick together. Derrick is a classy young man and has a bright future ahead of him. He comes from a good family and most importantly, the two of you really love each other. I don't foresee any problems but to make sure that there aren't any, we're going to contact the Johnson's together."

With tears of joy in my eyes, I tightly hugged my father. He always knew what to say and do to make his little girl feel better. He knew that I desperately needed his support now more than ever. My stomach was in knots when I arrived at the Johnsons. I was embarrassed for I knew that Mr. Johnson's worst fear finally came true. I got pregnant.

Jokingly Mr. Johnson said, "I always knew that you were going to make me a grandpa." Then Mr. Johnson hugged me and my father. "Charlene is an extraordinary young lady and I always knew that she was the one for my son. I assure you that my son is going to do the right thing."

"I never doubted it for a minute. Likewise, I always knew that Derrick was the one for my Charlene."

Derrick's mom was overjoyed. She always wanted to have more children but because of her difficulty to carry to full term, she gave up hope. She would later come to find out that her difficulty was the result of a botched abortion that she had, in an underground abortion clinic, when she was fifteen years old. It was a miracle that she had Derrick.

Forming a united front we all decided to go to Los Angeles to tell Derrick in person. Excited to see me, Derrick passionately kissed me in front of our parents. Embarrassed, I pulled back and screamed "Derrick!"

"That's enough of that you two…it's that type of behavior that has me preparing myself to be called grandpa." My father said jokingly.

"Dad, I thought we all agreed that I would tell Derrick first!" I sighed.

"My bad, I lost my head. Can I help it that I am a proud grandpa to be?" Everybody started to laugh.

"I knew it!" Derrick screamed, as he started pumping his right fist in the air. "I never miss my shot. You should be a little over three weeks by now. Soon, I was going to be making a surprise visit to Jersey if I didn't get my phone call from you." Derrick arrogantly said, as he held me in a bear hug.

We were all ecstatic like one big happy family until Derrick asked to speak to me privately.

Once alone, in an aggravated voice, Derrick started interrogating me. "Why didn't you just tell me this over the phone? Why did you bring our parents down here? I told you when I got you pregnant that I wanted you to stay in Jersey until I was ready to send for you. You thought that I would change my mind if you bought our parents down here?"

In shock, I stayed silent. I felt like I was gut punched. My heart felt like it was about to explode. I refused to answer any of his questions. I just stared at him in disbelief. It was as if I had gotten pregnant by Dr. Jekyll and not by Derrick. And now his alter ego Mr. Hyde was finally coming out. Derrick tried to hug me but I pulled back. Can you believe that he apologized for the bass in his voice and not for what he said? I just stared at him. I couldn't believe my ears.

Derrick suddenly fell to his knees and grabbed me around my waist. "I'm sorry baby. Please forgive me. Say something, I don't want to lose you. Please say something!"

I refused to answer him. Once loose, I ran out of the room. I went back to my hotel room and asked my father to please take me home. My father gestured as if he was going to ask me why but instead, he just called the airport to check on the next flight to Jersey. My father was an insightful man. He felt my pain and like a loving father, he just wanted to get me out of harm's way.

On the other hand, Derrick's father was not pleased. He was outraged. "Why did Charlene and her father abruptly leave?"

"I don't know. I didn't tell her to leave."

"Then, what did you say to her dammit! I demand…"

"You demand what? An explanation about what I discussed with my girlfriend. Listen old man, the creation of my baby was no accident. You don't have to worry. I know Charlene and the baby are my responsibility. It won't cost you a thing. I'm making my own doe now. I got this."

While yoking Derrick up with one hand, his father said in a sinister voice. "Young man, speak to me in that tone again and your mother will be preparing for a funeral instead of the arrival of her first grandchild. I'd rather she mourn for her loving son than live with having a disrespectful son."

"Darrell, please stop before someone gets hurt. You could end his career before it even starts!" Mrs. Johnson pleaded with her husband.

When Mrs. Johnson told me this over the phone my jaw dropped. I knew then that I needed to be the bigger person and to do some damage control. I invited Derrick and his parents over to my house for a cookout to keep the peace. I told my father and the Johnsons that I didn't want to get married right now so that Derrick could focus on his career in basketball. I also announced to them that I had accepted my scholarship to attend Jersey City State College and that I wanted to stay in Jersey City to be close to my family and friends. With a big smile, I turned to Mr. and Mrs. Johnson. "Now, that includes you two poppa and momma Johnson. We're family now. We don't need a piece of paper to say that."

We all hugged each other as we all started to cry.

Momma Johnson sighed. "I speak for both my husband and myself when I say that Charlene you're so precious to us. You're the little girl that we never had."

"Aww, momma and poppa Johnson, I love you too."

Mr. Johnson elbowed my father and sighed. "Well grandpa, I don't know about you but this grandpa sure can use a stiff drink just about now."

We all continued to celebrate and be jolly except Derrick. He just appeared to be relieved that he dodged a bullet. The get married and move to Cali as a family bullet. By the end of the night, he pulled me close and whispered in my ear. "Thanks ma, you know I got you…no matter what the future has in store for us. I promise…I got you covered."

To no surprise, Derrick is an awesome father. Derrick and Destiny are very close. I must admit that I'm a tad bit jealous of their relationship and not for the reason that people may think. Ever since I had Destiny, I've dreamed of the day that Destiny and I would become extremely close. Destiny has enriched my life beyond my wildest dreams. Through Destiny I was able to fill in the void that was placed in my life by not having my mother when I was young.

I'm also happy that Destiny is a daddy's little girl just like I am with my father. Derrick spoils her with love as well as with gifts. He encourages her to dream big and live life even bigger. Derrick is far from being a telephone dad. He's hands on. Destiny and I would stay weeks at a time with Derrick at his Saddle River estate. Not to disturb Destiny's school schedule, the limo driver would drop her off and then pick her up from school. Derrick and I would stay behind and have hot, passionate sex throughout the mansion until it was time for Destiny to return. Derrick rarely missed any of the parent/teacher meetings at Destiny's school. He didn't allow his celebrity status to interfere with the upbringing of Destiny.

I especially remember when we took Destiny and Jasmine's children apple picking. Destiny sat on her father's shoulders the entire time she picked apples. Can you imagine how heavy it was to carry a seven year old with a basket full of apples on your shoulders for four hours? I had to massage Derrick's shoulders all night long with rubbing alcohol.

Destiny was three years old when we decided to publically break up as a couple. We just wanted to keep our families, our friends, and the media out of our relationship. The pressure for us to get married was getting to be a bit too much, especially when he had gotten traded to the Los Angeles Lakers. The tabloids were reporting our every move. Secretly, Derrick and I were still together until the news media informed me otherwise in 2004. I was devastated to hear that Derrick had gotten engaged to some Asian chick named Mei-Li. In shock, I decided to send an email to Derrick instead of confronting him in person.

"Wow, player…you could've least warned a bitch. You always told me that you would keep it five hundred. Is this what you call keeping it real? I find it funny how they call you "The Truth" yet you live life far from the truth. I now see that you can't want more for a person than you want for yourself. Destiny is now twelve years old. We should've been gotten married. It's all good, though. You live and you learn. And oh…by the way, I changed my locks to my house as well as to my nana. Access is no longer granted, to either."

"Damn, I didn't mean for you to find out like this. When I got a chance, I was going to tell you in person. Mutha fuckas need to mind their business. Charlene, stop playing and just answer your damn phone! It's like that? It's really like that Charlene? You're just going to leave shit like this? Cool, I respect and understand your decision. I hope you know that you and Destiny are my heart. When you calm down, you know where you can find me."

"Whatever! When you're ready for a real woman, you know where to find me. And when you come for me, I pray that you find me in bed with a real man chowing down on what you oh so casually walked away from."

I guess Derrick didn't like that statement because pretty soon security was calling me to say that an irate Derrick was demanding that they let him into my townhouse complex. I laughed and told them if he didn't leave to do what they have to do, call the police.

Derrick tried his best to make friends of Mei-Li and I but I wasn't having it. In my eyes she was a home wrecker and I didn't want any part of her. Not wanting to drive a wedge between Destiny and her father, I encouraged Destiny to accept her father's new bride. If I openly acted out towards Mei-Li, Destiny would've followed suit. Knowing how my girlfriends were I told them to keep their opinions to themselves, particularly when they were around Destiny. Mei-Li is Derrick's problem and none of my business. I just don't want the relationship between Destiny and her daddy to change.

Now that Derrick got married on a bitch to some random chick, I decided to launch a hip hop clothing line named "2TRUE." I pulled out my Aunt Bird's old sewing machine and decided that I needed to be able to support myself in case Derrick started acting funny. When Derrick got married to Mei-Li, I cut him off from the pussy. He might retaliate by cutting me off from the money.

Destiny dibbled dabbled in modeling and often would tell me about all the money that the rap industry generated. Inspired by Destiny, I decided to design my own line of hip hop clothing and make her the model and spokesperson. Derrick's nickname was "The Truth" and I named my line "2TRUE." Legally I didn't know if I could name my line "2TRUE." It was a play on Derrick's nickname "The Truth." So I invited Terry over to my house for dinner and asked her for some legal advice. Hesitantly, Terry gave me some advice and directed me to a suitable lawyer to work with to patent my trademark and logo.

I called January's mom to further assist me because she could sew circles around me. I had Jasmine come up with a fresh new hairdo for Destiny and I was on my way. To further help me January and Terry spotted me some funds and became my silent business partners. Once out of the red I decided to open a "2TRUE" store downtown, by exchange place. Now five years later, I bought out Terry's and January's share of the company and became the sole owner of "2TRUE" fashions. I did it! I'm finally fulfilling my destiny and I love it.

I have a smart and beautiful seventeen year old daughter, a successful business, loving family and friends, and now, at the blessed age of thirty-five years old, I finally got married. I am Mrs. Charlene Wiggins. I'm married to newly retired, forty-five year old, former Marine sergeant Godfrey Wiggins aka "POPPA BEAR." He's fine, fine, fine. 6'2" and weighing 225 pounds, Godfrey is fucking gorgeous! Pure chocolate perfection, he has a salt and pepper goatee and sports a smooth and perfectly round bald head. And does he have muscles you ask? Hell yeah, Poppa Bear has…hella muscles!

If I wasn't sold by that then what about the line he hit me with when I first met him. "I want to cherish and take care of you for the rest of my life." He said, as he kissed my hand.

No, you don't hear me. I have waited seventeen years to hear Derrick say that to me. Yet, this stranger said it to me the first time he met me. I thought chivalry was dead until I met Godfrey. I was already hooked but baby, baby, baby when we first made love…I was sprung. This punnany was his signed, sealed, and delivered. No longer do I have a va-jay-jay, I now have a wet and juicy punnany.

Godfrey makes me feel like I'm eighteen years old again. I've never had my soul touched the way that he has touched mine. I finally can say that I'm over Derrick. I know that you think that I shouldn't have gotten married to Godfrey after only knowing him for six months, but waiting for Derrick to come to his senses wasn't getting me anywhere. I'm a thirty-five year old seasoned woman and know a good man when I see one. Sgt. Wiggins is a great man, loving man, and an intriguing man. He's a man that knows what he wants and goes after it!

He knows this woman's worth! Unlike Derrick, who strung me along for years and dumped me for a woman who was looking for a sponsor. I'm making my own money and I love it! As a newlywed of three months I must tell you that my feelings for him have quadrupled. He's strong, loving, funny, tender, smart, and sexy.

POPPA BEAR IS MY PRESENT AND MY FUTURE! HE'S MY BELOVED HUSBAND.

I'm so excited for January. She has worked so hard for this shot. I always knew she had it in her to take her career to the next level. Tonight, she deserves all of our support. I hope Monica shows up and doesn't let her down. I was shocked when she didn't show up to Derricks' extravagant 35th birthday party. I have never known Monica to miss a party. That is actually when I got concerned for her safety. Until Derrick told Destiny that Monica called him to wish him a Happy Birthday. Monica told him that she was out of the country on an interior decorating assignment. If that was the truth then what's with all the secrecy? All I know…, she better not disappoint January tonight. Monica has always been a drama queen. If the spotlight isn't on that bitch she grows another head.

CHAPTER 4

TWO IS COMPANY AND THREE IS DELIGHTFUL-(Monica)

Ever since the Freemans adopted me at the early age of six years old, I have known Charlene, Jasmine, January, and Terry. Neighbors, Jasmine, January, and I grew up together on the same dead end street located in downtown Jersey City. Aligned with an abundance of tall trees, our dead end street had rabbits, stray cats and dogs, raccoons, possums, squirrels, and even snakes. Living on our dead street made us feel like we lived in the suburbs. We would run around and play all day long, in the street, with no worries of getting hit by a speeding car.

We all had backyards but you couldn't see all of the action from your backyard and man was there ever action. For example, anyone that knew old Mrs. Grecco and her twenty-three year old daughter Kelly knew that they were racists. Harmless, you would often hear them complaining about how the "niggers" brought down the value of their property.

Well one day, Jasmine, January, and I were playing kickball in the street when Jasmine accidentally kicked the ball into old Mrs. Grecco's front yard. Well, all hell broke loose when Jasmine went into her yard to get the ball.

All you heard echo throughout the block was Kelly yelling at Jasmine. "FUCKIN LITTLE NIGGER, DON'T YOU COME INTO MY YARD!"

Jasmine ran back across the street crying and told her mother, who went across the street and approached Kelly. "Now, Kelly...I apologize for the children kicking the ball into your yard. I also apologize for Jasmine not asking for permission to enter your yard to get her ball but all that calling her out her name. Nah, you owe my baby an apology. She's just a little girl playing kick ball. She didn't mean any harm. She's only eight years old. No child deserves to get called out of their name like that and especially not mine."

"This is private property. Just take your ball and your little niglet and just go back across the street, where you belong."

"Nah, I didn't hear you correctly…can you please repeat what you just said to me?"

Kelly word for word started to repeat what she said and then it happened… Jasmine's mother connected with a left hook that would've made Joe Frazier proud.

Stunned, everybody on the block said "OH SHIT!"

Before Jasmine's mother could turn around she was surrounded by the police. Observing the entire scene from her front window, old Mrs. Grecco had called the cops when she first saw Jasmine's mother approaching her house. Jasmine's mother was taken to police headquarters and was later released. No charges were filed. Old Mrs. Grecco and her daughter Kelly later apologized about the misunderstanding and wanted bygones to be bygones.

Jasmine's mother was gangster, I thought to myself. I looked up to her. She had grit…she had courage.

Another example of the excitement that you would have missed, if you were to play in your back yard, was the day when someone blocked old Mrs. Grecco's driveway. Upset, she flattened their tires and then called the city to ticket them. January, Jasmine, and I tried to tell her whose car that was in her driveway but to no avail; she didn't want to listen.

Well, well, well when she found out that it was Father O Reilly's car and that he was visiting everyone on the block to get up close and personal with the community…let's say she turned bright red and didn't go to services for an entire month.

We all laughed so hard that January peed on herself. It was fun on our block. Everyone knew everyone and we all tried to live in harmony. Truth be told, we even loved the Greccos. They were harmless. They never physically hurt anyone. They were just practicing the old belief system that use to be the norm in America. As time went by, they quickly realized that it was better for all of us to try and get along. We all needed to stick together to protect the serenity of our little block against outside forces which consisted of everyone and anyone who didn't live on our dead end street.

I loved my new family, neighborhood, and girlfriends. Charlene, Jasmine, January, and Terry are my sisters and like sisters we would often argue and fight. Terry and I never really got along. We tolerated each other to keep the peace. Not to sound ungrateful, I appreciated how she had my back a couple of times but she just always rubbed me the wrong way. She thinks that she's so much smarter than everybody else. To politely say it, "Terry is a sarcastic BITCH!"

I always felt that Charlene and I were closer because unlike the others, we both could barely remember the images of our birth mothers. I also felt that Charlene and I were closer because we were the most attractive of the clique. Charlene was fair-skinned with grey eyes and I was chestnut chocolate with green eyes. My green contacts look so natural on me that I forget that my eyes are actually brown. We were America's most envied. Fascinating, smart, and sexy, we had it going on. Both girls and boys wanted a piece of us. Most importantly, men with money desired us. We would get mad free shit because we were so fly. When we allowed Jasmine to tag along, men use to get erections just by gazing at us. We were some fly ass bitches!

Jasmine was sexy but she was as ding-y as a doorbell. Her theme song should've been "If I only had a brain."

January was and is my peoples but she could stand to lose a couple of pounds. January has a pretty face and a beautiful disposition but frankly, she is too fat. She wasn't sloppy or nothing. She was just too damn fat. If she would lose fifty or sixty pounds, I know that I could convince her to kick Terry to the curb and just hang with the three of us. Terry cramps our style, she's a herb.

Terry would be considered as gorgeous as Charlene and I, if she wasn't so damn snobby and self-righteous. She was always trying to preach to us about doing the right thing. I don't know who told her that she was God's right hand woman. Terry needs to take a chill pill or just let me lick that clit a little and then maybe she would loosen up. I bet she's a straight up super freak in bed. That's why she tries so hard to appear to be cold as ice.

The Freemans saved me from a life of uncertainty and poverty. My birth mother was useless. She didn't even know who knocked her up. I could have a rich father and because this bitch couldn't get her story straight, I'm left without knowing him. Someone called D.Y.F.S. on her when they noticed that she didn't enroll me into school. People are too god damn nosey. They need to tend to their own gardens, if you ask me. That's why I keep my secrets close to my chest and I never let my right hand know what my left hand is doing, it's better that way. That is why when I searched for my birth mother, I didn't tell anybody. I didn't want someone to have one up on me.

I found out that my mother died of a drug overdose ten years ago. Shit, if it wasn't for the Freemans; I probably would've been dead too. I'm grateful for the Freemans. I was and am just perplexed by them. They were always fucking working! I don't even understand why they even adopted me? I spent more time under Jasmine's grandmother and January's mom than I did under my own adopted mother. I knew that my parents loved me because they always kept me up with the latest fashions and gadgets. The only thing that used to get me upset with them was that they were so fucking stingy with the money. SHOW ME THE MONEY!

I must admit that they did hit me off with some doe but just not what I wanted. They use to tell me that they were trying to teach me how to v-a-l-u-e money. Yeah, they taught me how to v-a-l-u-e money alright…how to save mine and spend someone else's. I really learned the most about how to get money from my father. He used to sneak and give me extra money because he thought that I heard him on the phone begging his mistress not to dump him. Of course I heard him but I kept telling my father that I didn't hear anything. The entire time that I said that to him, I would smile and hold my hand out until I was satisfied with the amount of money that he would give me.

Now, that is what I call a herb. Every time the girls would come over to my house, I use to catch him sneaking a look at January's fat ass. I bet he used to jerk off thinking about her. My father taught me early on that men were perverts and would gladly pay to maintain their life of perversion. That is why I use both men and women to get what I want. They will gladly pay for it and I will gladly take it!

I thought that my life couldn't get any better until freshman orientation when I saw Derrick. OMG! He was fine, fine, fine and I wanted him to be mine, mine, mines. Fuckin', Charlene called "dibbs" faster than me and felt that Derrick was hers for the taking. Now, I knew that "dibbs" meant hands off but there should've been an exception to the rule, especially when it came to Derrick Johnson. It was bad enough that Jasmine had her hooks into Eddie, who was the sexiest dark skin brotha that I've ever met before in my life, but for Charlene to call "dibbs" first on Derrick … no … no …No, a penalty flag should've been thrown on that play. Derrick was out of her league but like a loving sister, I let her have him to keep the peace. Not to brag, I had my hands literally full anyway with a couple of numbers that's why I was so slow on calling "dibbs."

I would've probably gotten over my attraction to Derrick if he didn't approach me a week prior to the senior prom, to accompany him to his house after school.

Yes, I said it, he approached me.

The clique went to New York to find some prom shoes for January. January had huge feet. She wore a size 12EEE. It was always hard to find her fashionable dress shoes. I didn't go with them because I was waiting for my shoes to be delivered. I missed the delivery twice and if I missed it this time they were going to send it back.

In a cocky voice, Derrick said. "I always knew that you wanted to fuck me and before I go away to play pro-ball, I want to grant you your deepest wish."

"What makes you so sure that I won't tell Charlene on you?"

Smiling Derrick leaned close to me and whispered in my ear. "You've been fucking me for years with your eyes. You're not going to miss out on the opportunity to experience the pleasure that I can give you and better yet I bet your pussy is wet right now… just thinking about it."

"It would be better if you came over to my house. My parents have inventory to count at the shop and they won't be home for hours. If we got caught, it would look better if I was at my house. How would I possibly explain to Charlene, why I was at your house? I can always say that you came to my house to wait for her and January, to come back from New York. And most importantly, I didn't want to miss my shoes." I smirked.

"Cool!" Derrick said, as he followed me to my house.

My room was extremely sexy and provocative. Paying attention to every detail, I personally painted my walls lavender and the ceiling and crown moldings white. I had all white furniture to brighten up my room and sheer burgundy and lavender curtains. Always pampering myself, I had burgundy 500 count satin sheets and four extremely large deep burgundy and lavender satin pillows. To add an extra soft touch of elegance, I generously draped sheer burgundy and lavender panels over my full size canopy bed. From a distance, this made it hard to tell if I had an overnight guess. Safer than incents, I would always burn lavender scented oils in my oil burner which was useful in covering up the lingering scent of sex. Experienced in granting one's deepest desire; I felt like I was a Jeanie in a bottle, so when Derrick said that he wanted to grant me my deepest wish… let's just say that I was taken back.

"Well, excuse me as I go take a quick shower. You're welcome to come and join me," I said, in my most inviting voice.

"Now, that's what I'm talking about!" Derrick said, as he quickly followed me to my bathroom.

Before we stepped into the shower, Derrick pulled me close and passionately tongue kissed me for about ten minutes. Afterwards in a deep sexy voice he said, "I'm hungry. I can't wait to taste your goodies."

"Now, that's what I'm talking about." I said, as we burst into laughter.

We stepped into the steamy shower and started to lather up. He washed my cookie while I washed his long, thick, and oh so pretty circumcised dick. Hairless because he shaves down there, I was happy to see how he maintained himself. I kept my cookie in a low triangle cut. It's nature with a twist.

Suddenly, this 6'5" bronze statuesque man picked me up and pinned me against the wall of the shower and started eating me. OMG! I thought. "AH! AH! AH!" I exclaimed as Derrick's sticky tongue slowly massaged my clit from the bottom to the top. "Oooh, oooh Derrick that feels soooo good," I muttered, as I was digging his head game. Devilishly grinning, as he then changed his speed and technique, Derrick became obsessed with the tip of my clit. His massive tongue tortured my clit to no end. "Ahhhhh, ahhhhh, oooooh, oooh, ooh!" I whimpered in pure ecstasy.

Starring at me the entire time, he just drank every drop of my lava juice as he then stuck his elongated tongue inside my kitty cat. "UMMMMMM," he moaned in delight.

Derrick is no joke. Engulfing my entire clit in his mouth, he started finger popping me with his long and oh so talented middle finger. "YEAH, UMMM, YEAH, RIGHT THERE…, AHH, AHHHH, AHHHHHHHH," I exclaimed, as I came all over his face. "Damn, you can eat a mean pussy," I muttered as I tried to come back down to planet Earth.

Smiling, Derrick just grabbed me and started doing what most men do after they eat you. Yeah, you called it. He started tongue kissing me. Wanting to return the favor, I playfully pulled away and started kissing his chest, his stomach, and then bingo, I grabbed his dick. I hungrily licked and gently sucked his plump and juicy balls. Once I had my fill, I s-l-o-w-l-y licked my way up his long and thick rod until I reached his swollen head. Going around and around in circles, my tongue teased his head until it cried a river of pre-cum. "UMMMMMM, you taste good," I purred as I licked along his slit and then sucked every drop. I was about to turn this mother out.

"YEAH…, YEAH…, DON'T STOP," he moaned, as he sampled my head game.

Impassioned, I gagged trying to swallow his dick whole. I love it when a lover keeps themselves up. It makes it so much more enjoyable for both parties. I could tell Derrick was an experienced lover by the way he ate my kitty cat and how after thirty minutes, I still couldn't get him to nut.

He gently took his dick out of my mouth and asked me. "Are you on the pill?"

"Yes…, for three years now."

"Good, now turn around and let me see that tight ass!"

Derrick gently bent me over and slid his thick 9" dick inside of my wet pussy.

"OOOHHHH, AHHHHH!" I moaned, for his dick felt more like eleven inches.

"YEAH… YEAH, back that pretty ass up!" Derrick barked in a deep and sexy voice, as he stroked my nana. Deeper and deeper, in and out, and around and around he went in. "Yeah, oooooh yeah…, you want this dick… don't ya?" He muttered, as he straight punished my puss.

"UMM…, UMM…, AHH YEAH, GIMME…" I cried as he sent my nana to seventh heaven.

A skillful lover, without difficulty, Derrick instantly found my g-spot. I just loved how he held his entire dick inside of me pressed against my g-spot. As the massive vibrations sharpened, I would purposely clamp my pussy muscles around his dick. The intensity was awesome. Too much to bear for both of us; we both yelled, in delight, "AAHHHHHHHHHHHH!"

Damn! I'm slipping. I thought to myself. I've already came twice while he just had his first nut.

"Boo, you got me." Derrick laughingly said, as he pulled out of me. "We need to go to your bedroom so that you can fully feel my magic stick. I bet he can make you see stars," he said, as he quickly freshening up before stepping out of the shower.

"We will see who will be seeing stars. I love it when I am challenged." I said, as I quickly freshened up my honey pot as well.

After we dried off, Derrick picked me up and carried me to my bedroom. He placed me, on my back, in the center of my bed. Derrick climbed on top of me and just inserted his erect dick inside of me. He started fucking me deep and hard like I like it.

"Yeah, yeah," I sighed, as he fucked the shit out of me.

"EAT THAT DICK! EAT THAT DICK!" Derrick yelled, as my pussy instantly drowned his dick. "Oooh, oooh!" He moaned, as he then slowed down to enjoy my hot milky cum all over his dick.

He deeply and slowly fucked me, as he licked my perky nipples. The sound of his dick going in and out of my pussy was intoxicating. I was getting stimulated from three different areas: his tongue licking my nipples, his dick stroking inside of my pussy, and his two fingers vigorously stroking my clit. I started to feel those sharp and intense spasms build up inside of me again, as he continuously worked his fingers on my clit.

"YEAH…YEAH…RIGHT…RIGHT…AHHHHHHHHHH! AHHHHHHHHH," I yelled at the top of my lungs, as I climaxed. Drunk with pleasure, I thought that I was seeing stars.

"YEAH, YEAH, I'M GOING TO MAKE YOU FALL IN LOVE WITH THIS DICK! YOU'RE ALWAYS GOING TO WANT THIS DICK!" Derrick exclaimed, as he then filled my nana with his hot spunk.

I moaned, "Always" as my body started trembling. I realized that he was right. We've been consistently fucking each other for the past seventeen years, even when he got married to his wife Mei-Li.

Derrick, Mei-Li, and I would have ménage a trois.

Yes, you heard me correctly. We would have ménage a trois.

His wife was fine and freaky. Mixed with Chinese and Italian, Mei-Li was 5'3" and weighed 130 in pounds. Her beautifully put together body had a 28D bust line, 23" waist, and 28" hips. Having long, straight, jet black hair that went past her waist, Mei-Li looked more Asian than Italian but you could still see a glimpse of her Italian side with that juicy butt of hers.

She had me in a trance ever since Derrick introduced her to me, and when I ate her I was sold. Mei-Li would squirt into my mouth mint flavored lava juice. Later, I discovered that she would always insert a peppermint depository in her nana a half an hour before she would have sex. She said she likes to consider herself as being a human after dinner mint.

Sold on each other, Mei-Li and I started seeing each other without Derrick six months ago.

Strung out on Mei-Li, Derrick stopped sleeping with me solo and would only hook up with me at the request of his freaky wife. "Monica, I really dig Mei-Li and want our marriage to work. I hope you understand that it has nothing to do with how I feel about you."

WHAT THE FUCK DOES THAT BITCH HAVE OVER ME? I thought to myself. After all the years that I've given Derrick; he just decides to up and outsource on a bitch, marry someone other than Charlene or me. Now, I understand why everybody is upset at the companies who outsource to other countries instead of hiring people from within our country.

She's attractive and all, but to marry her over me? Nah, I'm the original queen-bee. Mei-Li has nothing on me. Derrick should've married me and made Mei-Li his little side piece, not the other way around. I think that I'm getting the short end of the stick. Derrick will live to regret the day that he dissed me.

One night after Mei-Li and I had great sex, she started talking crazy. "I didn't mean to do it but I fell in love with you, Monica. I want to leave Derrick and move to Atlanta to be with you. I want us to get married and have a baby. Derrick doesn't want to have any more children and I want to start a family."

I tried my best to talk that crazy bitch out of it but she wouldn't listen. She was open. How open? Well, you tell me.

Four months ago, Mei-Li found my three month supply of birth control pills and flushed them down the toilet. She wanted me to consider getting artificially inseminated by her brother, so that the baby would look like both of us. I didn't take her seriously until Derrick called me in March upset that Mei-Li wanted a divorce. Wow, talk about show and prove. Mei-Li is either gangster or she's just plain stupid. She got Derrick to marry her and now she wants to divorce him. Personally, I think she's stupid. Then again, I guess she knows that this right HERE is the SHIT.

Derrick needed me to hook up with him to soothe his bruised ego. He believed that Mei-Li must've found another man that could fuck her better than him. Derrick sent his limo to pick me up and whisk me away to his breathe taking estate in Saddle River, New Jersey. He left Mei-Li in LA to give her space. He felt that maybe with some distance between them that she might change her mind.

When I got to Derrick's house, to my surprise, Eddie was there. They were playing pool in Derrick's game room. Eddie dropped by to speak to Derrick about Jasmine. She was pressuring him to get married, again. Eddie smiled and licked his lips as he stared me up and down. "Damn, Monica! I didn't know you two got down like that. Why was I the last to know and can I get down?"

"Now Eddie, what would Jasmine say about that if she heard you?"

Smiling Eddie said, "I was only kidding… Monica. It was just a friendly joke amongst friends."

Derrick and Eddie were drunk as skunks. They drank an entire bottle of Hennessy and were working on their second one.

Derrick in a soft and sexy voice asked, "Baby, am I man enough for you?"

Shocked to hear Derrick talk to me like that in front of Eddie, I answered. "Yes."

Smiling coyly, I leaned over and planted a kiss on his cheek. What can a say, I've been fucking dude since we were in high school. I do have a soft spot for him.

All of a sudden, Derrick pulled my black tights down to my ankles, bent me over the pool table, and started eating me. He licked my kitty cat and tossed my salad. Excited and pleasantly surprised, my kitty betrayed me and got wet. Derrick then started to fuck the hell out of me from behind.

Yes, he started fucking me in front of Eddie.

At first I screamed, "STOP!" Then I screamed, "YES! YES! YES!"

While Derrick was straight fucking me, from the corner of my eye, I saw Eddie jerking off. Eddie's big chocolate cock turned me the fuck on. It reminded me of a Hershey candy bar and I had a sweet tooth, especially for chocolate.

"AHH, AHHH!" I exclaimed.

"I'M CUMMING!" Derrick shouted, as he came inside of me.

"UGHHH," Eddie grunted, as he came on top of Derrick's bear skin rug.

We all started laughing. I took two shots of Hennessy and said, "Let the games begin."

Derrick threw Eddie a condom. "I bet your pussy ass won't last fifteen minutes in her without blowing your top off."

"Word, it's like that! Bet." A smiling Eddie said, as he quickly placed the condom on his fat dick.

He then bent me back over the pool table and started to work. I thought fire was shooting up my ass, for Eddie gently inserted his fat dick into my asshole. Eddie slowly worked his steel rod inside of me. At first I wanted to scream but then it started to feel so good. Eddie was playing with my clit from behind with two of his fingers while he was gently fucking my asshole with his dick.

"UMMMMMM, UMMMMMM!" I moaned.

"Yeah, daddy knows what you like." Eddie muttered, as he pleasured me.

"UMMMMMM, UMMMMMM!" I moaned.

Then as Derrick predicted, Eddie came. How delightful... indeed how delightful?

When I originally moved backed to Jersey City, I missed Atlanta. I missed the weather, the people, and the vibe. In Atlanta, no one really knew me and I liked it that way! When I would introduce myself to people, I would often give them an alias. It was safer that way. See, living in Jersey City, everybody knew everybody. That was the main reason why I left Jersey City in the first place. I wanted to start a new life... in Atlanta, THE BLACK MECCA. I love to party and bullshit. Most of all, I love gettin' that money. And damn, I did my numbers in Atlanta.

Derrick would never visit me in Atlanta. A control freak, he would send a limo for me when he wanted to see me. The limo driver would take me to the airport and then I would get onto his private jet. Derrick was extremely private. Always on center stage, he wanted to keep some aspects of his life personal. He claims to hate the limelight but I know otherwise. He just doesn't want to get caught in his own lies. I can understand that.

I never told my family or friends in Jersey City that in Atlanta, I was an exotic dancer. When the economy took a bad turn, it hit the real estate market like a tsunami. Personable and super sexy, it was easy for me to go from being a realtor to become an exotic dancer. I called myself Tasty... I'll let you guess why. I gave up my apartment and moved in with an exotic dancer named Reindeer. She was called Reindeer because she had a PHAT ASS. As early as I can remember, I've always been torn. I love the look and taste of a woman's body but at the same time, I also love the look and taste of a man's body. What can I say, I'm a peoples' person.

I would often travel back and forth to New Jersey from Georgia. When I was in Jersey, I would either stay at Charlene's place or with my parents. Since Charlene got married, I got the vibe from her husband that I was no longer welcomed. Charlene never said that I couldn't stay at her place but I got the memo. I knew what time it was. Refusing to pay rent anywhere, I decided to move back home with my parents.

That's how shit got started between Chad and I. In Atlanta, I had connects when it came to copping but in Jersey City so much had changed since my younger years that I didn't know who I could trust. So, I called Chad. "Let me cut to the chase, where can a girl get some Lady Snow?"

"Lady Snow, why would I know where to get that?" Chad said laughing.

"Don't fucking play with me mother fucker, you own a bodega in Crown Heights. You know where? I'm not January! You can't fool me." I jokingly said, hoping he could help a sister out.

Now, hysterically laughing, Chad responded. "I think you've been watching too many movies, mami! Hang up the phone and come see me at my loft. I will see what I can do. I can't make any promises but for a friend of January's, I can at least see."

Surprisingly, Chad was a gentleman. "Would you like some wine or something to eat?

"No thank you."

"So, how was Atlanta and why in the earth did you go back to Jersey City of all places? You should've moved to Brooklyn. I could've hooked you up. I'm the man around here."

"Atlanta was great but I got a little home sick. Truth be told, I missed my peoples." I responded, as I licked my lips. "What it do?" I asked, as I wanted to cut out the small talk.

"Oh, I see what you want." Chad said, as he placed a sandwich bag of coke on his glass coffee table.

Smiling like a mutha fucka, I could barely get my question out of my mouth. "How much do you want?"

"Your money is no good here."

"Well, what's good?"

With a devilish smile he said, "You are…?"

I snorted some coke and fucked him all night long. I was so fucked up that I didn't know whether I was coming or going. Damn that was a wild night! Chad is way too cool and freaky for January to keep up with. Whether I would fuck him or not, he would let me cop with no strings attached. Chad needs a hot chick like me to fulfill all of his sexual fantasies. January needs to lose some weight and hang with me and my crew in Atlanta, for a couple of days, before marrying dude. Chad is a ladies man. One woman will never be enough for him unless the one woman was me.

Recently, I bumped into Chad's sexy twin sister Venus while getting a shape-up at his barbershop. Pleasantly surprised, I was happy when she actually spoke to me first. For a long time, I had a secret crush on her. I've tried to hook up with her on a couple of occasions but it didn't pan out. A diehard New York Giants fan, she commented on my outfit. I was wearing a cute little mini dress that was made from a New York Giants football jersey. She thought my dress was dope. I pretended like I was also a diehard fan of the Giants. In truth, not only did I not watch football but the dress didn't even belong to me. I stole it from a stripper in Atlanta named Mercedes. Having the luck of the Irish, I held my own while we talked about football. We exchanged numbers and she promised to call me when she was free.

OMG! This bitch is fine as hell. Venus is handsome like a mutha fucka! She has dreamy hazel eyes, curly black hair, a sexy voice, thick luscious lips, and a muscular body. If she wanted too, she could pick me up with one hand with no problem. Venus is the opposite of Mei-Li. Mei-Li is more like a super model, you know...girly. Venus is street. Venus is hood. I think that I'm attracted to Venus because she's a challenge. She doesn't try to hit on me like everyone else. You know what it is? She's the female version of Derrick, just cockier. I would have the best of both worlds if I got with Venus. Shit, I want her! Now, what is a sister to do? Since I had already fucked her brother, I guess I have no other choice but to first ask for his permission.

"Let me get this straight. You want to know, from me of all people, whether or not you're my sister's type. To put it politely my sister ain't fucking with bitches that get high and smoke. She doesn't get down like that. Now, if I'm not mistaken... don't you do both?"

"I'm getting older and all that drug shit is played out. I don't mind giving it up for Venus. Do you have a problem with me possibly hooking up with her?"

"You ain't my girl! This is America! You're free to fuck whomever you want. Just as long as you remember that you never came to my loft. From this day forth, I'm January's fiancé and nothing else to you. I never fucked you...comprende?"

"I understand."

Chad and I agreed to never sleep with each other again and to keep our little secret tight to the chest, no matter what.

For the past three months, Venus and I have been exclusively seeing each other. Agreeing to take things slow, we're not in a rush to have sex. I told her about my wild past and explained to her that I needed some time to set some shit straight. She said that she understood and told me to take all the time that I needed. On our first date, Venus took me to Cherry Grove, New York located on Fire Island. Cherry Grove is most popular for it being one of the nation's first and oldest lesbian, gay, bi-sexual, and transgender communities. It's an uninhibited party community that has beautiful beaches and enchanted greenery throughout. Gay and free, it's like Greenwich Village on an island. The Grove has no paved roads and the cottages and beach area are only accessible by using a series of wooden boardwalks. I would've never in a million years dreamed of going to such a place, let alone with Venus.

Venus is about two things... making money and her family. She's the truth unlike Derrick the fake! She wants to build with me and only me. I love it! She has even reserved one of her family's private villas for me to stay at for a couple of months.

"Spending some time in the Dominican Republic will help you to understand me better. It will also clear your mind, so that you can return to the states better prepared for the uphill battle that you're about to embark on. People do not like change. People will not believe that you want and deserve better for yourself. I will weather the storm with you as long as you keep it real with me." Venus said lovingly, as she dropped me off at the airport.

"Always baby," I responded, as I started to feel a little emotional. I really need a person like Venus in my life, right now. She won't let anybody harm me. Unlike Derrick, she speaks to me every day. I'm not something to do. I'm her woman. She's far from being a push over like Mei-Li. She keeps me in check. If say or do something that she doesn't like, she lets me know immediately. For the first time in my life, I think that I can whole heartedly try this lesbian thing. I think that I can give up men.

I haven't spoken to the girls in a couple of months. I wanted to call January to tell her about Venus and me but I changed my mind. I will see them all tonight, at the premiere. I'm going to look FABULOUS.

CHAPTER 5

I LOVE CHARLENE, SHE'S JUST NOT EXOTIC ENOUGH-(Derrick)

It has been a blessing and a curse to be the son of Darrell and Angela Johnson. Any and everything that has happened to me in my life can be retraced back to that statement. I was blessed to have talented and famous parents, who gave me my athletic ability and natural charisma. I have had the best of both worlds. As a child I have lived in the states and abroad. My family has lived in Italy, Spain, China, and of course The United States of America. Being fluent in all these languages made me a golden child.

My father has played professional basketball ever since he was eighteen years old. He was twenty years old when he got my mother pregnant and thought that the honorable thing to do was to marry her. Four miscarriages later, my father realized that he could've waited to get married. Both my father and mother would attest to you that they were not in love when they got married. It was clearly lust and money that originally attracted them to each other. My mother was an up and coming actress and my father was the latest and greatest shining star of professional basketball. Against the advice of his family and friends, my father married my mother without a prenuptial agreement and there you have it. It was cheaper to keep her.

As a child my mother's number one priority was to ensure that, as a grown man, I'd be hung like a horse. My mother use to literally suck my dick until I turned six years old. I have vivid memories of her sucking me off. I thought it was normal until I turned ten years old and realized that I have never heard any of my classmates talk about their mother going down on them.

My parents told me not to tell anybody. To hear my father tell it, I was "blessed to have such a thoughtful and loving mother. Most mothers wouldn't care about their son's dick size."

Can you believe these people? They were sexually abusing their son and in their warped minds they were justified because I ended up having a super long and fat dick. Up until I was twelve years old, I got weekly dick inspections to make sure that everything was in order.

A bitch gotta have world class skills to get me off with her head game. That is why I never ask chicks for head. If they go all in I'm with it but most of them don't know what they're doing. I could remember my mother licking her lips and instantly my dick would get rock hard. If that wasn't enough to fuck me up in the head, my father used to take me to Asian massage parlors at the ripe age of twelve.

"Son, I don't want your first piece of pussy to be able to trap you like your mother did me. No son of mine is going to be pussy whipped. I want you to be taught by a professional so that you will be able to handle the peer pressure that is involved when a superstar has sex." My father believed in his warped mind that he was preparing me mentally for my career as professional basketball player. "Groupies are certain to try and latch on to you, son. Fuck them mind, body, and soul. Fuck their minds with your smooth talk, fuck their bodies with your tongue, fingers, and your dick, and most of all give them an expensive gift that will leave them with a pleasant memory and forever fuck their soul. If you follow my advice to a tee, you will not get any loose lips or worse lawsuits."

These women use to take turns on turning me out. At twelve years old, I was 6'1" and weighed approximately 200 pounds. I had facial hair and a deep voice. I could reasonably pass for being eighteen. Because of my sick parents, I was groomed to be a super freak and a super freak I was. These women would let me do whatever I wanted to do to them. I fucked their mouths, breasts, pussies, and asses. We used hot oil, wax, warm milk, honey, chocolate syrup, whip cream, cherries, bananas, ice, whips, handcuffs, feathers, masks, and etc. I was living foul and I liked it.

So when my family and I returned to the states to play basketball at Saint Mary's High School, I was thrown back…

…I was thrown way back when I met and fell in love with Charlene Jones. Unlike my parents Charlene and I shared real love. Unlike my parents Charlene was nurturing, supportive, loyal, trust worthy, bold, honest, beautiful inside and out, smart as a whip, and unselfish. My parents represented the total opposite. They were child molesters, liars, cheaters, morally ugly, and selfish. That's why I purposely got Charlene pregnant. She represented everything that I wanted in a mate and in the mother of my child.

Unlike my father, I was first in love with Charlene. I wanted Charlene not just any random chick to be the mother of my child. I wanted my child to have a real mother and not a surrogate. Just because you give birth to a child, it doesn't make you a mother. A real mother would've never allowed what my mother did to me to have happened.

Charlene was a lady in the streets but a freak between the sheets. She was passionate about life and loved her family and friends. She made me feel like I was invincible and that I could conquer the world. I didn't marry her for lack of love. I didn't marry Charlene because after having a childhood like I had… she just wasn't exotic enough.

I would've cheated on her. Charlene deserves to have a faithful husband. I knew I couldn't be that for her. Once Charlene told me that she was pregnant, we tried for three years to have a long distant relationship. She wanted to finish college before moving to LA and I wanted her to stay in Jersey City with her father and girlfriends.

My parents were constantly pressuring me to marry Charlene, especially my father. "Son, Charlene is a good girl and she deserves to be titled as being your wife and not just your baby mama. Trust me, I wouldn't steer you wrong."

Though they were right, I did the opposite because the advice came from them. I never told anyone about what they did to me when I was growing up. There were times when I considered telling Charlene, but she loved them dearly and I didn't want to change her opinion of them. I would just tell her that Destiny wasn't allowed to spend the night at my parents' house without her presence. You never know what those child molesters were capable of doing. I believe if I had told Charlene the truth about my parents then maybe we could've made it. I realized too late that I could never live a normal life. I was a product of my parents, a slave to the flesh.

Me being the man that I am, I naturally gravitated towards my own kind. Monica Freeman is my fuckin twin. She's fuckin freaky as hell! Unfortunately, she's Charlene's best friend. She ain't the type of bitch that you marry or have kids with but she's a beast in bed. She's a creative and passionate play thing. In a sick twisted way, she reminds me of my mother. Both Monica and my mother are beautiful and fashionable. However those aren't the only two traits they share, I ain't saying that they're gold diggers but well you know the rest. That's why I make sure that I hit both of them off. You know… keep them happy no problems.

If Monica was smart she would've taken all of the money that I have given her over the years and bought herself a condo, in Atlanta or in Jersey City. She's not as savvy as Charlene. Charlene plays it smart with me. She doesn't ask me for anything. She knows that I got her back. My mother and Monica believe that only a squeaky wheel gets oiled. If they really knew me like Charlene, they would know that I am like my father. I am always going to do the honorable thing. Other than marriage, I did right by Charlene. Charlene and Destiny are set for life.

Charlene and I were still sleeping together until I married Mei-Li. Part of me wanted her to be like Monica and just go with the flow. The other part of me respected her even more when she told me that she could no longer sleep with me because I was married. My parents had always hoped that I would marry Charlene. They thought that I needed some time to get some more shit out of my system before I could settle down. Deep down, I also thought that someday that I would get it together and marry Charlene. Charlene and Destiny are my world. I would kill somebody over my girls.

Destiny is smart and beautiful like her mommy. Charlene has done an excellent job with shaping her into a lovely young lady. I didn't want her innocence robbed from her like mine was. So I stayed crisscrossing the country to stay close to her. To insure that I stayed an influential figure in Destiny's life, during my off season I would reside at my New Jersey mansion. Destiny and Charlene had their own rooms and would stay over from time to time. When I got traded to the Los Angeles Lakers in 1996, I began to spend more time in LA but still managed to find time for my baby girl.

The Lakers secured a bunch of young talent that year and didn't know quite what to do with me. I went from being a starter with the Clippers to a bench warmer with the Lakers. I was devastated. Averaging 15 points off the bench, I was determined to prove that I had game. I finally got my chance to shine in my 1998-99 season when I became a starter, averaging 23 points per game. I busted my ass to become a starter and it was only the tip of the iceberg. When we won the 2000 NBA Championship, for the first time in my professional basketball career, I was humbled. I was in love again with the game and didn't want to let go of this feeling. When we won the 2001 and 2002 NBA Championships, I helped to secure the franchises' its first "three-peat," I surpassed my parents' expectations and became an Icon.

My parents were sweating me big time and I could do no wrong until I introduced them to Mei-Li. They loved Charlene and refused to give Mei-Li a chance. If my parents would've shown some remorse for fucking my head up during my childhood, maybe I would've been able to move past the bullshit and marry Charlene. They didn't and I'm not, so why are they so shocked that I want to marry Mei-Li?

They even refused to attend my wedding. "We're not going to stand by and watch you make the biggest mistake of your life!"

"Mei-Li is a gold digging whore and she's going to ruin your life!" My mother shouted, as she pleaded with me to call off the wedding.

Can you believe it? My father actually cut me out of his will.

"I see that all my work was in vain. You can lead a horse to water but you can't make it drink. Son, I truly feel sorry for you. You're a fool for not marrying Charlene." My father said, as he shook his head side to side in disbelief.

My father has some balls when not only did he not marry for love; he introduced me to a world of perversion! I haven't spoken to my parents since the wedding. Go figure, they want to wait until I was an adult to act like real parents.

Mei-Li is exotic as hell! She was working at the ad firm I had hired to market and promote my sports bars. She played hard to get but after six months of chasing her, she finally agreed to let me take her out on a dinner date. She acted like she didn't even know that I played basketball for the Lakers until she was assigned to my project.

"Personally, I think that you're overrated as one of the greatest basketball players since Jordan. You're good…just not the greatest."

"Ouch, so I take it that you're not impressed by my stats. What does one have to do to impress you?"

"You have to find that out on your own. If I made it that easy…I wouldn't be worth the chase."

Mei-Li was beautiful, smart, and fiery. She had a pleasant disposition and was always optimistic and smiling. She reminded me a lot of Charlene, just more exotic. I threw a dinner party to introduce Mei-Li to my family and friends. Everybody seemed to like her, except my parents, who told her so to her face and then proceeded to question her true intentions by me. My mother actually slapped Mei-Li and called her a whore and an opportunist. Embarrassed, I threw my parents out of my house and apologized to Mei-Li and my guests. In 2004, after knowing Mei-Li for only eight months, we got married.

Unlike my father when he married my mother, I had my attorneys draw up an iron clad prenuptial agreement. Before any planning of a wedding could take place Mei-Li's attorneys had to first approve the final draft. Like I said before Mei-Li was smart and beautiful and reminded me a lot of Charlene, but Mei-Li was no Charlene that's why I had her sign a pre-nup. I would've never asked Charlene to sign such an agreement if we had gotten married because Charlene and I understand each other. To have someone in your life that truly gets you is priceless. Charlene knows no matter what that I got her back. She never took me to court over Destiny and loved me enough to give me my baby girl. Most chicks would've threatened to have an abortion if I didn't marry them or they would've taken me straight to the cleaners. Charlene did neither and I will always love and respect her for that.

Eddie Montgomery is not just my best friend, he's my brother. Eddie can be a play fiend at times but he is harmless. He makes me laugh and is the only man that I would trust around my girls. Most men are not to be trusted around your woman. When a man wants to get at you he goes after your woman. Women just don't understand that men look at them as chess pieces. The best way to get checkmate is by sleeping with your boy's woman. So ladies, when your man's so called best friend comes on to you; it's more about the power play between him and your man than it is about you being so irresistible. If he valued his friendship with your man, he wouldn't have even thought about stepping to you in the first place.

It's hard to find someone who can put up with my ego and keep it moving. I know I've got a BIG EGO. Eddie is my peeps and knows everything about me, except for my relationship with my parents. Eddie and I have shared drinks, women, and goals. We just don't do the advice thing very well. I can't see myself taking woman advice from a man who doesn't want for himself. Jasmine has always been the driving force behind him. He's just too damn drunk to see that Jasmine has stood by him and has given him three beautiful children. He needs to marry her before it is too late.

When it comes to describing Mei-Li, the term exotic couldn't be more appropriate. Mei-Li is breath taking. Mei-Li is what happens when you take two cultures and blend them together in harmony. Mixed with Chinese and Italian descent, Mei-Li has brown almond shaped bedroom eyes that needless to say… beckoned you to come and see about her. Her long silky jet black hair went past her 23" waist as to invite you to look at her voluptuous bottom, which was perfectly shaped like an upside down heart. That's why when I met Mei-Li I knew that I couldn't let her get away.

Head over heels and intoxicated by her beauty, I remember the first time I hit that. I was walking around as if I was high on drugs for days after tapping that sweet ass. You women tickle me with all your game playing, though. You know you want to get a nut off just like us. Mei-Li made me wait six months to take her out on a dinner but gave up the goodies by the end of that same dinner date. Yeah, blame it on the alcohol.

When I picked her up in my black stretch it was written all over her face that I was going to hit it. I knew she had to be a closet freak. She tried too hard to play like she wasn't interested. With her hair pinned to her left side, Mei-Li wore a red freakum dress and some 4" red stilettos. It was serious. I could see her nipples standing at attention because she wore no bra. Mei-Li's 130 pounds hung on her petite 5'3" frame beautifully. She made the dress instead of the dress making her. Her outfit was screaming take me but I played it cool. I am a gentleman, ya heard.

I temporarily closed my Los Angeles sushi restaurant that night for our date. Dimly lit with vanilla scented candles, the restaurant was filled with white lilies and roses. To further set the mood for romance, I had a violinist play classical music all night long. (I did my research and found out that she played the violin.)

"I'm truly impressed. I know that you call yourself the truth but I thought that you were just tooting your own horn. I had no idea that you were actually telling the truth."

"I was hoping that you'd be doing the tooting." I laughingly said, as I poured her a glass of wine.

"Well, I'm not familiar with the tune." Mei-Li responded, as we both took a sip of our wine and smiled.

"I'm sure that I could teach it to you."

"I bet you could," she said licking her lips.

After our delicious meal, I offered to fly her to Las Vegas on my private jet to go dancing.

She declined and said in a sexy voice, "I'd rather go over to your condo for a night cap." As soon as we entered my condo, she laughingly said to me, "You better not be a dial a joke."

I responded, "I'm a professional you're in good hands with Mr. Johnson."

I picked her up, carried her to my master suite and placed her on my enormous custom made bed. Being 6'5", custom was the only way to go for comfort. Decked out in gold and black my suite was tastefully furnished and laid out from floor to ceiling. I had a black marbled Jacuzzi in the right corner of the room and a black marbled fire place at in the other side of the room. With two 60" and three 42" flat screen televisions mounted throughout the room with surround sound, I had a hidden video system set up to video tape any and every sex act that took place in my bedroom and/or in my bathroom. I wasn't about to fall victim to some bitch screaming rape. I've heard of guys being caught up in that situation, it's not a good look.

As Mei-Li dress dropped to the floor, I thought I died and went to heaven.

Seductively she asked me, "Do you mind if I take a quick shower?"

"Of course not," I replied, "as long as I can join you..."

She agreed and we showered together in my massive frameless glass shower. I was a gentleman, I didn't touch her. To tell you the truth, I was actually nervous. I think other than Charlene this has been the closest I've come into contact with marriage material in years. I adored everything about her. Her walk, her talk, her smell, her everything, and I wasn't ashamed to admit it. When we got out of the shower and dried off, Mei-Li wrapped herself in a plush thick towel as I went about pouring us some more wine.

"Would you care for a massage?" I asked, as she sipped her wine.

"Yes, I adore massages if they are done correctly."

"Don't worry, like I told you before I'm a professional. You're in good hands." Now, let the games begin, I thought to myself as I licked my lips with anticipation.

Mei-Li lying on her stomach looked heavenly as I reached for the bottle of oil. I poured the oil in my hands and warmed it up before I began applying it to her flawless skin. She moaned as I expertly massaged the oil into her shoulders. With precision, working my way down towards her lower back, I gently kneaded her muscles to relax her even further before I made my tender assault on her ass and legs. Her moans filled the room, as she oozed into another dimension. I am a patient lover and all I wanted was for her to loosen up so that she could feel every inch of her body being flooded with exquisite pleasure.

Turning her onto her back, I focused on her perky breasts and her pretty stiff nipples before sliding my hands down her smooth flat stomach to greet her shapely thighs. Soft whimpers escaped her pouty lips while I looked to indulge another fetish of mine. Grabbing her perfectly manicured size 5's I began to suck and lick on her toes. I had Mei-Li exactly where I wanted her, in the palm of my hand.

Then I parted her legs to see her pearl tongue standing proudly. It was adorable. Totally bald, her pussy was already wet. I lashed my serpent tongue back and forth across her stiff clit. As she squirted into my mouth, I swallowed every drop. "UMMMMMMMM," her juices tasted like strawberries. Greedily, I drank all of her juices then began licking her clit in circles.

"OH MY GOD...UMMMMMM...OOOOOH," whimpering and trembling, Mei-Li moaned in ecstasy. "AHH...AHH ...AHHHHHHHHH!" Mei-Li roared, as she climaxed.

My nasty ass drank up everything that she gave me and then I started my assault all over again. After she reached her second climax, I put a condom on my rock hard dick and mounted her. I didn't want her to do anything. I just wanted her to enjoy herself as I worked my magic stick in and out of her creamy pussy. Hearing her moan and groan, it reminded me of the women at the massage parlors. I couldn't help but make the correlation. I was in loooove!

I stroked her for hours and then I pretended that she made me tired. She had experienced at least three orgasms before I took it down. I didn't want to reveal all of my tricks. I just wanted to give her a little taste to make her want to come back for some more. I had to show some dick control. My mission wasn't to get off. My mission was to capture my future wife.

Being the freak that she was, I wasn't at all surprised when Mei-Li suggested that we invite Monica to join us in our sexual-escapades. A month after our wedding, Mei-Li revealed to me that she had always been bi-curious. She also admitted to me that she was attracted to Monica. Excited like a kid in a candy store, I confessed to Mei-Li that I had slept with Monica in the past and that she would probably be down. Ever since that day, five years ago, the three of us have been having awesome threesomes.

Six months ago, I noticed a sudden change in Mei-Li. She seemed distracted. I expected after five years of marriage that there would be some changes but this wasn't one of them. The closer I got to retirement, the more she wanted to work. I suspected she had another nigga. It would serve me right, considering all the hearts that I have broken over the years. It was becoming clear that something was on Mei-Li's mind. She could often be found staring at a wall lost in thought. Then she hit me with a low blow while we were lying in bed one night.

"I want to have a baby."

"I told you before we got married that I didn't want any more children. It was even stipulated within the pre-nup that you signed. You not only understood but you accepted my decision. Why the sudden change of heart?"

"Can't I just have a change of heart?"

"No! You signed away that option for more money. No one twisted your arm."

"Well, if you really love me like you say that you love me, then you would change your mind."

"LOVE HAS NOTHING TO DO WITH THIS! Not only did you fuckin agree to the no baby clause, you said that you were happy about it because you didn't want to mess around and get fat trying to have a baby. WHAT THE FUCK IS REALLY GOING ON MEI-LI? IS THERE ANOTHER MAN?"

"I HAVE THE RIGHT TO CHANGE MY MIND! I WANT TO HAVE A BABY!" She yelled, as she stormed out of the room, while attempting to make a phone call on her cellphone.

I guess she called her attorney because she came back into the bedroom and apologized. The crazy bitch even wanted to have sex. I told her that I had to get up early in the morning for a business trip and rolled my ass over. I went the fuck to sleep. You can call me a sweet bitch if you want to but after that performance that crazy bitch gave, I was not about to fuck her.

A couple of months went by and then I got the shock of my life. I was served papers. Mei-Li wanted a divorce. Before I said or did anything that I would regret, I just left Los Angeles and went to stay at my Saddle River estate. She might change her mind, I thought to myself. If Mei-Li really wants me to believe that she wants a divorce because she wants a baby, then she got me mistaken for a fool. I know it has to be over another lover and if so she's stupid. Mei-Li should know me enough by now to know that she could keep her lover and still be with me. All she has to do is act like she knows who comes first… me. My father prepared me well. It's cheaper to keep her. Thanks dad.

CHAPTER 6

HIT IT AND QUIT IT-(Mei-Li)

My name is Mei-Li Johnson. I'm currently the wife of NBA legend Derrick "The Truth" Johnson. I work for a prestigious advertisement and marketing firm in Los Angeles, California. I was born and raised in Beverly Hills. My parents are Mingzhu and Salvatore Giovani. My mother runs a private practice as a psychologist while my father is one of the most successful plastic surgeons in LA. My thirty-five year old single brother, Sal Jr., works with my father. He looks identical to our father while I favor our mother. Five years younger than my brother, I am fluent in Italian, Mandarin, and in English. An overachiever, I will be the first to admit that I can be extremely ruthless when going after something that I want. I believe in making a plan and executing it with precision. There is no room for failure.

A stern disciplinarian, my mother was strict while my father spoiled me. I was his cute little creation. He instilled within me that it gets no better than me. He was always showing me off to his friends and colleagues. My mother felt that I lacked motivation and felt that it was her job to literally whip me into shape. She used to tear my butt up. I think deep down she was jealous of the fact that I was prettier than her.

Slightly overweight by Hollywood standards, my mother was always on a diet. She was 5'3" and weighed 150 pounds. Always doing something to alter herself to keep up with the Hollywood lifestyle, my mother went and got breast implants, regular Botox treatments, and liposuctions. She made her cup size go from a 32B to a 32DD. She even permed and dyed her long jet black hair honey blonde. I think she's the one that needs to be talking to someone.

Because of her chosen profession my mother thought that she knew

63

everything. You couldn't tell her that she didn't have the inside track on what people were thinking. She was always making shallow accusations.

Clearly her favorite, my mother let Sal Jr. dictate the minute details of his life while she sought to control my every move. I could remember how she enrolled Sal Jr. into singing and ballroom dancing classes while I was stuck with violin lessons which were something I always hated. My mother never asked me, what did I want to do? She felt that because she was a psychologist she was better equipped to make my decisions for me. Plain and simple, she just didn't care about what I wanted to do. Clearly, this is an example of how a little book knowledge can go to somebody's head.

Now, my father was a character. Handsome and charming, he was very popular with the ladies. He was always telling jokes, singing, and dancing. My father was 5'10" and weighed 175 pounds. Fit, you could always find my father working out at the gym. Pale in complexion, my father had shoulder length, curly black hair that he would wear slicked back with some gel and mousse.

Besides ballroom dancing, my parents really loved gambling in Vegas. They would travel to Vegas weekly to lose a shit load of money. You would always hear them arguing about how bad a poker player my father was. Anything that my father wanted to do, my mother would allow him to do. It wasn't unusual for him to get thousands of dollars in markers. Now, can anybody please explain this to me? How does a person, who thinks that they can read minds, walk around acting like they don't have a mind of their own?

My relationship, with my parents for the past couple of years, has been strained because I married outside of the "preferred" races. (You know Italian, Caucasian, and Chinese men.) I, instead, chose to marry Derrick, an African American.

Old fashioned my parents argued, "We don't like this ball player for you. We wanted a "traditional" son- in- law like a doctor or a lawyer."

On the day of my wedding, my mother expressed her disappointment by wearing a black veil. "You better not give me any grandchildren. I will disown them."

"I wouldn't mind grandchildren if they favored our side of the family. Other than that; I agree with your mother." My father said as if I had the power to control how my child would look.

Frankly, coming from two highly educated people, they didn't make any sense to me. Derrick net worth is twenty times that of my parents. Does it really matter that he's an African American and played basketball? He's filthy rich!

Fortunately, I had the blessings of my brother. "I can tell that he genuinely cares for you. You two make a cute couple. I say go for it. Money and good looks, I wish I could be so lucky."

Hmm, something tells me that my brother wishes that he had Derrick for himself. I mean, I have never seen my brother bring home a chick to meet our parents before. He claims that he's too busy at work to have a social life. Well, I know my mother is happy about that. As long as he doesn't have a significant other, her precious son will stay home longer

I practically live in a gym, I have to do something to keep my money making figure. Only the finest designer threads touch my back and my travel habits would put Columbus to shame. I'm a bi-sexual woman who actually preferred women to men before meeting Derrick. Up until then, I lived a secret double life so not to widen the relations between my parents and me. I had a typical college life. I experimented with drugs and sex like everybody else. Regrettably, I even worked as an exclusive escort for awhile to support my heavy drug habit. That is how I had originally met and slept with Derrick's parents. When Mr. and Mrs. Johnson would visit Los Angeles they would contact my agency, specifically requesting for me. So when they saw that their precious son was going to marry me, they flipped the fuck out. They even offered to pay me two million dollars to leave Derrick alone. I rejected the offer because Derrick was worth a whole lot more. And besides, I started to like the idea of being married to a rich and famous basketball player. Wouldn't you?

No matter where I went people wanted to get next to me because I was married to Derrick Johnson. It was the best drug that I have ever had in my life…, FAME. Fame can make you lose sight of reality. It can make you think that anything else wasn't worth living for. Once my parents got a taste of the FAME that came from being apart of Derrick's inner circle, they were hooked. They started inviting us to join them on vacation and to family gatherings. They were even pressuring me to start a family. My mom and I even started to hang out together and go out on shopping sprees. Who would've thought? We were actually acting like we liked each other…even worse like we loved each other.

I like dick but I knew that I loved pussy more. So when Derrick and I started doing ménage a trois with Monica, I was caught in my own web of deceit. I wanted Monica all to myself. I realized just how deep my feelings were for her when I almost had to kick somebody's ass over her, at a bar in the village. I walked into the bar and saw this chick hanging all over Monica. "Bitch step away from my girl!" I shouted, as I was about to have my first real fight.

Monica and the girl turned around to face me and instantly started to laugh.

Once I calmed down, I found out that the girl knew Monica from Atlanta. Her name was GiGi. Because of the noise in the crowded bar, GiGi had to lean in close to Monica which I mistook for something else. She was telling Monica about some stripping gig that she had lined up in the city.

"Slow down rocky," Monica playfully said, as they cracked up laughing at me.

"Okay, you want to laugh at me. I guess you don't want the surprise that I bought for you?" I said, as I dangled a little box in front of her face.

"I'm sorry baby, I want it! I want it!" She eagerly exclaimed, reaching out both hands for it.

"Then close your eyes and count to three." I said, as I then placed a two karat princess cut diamond on her ring finger. "Now, open your eyes."

"I love it baby! It's beautiful!"

"It's a promise ring. As long as you wear my ring, you promise to be true to me."

"I promise to be true to you, as long as you will have me." Monica declared, as she then passionately kissed me in front of GiGi.

We commenced getting toasted.

Then GiGi reached into her purse and pulled out some E pills, "Now the party can really started."

We were fucked up. GiGi invited us to stay at her motel until we came down from our high. The motel was located around the corner from the bar. It was a dump but it at least had a clean full size bed and bathroom. I had to piss like a race horse. All that I could remember about the room was that it had some tacky orange and black striped wallpaper.

I was so high, so hot, and so fucking horny! I had to take a cold shower to try and cool off.

Once out of the shower, with only a towel wrapped around me, Monica proceeded to tie me up to the bed post while she whispered in my ear, "Enjoy the show baby."

Piece by piece, Monica and GiGi started taking off their clothes. Once naked, they proceeded to kiss and lick me all over my body.

"OOOOH, OOOH BABY," I sighed, as their plush lips and sticky tongues titillated my body to no end. As I felt my pussy throbbing and my sensitive nipples get teased, all I could do was cry out in ecstasy. I don't know if it was the combination of the alcohol and pills or the fact that they were turning me out, all I know is that I didn't want them to stop. "UMMM BABY!" I sighed, as Monica climbed up on top of me and sat her pussy on my face. Trying my best to please my baby; her crazy ass girlfriend started eating me out. What the fuck was this girl doing? I thought to myself, as I licked on Monica's stiff clit.

"UMMMMM, AHHHHHH," Monica purred.

"UMMMM…yummy…yummy," GiGi moaned, as she buried her mouth even further into my muff.

This bitch even put her tongue inside my asshole. I just met this bitch! What the fuck was I doing? While these thoughts coursed through my mind, I started to go into convulsions. Wailing at the top off my lungs, "AHHHHHHH, AHHHHHH," I was having an orgasm. The more I screamed the faster and the harder GiGi tongued my clit. "STOP, STOP I BEG YOU!" I pleaded, as she continued to lick and suck on my pussy.

Fully engulfed in lust, all I could do was take it out on Monica. I thrashed her clit with a fury of licks.

"YEAH BABY…YEAH BABY…RIGHT…RIGHT…AHHHHHHH, AHHHHHHH!" Monica howled as she exploded.

Once Monica untied me, I reached inside my purse for my strap-on. I'm always prepared when I plan to see my Monica. Hot blooded, she's always ready. As I bent Monica over and inserted my dildo inside of her, GiGi started to lick my nipples. I wanted to tell her to stop but it felt so damn good. As her tongue sent tingly sensations throughout my body, I started to slam dick Monica. Deeper and deeper, I just hammered her pussy.

"HARDER! HARDER!" Monica shouted.

The deeper I fucked Monica the faster GiGi would lick my nipples. Then she started sucking them while she rubbed her clit with her right hand. Moaning and groaning, GiGi would twirl her hips around and around as she sent shivers down my spine. This bitch was turning me the fuck on.

At the same time, all three of us yelled, "AHHHHHHHHHH, AHHHHHHHHHH!" We simultaneously reached our climax.

Monica and I plopped onto the bed while GiGi retreated into the bathroom to take a shower.

"Did you enjoy yourself baby?" Monica asked innocently.

"Yes, I enjoyed myself but how well do you know this GiGi chick?"

"I never met her before a day in my life. I set it up through this escort agency."

"ARE YOU CRAZY?"

"Yeah, I'm crazy for you." Monica responded as she couldn't help herself from laughing at me. "If you could've seen the expression on your face when GiGi started to eat you, it was priceless. That is why I had to tie your fast behind up. I knew that you wouldn't be down to get with a stranger. You could be such a herb at times."

If Monica only knew, I chuckled to myself.

Monica and I shared a nasty coke habit that started to get out of hand. The habit was so nasty that Derrick started drilling me with questions. He said that he could tell that something was bothering me. Yeah, something was bothering me alright, I wanted to tell him. I needed some more coke and I was tired of his ass. I was tired of hiding my love for Monica! Monica and I would have kinky cocaine fueled sex. We were insatiable. I really knew that things were getting out of control when Monica stole some money from her roommate. If I'm not mistaken, I think her name was Reindeer.

"The bitch owes me this money!" Monica screamed at me from the top of her lungs.

We argued all night long. "Monica if you need some money, I can give it to you."

"This has nothing to do with you! That bitch had this coming. She ripped out a couple of pages from my black book. She stole from me and I expect to be compensated for my loss. You wouldn't understand."

She was right. I didn't understand. After she calmed down, we agreed that we needed to split up for awhile. I begged Monica to get as far away from Atlanta as she could before Reindeer realized that her money was gone. That's why Monica left Atlanta in such a rush and headed back to Jersey City. We agreed that we were both moving way too fast and needed some time apart to get clean. We needed to reclaim our lives and to get focused. Our love was the real thing. So, we promised each other that we would start a family together once things settled down with my divorce.

When I originally got married to Derrick, I knew I had to devote at least five years to our marriage. I signed a pre-nup for a guaranteed 10 million dollars if I stayed married to him for at least five years. I have reached my five year mark and I'm not happy with Derrick anymore. I want out! Not only do I want out but I also want more money to get out. Derrick has just retired and is about to blow up as a sports caster on a popular cable network. I want to get some of that money. I'm not going to stay with Derrick and continue to be his little Asian sex toy. I want more for myself. By no means am I trying to give the wrong impression of Derrick. We got along. He was a good husband and I did learn to love him. If we never invited Monica into our bedroom; who knows, we could've made it. However, we did and now I just want my money. I don't want to share Monica with Derrick anymore, let alone anyone else. Between the money that I make from my job and will receive from my divorce settlement, we will be set for life.

Can you believe that my parents are planning to disown me if I go through with this divorce? They told me that I was stupid and needed to rethink my decision. My parents have some nerve. They were angry with me when I married the man and now they're angry with me because I want to divorce the man. There is no pleasing them!

Once my divorce from Derrick is final I plan on taking my relationship with Monica to the next level. The only glitch I see with that is Monica. I'm not allowing her to have any more dealings with Derrick. I don't care how long she has known him I want him out of the picture. We can't start our new life together with Mr. Ego in the mix. Recently, I accepted a promotion in San Francisco so that we could move and have a fresh start together. I plan to make her my wife. Yeah, I like the sound of that. Once we settle down in our new town I want Monica to get artificially inseminated with my brother's semen so that our baby could look like both of us. I get so excited just thinking about it. I have it all mapped out, all I need is for Monica to actually say YES!

It's been four long months since I've seen her. We Skype each other but that's it. Until the divorce is final we have to keep our relationship on the low. Derrick's lawyers are playing hardball with my lawyers and are probably having me tailed. When the time is right I'm going to go to Jersey to tell Monica, in my Alicia Keys voice, "If you ask me, I'm ready."

CHAPTER 7

I JUST DON'T WANT TO DO RIGHT-(Eddie)

I've tried all of my life not to make the same mistakes my parents made, yet what did I do? I repeated some of theirs and made a few of my own. I walk around acting like I'm single and free when I damn well know that I'm actually very much taken. I love the family life that I've built with Jasmine and our three children. It's just that the activities that I do behind closed doors totally undermine all that I've built. I sure am a fuck up just like my father.

The highest grade level that my father completed was 12th grade, so I decided to set the bar higher for my brothers and got my associate degree in business, at Hudson County Community College. I knew that my true passion was in cars and not in the corporate world. I liked wearing suits and making money; therefore I thought those two things would sustain me. I realized too late that I hated the corporate life and had a passion for working with cars, period. What a waste of time and money. I could've gone straight to automotive school instead of taking my little detour. I've been working in my uncle's garage ever since I could hold a wrench. I didn't need a degree in business to tell me that I loved fixing cars.

When my father says he's proud of me I have mixed feeling. I still hold some resentment towards him for chasing away my mother with his cheating ways and abusive behavior, yet I'm glad that I had my father because obviously I had a shitty mother. I mean that bitch just up and bounced on us and never looked back. Either way you look at it, I just can't get a break.

My father drinks too much beer and I drink too much Hennessy. My father shoots dice and plays the street numbers while I like to play the lottery, poker, spades, and pity pat. My father is a womanizer and I am a womanizer. My father created five children that I know of and I have created three children that I know of. The only thing that I've done right is that I've chosen Jasmine to be the mother of my children. Unlike my three dollar bill mother, Jasmine would never abandon our children. She has built her life around the children and me.

For years I felt conflicted about my father with his selfish ways yet I've come to admire him for having the courage to do him. Now, having a family of my own, I understand what my father was going through. Just like me, he couldn't resist all the attention that the ladies were giving him. He loved the ladies and his family. He just couldn't handle both because his guilt would lead him to beat and mistreat my mother. I could never imagine myself raising my hand to hit my Jasmine. She's my cuddy. We practically grew up together. Jasmine is only 5'3" and weighs approximately 146 pounds. I'm 5'9" and I weigh 230 pounds. We're entirely in two different weight classes. I can keep her little ass in check without beating on her. I've learned firsthand that beating on a woman can get you incarcerated and/or cause you to lose your woman, it's not worth it.

My father was smooth. He hypnotized women with his sense of style and was the only black man that I knew in the hood who subscribed to GQ magazine. At first look, you wouldn't have guessed it. Especially, being that my father worked around cars all day long. At the garage, my father could always be found covered in motor oil, wearing a pair of raggedy overalls with an old pair of boots. Off duty, my father would dress his ass off. He especially loved wearing suits. Dressed to impress, my father would drive around in his old white Cadillac Coupe Deville.

My father would always stress to my brothers and I about appearances. "Women look down on a brotha when he looks dingy all the time. They assume that he doesn't have a job or that he's a bum. Working as a mechanic is how I pay my bills; it doesn't make or define me, the man. It's an honest living and it takes a lot of knowledge and patience to be a mechanic. You see how your uncle always looks filthy? Whether he was on or off duty from the garage, he always looks stank. He's a fool. I better never catch any of you following behind that fool!"

So fresh and so clean, clean… My father couldn't keep the bitches off of him. Employed, well groomed, and singlehandedly raising five sons on his own, my father was a hot commodity. He was dark in complexion and kept a tight afro. Muscularly built, he was 5'9" and weighed 200 pounds. My father was a low budget Billy Dee Williams. I believe that I got my work ethic and my sense of style from my father. I definitely got my love for cars from him.

No matter how late, my brothers and I use to wait for my father to get home from one of his late night trysts. He would whip us up something good to eat in the kitchen and talk to us about life. We would play the dozens and watch a little television. He would often encourage us to dare to be whatever we wanted to be. "Live life with no regrets! I regret that I didn't try my own luck at having my own garage. Instead, I settled for working for your stingy uncle. I guess in the end that I was the fool and your uncle was actually the smart one."

Now, when it comes to my mother…well, I don't have any respect for that bitch! How do you just abandon your five boys with a man that you felt "terrorized" you and never look back? She could've at least kept in contact with one of us. She didn't even give my father some financial support. If the roles were reversed, I bet she would've sent child support after his ass. That bitch just washed her hands of us and probably said to herself good- riddance. The youngest, Rodney was eight years old, Phillip was nine years old, the twins Robert and Ricky were eleven years old, and being the eldest I was fifteen years old when my mother left. If it wasn't for the generosity of Jasmine and her grandmother, Ms. Wright, I don't know what would've become of me. When I graduated from high school, I moved in with them. Ms. Wright didn't charge me any rent and refused to take any money from me when I would offer her some. This helped me as I went to college and as I worked two part-time jobs to financially help my father raise my little brothers.

And where the hell was Joanne Montgomery, mother of five boys? … Nowhere to be found.

Since Jasmine and I moved our family to Avenel, New Jersey two years ago, surprisingly I have been a good boy. All I do now is run my very own detailing shop/garage, help raise my three beautiful children, and tend to their mother my childhood sweetheart. I would be the first to admit that I have dogged Jasmine something terrible over the past twenty-five years. Now, I'm a changed man. Well, I was up until three months ago when I hung out with my best friend Derrick, at his Saddle River, New Jersey estate. I was doing pretty well, considering. Shit, since freshman year in high school all we did was drink hard, party, gamble, and fuck bitches. No drugs were allowed. We were athletes, young guns, and everyone wanted a piece of us. We were ghetto superstars.

At the end of our senior year in high school, Derrick knocked up Charlene. They had a beautiful baby girl named Destiny. Three years later, Jasmine gave birth to our first son, Eddie Jr. Two years after that Jasmine gave birth to Eddie III and then two years after that, Jasmine gave birth to our little pumpkin Jackie. By the age of twenty-five, Jasmine and I had three children. Feeling trapped, I started drinking, gambling, and sexing even harder than I ever did when I was in high school. I just felt overwhelmed with Jasmine constantly asking me about when we were going to get married. I felt my world was caving in all around me. PSYCH! I had you going for a minute. To tell the truth, what I do has nothing to do with Jasmine and my children.

I just love, love, love drinking Hennessy, playing poker for money, and I especially love having sex with big bitches. They just can't get enough of chocolate thunder. You would think that I would be satisfied with just having Jasmine. I mean she has body, body. I especially love her 32DD breasts. She looks like she comes straight off the pages of a King magazine. With her long jet black hair that cascades past her hips, Jasmine is one fly ass chick. What drives me crazy about her is how emotionally needy she is. Jasmine is funny, pretty, and witty. She's just too damn needy. I'm glad the children help keep her distracted enough for me to do me.

Like I said before, I have been good up until my dumb ass went over to Derrick's house. Recently, Derrick and I have been having awesome threesomes with Monica. I can't believe her head game. She puts bobble heads to shame.

Jasmine doesn't give or allow me to give her head. She says that it's disgusting. She has to kiss the children. She wouldn't feel right kissing them, knowing that she was going down on their father. Before her grandmother died her other excuse for not giving me head was that she kissed her grandmother every day.

I just smiled and said "Okay dear," knowing the whole time that she was full of shit. Ladies remember what sweet teddy bear Eddie is about to tell you. What one woman refuses to do, ten more women would leap to do. Okay, remember that statement when ya'll deny your man a simple request for head service. Thank you very much and you're welcome.

I remember when I was dating this scrumptious woman named Sheila Woods. She was this big, juicy, red bone chick that I had met in family court, four years ago. I was accompanying my baby brother Rodney to family court for moral support. She was the judge handling his child support case. She was gorgeous. Sheila was 5'8" and weighed approximately 350 pounds. Check this chick out, she had a 48DD bust line, 48" waist and 54" hips. Solid, this voluptuous woman had it going on. Shaped like an hour glass, all I could do was stare at her.

How did I get a judge, you ask?

Well, once court was in recess, Judge Woods asked "Mr. Montgomery, Mr. Eddie Montgomery... I believe. Would you please come with me inside my chambers so that I could speak with you, for a moment?"

I assumed that it had something to do with my brother's case, so I obliged. Damn, I had no idea! She told me that she was attracted to me and that she wanted to suck my dick. It's alright; I know you think that I'm lying. Derrick didn't believe me either but I'm telling the truth. She wanted to suck my dick and I let her. She was a monster. She devoured my dick whole and sucked the dear life out of me. She gently licked my balls and softly sucked them in her mouth while she jerked the shaft of my dick with her hand. Ladies take note because this technique will drive any man crazy.

"Yeah, ewww yeah," I sighed, as she tea bagged me.

Then she started licking my shaft as she made her way up to the tip of my fat head. She slowly licked the slit of my head as to set me up for the bang, my legs started to shake. Slurping all over my head, she moaned in delight, "UMMMMMMM." She then placed my head into her hot mouth and started sucking it like she was in the Olympics, trying to get the gold medal for the U.S.A. Being a greedy mother fucker, with all my might, I was fighting not to come. I was representing the U.S.S.R. and losing was not an option.

Then all of a sudden, I felt light headed. "I… I am about to come!" I exclaimed, as she vigorously kept sucking my dick. "UGHHHH… UGHHHH," I came inside her mouth.

I was shocked. She drank every fucking drop and said "UMMMMMM, I see you have a sweet tooth… you taste delicious."

Ever since then my friend, we had been dating up until I moved to Avenel, New Jersey with my family.

Shit! Sheila could give a mean head and I loved dining on her fat pussy. Don't even mention her back shots. What! Her ass was so big and perfectly round that it looked unreal. It was as if she had two basket balls in her back pockets. I could do whatever I wanted to her and she loved it! In my Rick James voice, "She's super freaky, ya'll!" I was contemplating leaving Jasmine for her. This bitch was intriguing. I never could get enough of her. She was always on my mind and obviously, she felt the same about me because she introduced me to all her family and friends. I really, really knew that she felt the same way about me when she proposed to me.

Wearing nothing but a G string, she said in her Judge Wood voice "Mr. Montgomery would you do me the honors of becoming my lawfully wedded husband?"

"Damn baby…, you know that I want to say yes! And you know that things are complicated for me at home. If you can just give me some time to straighten out some of my affairs, I promise… that we can make it happen. I love you and I don't want to lose you." I said, in my Priest voice. Priest was the lead character from the 1972 movie "Super Fly." He was the man with the master plan when it came to bitches. I desperately needed to channel into him to help me get out of this mess.

Sheila gently gave me a quick peck on the mouth and then sighed, "I knew that you were going to say that. I understand things better than you think. I see it in court all the time. Bitches dangle their children in front of good men to keep them. I know how close you are with your children. You don't want to leave them like your mother left you and your brothers. One day you will realize that you're not like your trifling mother. You deserve better. You deserve to be with me. I will wait."

Wow, she knew the constant battles that were going on inside of me and was willing to wait it out until the end of the war. I didn't know what to say. I just held her tight as I mentally reminded myself to get back my copy of "Super Fly" from my little brother. I just hate when you lend your shit to mutha fuckas and they don't return it.

Derrick would often let me use his gatehouse to be with Sheila. I knew that I needed to do some damage control. I needed to do something special, something fly. So the next night, I took her to Derrick's gatehouse where I had a variety of flowers placed throughout. An excellent cook, I prepared an intimate steak dinner for two.

Amazed that I knew how to cook, she started to cry. "I never had a man cook for me before."

"I never had a woman who understood me like you before. I really love you Sheila ..." I said as I wiped away her tears. I tenderly pecked her nose, her pouty lips, and her chin as I made my way towards her succulent neck. Once at her neck, I sucked the shit out of her neck as if I was sucking a smoked neck bone. She liked it when I got a little rough.

"Oh baby, I... I love you too," she moaned.

Unzipping her black one piece dress, I slowly glided it down her thick bootylicious frame. "Damn, you're sexy!" I said, as I removed her bra to give her girls some attention. Gently holding her swollen melons together, I lavished her erect, honey colored nipples with a tongue lashing.

"OH! OOH! OOOOOOH! OH BABY," she purred, as I adorned her super sensitive nipples with my masterful tongue. Steadily licking in circles each nipple so not to have the other one feel neglected, I pleasured my baby to no end.

As she purred louder and louder, my dick could hear her pussy call him to come hither. Ignoring her calls, I aggressively started sucking on her stiff nipples. "UMMMMMM," I moaned, as milk came out of my baby's heavy breasts. Yes, my sexy momma bear's breasts lactate for her sweet teddy bear. Sucking on them until the last drop of milk came out, I knew that I had to move on. I could no longer ignore the calls from my baby's nana. She was getting impatient. While Sheila stood before me, I slowly pull down her thong with my teeth. Once at her hairy bush, I just dove in. Already wet from anticipation, the man in the boat was erect and saluting me.

"OOOH...OOOH," she moaned as I savagely licked and sucked on her clit. All you could hear were the echoes of her moaning and the swishing of her pussy juice as I devoured her pussy.

"Yeah baby…yeah baby, get your shit off," I muttered, as I happily stayed inside her forest while I tantalized her little red riding hood.

"OOOOH, OOOOH, OOOOOH! TAKE ME EDDIE… AHHHHHHHH!" She roared with desire, as she came inside my mouth.

"Umm, I love to eat you. You're my favorite dessert," I jokingly said as we left the living room and made our way to the bedroom.

Once in the bedroom, I mounted her. As I slowly inserted my swollen head inside her pussy, she begged me to make slow love to her. Willing to oblige, I slowly stroked her fiery hot pussy.

"Damn," I grunted, as the walls of her pussy hugged my dick. "Ah yeah, this is some good shit."

"OOOH, OOOH, UMMMMMM, UMMMMM!" She moaned, as I steadily made long and deep strokes.

"I could stay in this pussy forever!" I exclaimed, as I lifted one of her legs up in an angle so to get in even deeper into her hot oven. Once I positioned myself, I rammed my dick way inside of her and just held it there. "AHHHH, AHHH!" I shouted, as the feeling was too intense.

"UMMMMM, YEAH, BABY!" She cheered, as her eyes rolled up into the back of her head.

"IS THIS MY PUSSY," I shouted. "IS THIS MY PUSSY?"

"YES BABY," she responded as a tear came down her moon shaped face.

And then things got tricky, she started to fuck me back. In rhythmic motion, we fucked as if we were in the jungle. With the deafening sounds of our bodies swishing in the river of her pussy juices, we both moaned and groaned to no end.

"I'M ABOUT TO CUM! UGHHHHHH," I shouted, as I pulled out to snatch the condom off my dick so that I could come all over her face. Hold up, before you say that I'm a nasty mutha fucka. I have to straighten you out. She likes it when I come all over her face. I don't know why and I don't ask any questions. For the first time in my life I didn't feel the need to be with other women. I just wanted to be with Sheila.

I was this close to leaving Jasmine before her grandmother died, but I couldn't leave her alone with the children. Especially, when her grandmother had left her a paid and clear house, an insurance policy worth $250,000 and a fat savings account, I'm not crazy. I mean, Ms. Wright was so good to me and besides, I have been with Jasmine ever since we were in grammar school. Sheila will understand. She's a family court judge she knows the drill. My family needs me therefore I'm making the right choice. No regrets, I said to myself while I tried to convince myself that I was indeed making the right choice.

"Man, you better hurry up and marry Jasmine before she leaves you. Jasmine is a keeper." Derrick surprisingly said, as he offered his two cents.

Personally, I never remembered asking him for any advice about my dilemma. In the past, I just asked to use his gatehouse from time to time, nothing more and nothing less. "Well, well, well, since we are giving out woman advice...Why didn't you marry Charlene? She is definitely a keeper compared to Mei-Li. I personally don't see what you saw in her. I think that you would've been better off with Charlene." I snapped back at Derrick.

"JUST WORRY ABOUT JASMINE...! I GOT MY OWN FINANCES TO TAKE CARE OF CHARLENE, MEI-LI, DESTINY, AND ANY OTHER FEMALE IN MY LIFE. ON THE OTHER HAND, YOU GOT THREE CHILDREN AND YOU AIN'T GOT YOUR OWN SHIT. YOU HAVE BEEN LIVING OFF OF WOMEN EVER SINCE I MET YOU. IF YOU KNOW WHAT I KNOW, YOU NEED TO STAY WITH JASMINE AND MARRY HER BEFORE SHE REALIZES THAT SHE HAS BEEN HOLDING YOU DOWN ALL THESE YEARS AND NOT THE OTHER WAY AROUND!" Derrick barked in a huff, as he obviously had his panties all up in a bunch.

On that note, Derrick and I agreed to never give each other woman advice. Especially, when it comes to Mei-Li, Charlene, Sheila, and Jasmine; we both get too touchy. If Derrick knew what I know, he was blessed that Charlene was a stand up type of chick. Mad dudes use to try to kick it with her. She dismissed them without a blink of an eye. Our entire team dreamed about fucking her, including me.

Still, upset about Mei-Li filing for a divorce, Derrick recently reached out to me. "Man, I wished that I had married Charlene before she married Godfrey. I apologize for the time when I made those low blow remarks about you not having your own finances. I was just trippin. I just wanted you to marry Jasmine before it was too late. I have travelled around the world and back again and I have slept with women from just about every nationality. I still find myself comparing them with Charlene. I fucked up. I should've listened to my parents. You and Jasmine have three beautiful children and a life that you built together. Don't let a big butt and a smile, ruin that."

Knowing he meant well, I just said "thanks" and I changed the subject. "Where is Monica? I was surprised when she didn't come to your 35th birthday extravaganza last month. Jasmine says no one has seen her for the last two months. Do you think she's going to come to the premiere tonight?"

"Everything is good. She called me on my birthday and wished me a happy birthday. She told me ahead of time that she was going to be away on a business trip. And as for the premiere, who knows when it comes to Monica? She's not my chick. I just hit it…time to time. Lately, I've been seeing this model chick from Brazil. Mei-Li is still moving forward with the divorce and I'm just chilling. Bitches come a dime a dozen!"

Derrick and I are one and the same…WE JUST DON'T WANT TO DO RIGHT!

CHAPTER 8

I HAD A DREAM-(JASMINE)

I often dream about my mother...Jackie Wright. She was a petite woman known for her radiant smile. She had a honey brown complexion and long jet black hair that she would sport in a bun. You just couldn't ignore her pure beauty. She was spontaneous, enthusiastic, and passionate about life. Everyone just loved being around her. She was inspirational. Well, I know she inspired me. She saw that I had a gift to do hair and would allow me to experiment on hers. Now that was truly walking by faith and not by sight. I would never allow my daughter to do my hair.

My mother had a sweet angelic voice and a gigantic heart. She was also a fire cracker that would set it off if you weren't careful. She died entirely too young. She was only twenty-eight years old when she died... of AIDS. Bright eyed and bushy tailed, I was only ten years old when she died. I was devastated. I had hoped that she would've lived long enough to see the doctors come up with the cure. Who would've known; that she would first need the cure for a broken heart.

My father didn't attend my mother's funeral at the request of my grandmother. She would only allow him to privately view my mother's body before the wake. My grandmother wanted the focus to be on her daughter and not on the man that infected her daughter. I never got the chance to tell my father that I loved him and that I needed him, desperately, to be a part of my life. I sometimes feel as if I am trying to fill in the void left behind by my father with Eddie. Good or bad, I don't ever want Eddie to be out of my life.

In a couple of days I will be celebrating my 35th birthday. I have three beautiful children. My oldest, Eddie Jr., is fourteen years old, my middle child, Eddie III, is twelve years old, and my baby girl, Jackie, is ten years old. She's the same age that I was when I lost my mother and started dating her father. I've lived longer than my mother yet not as long as my grandmother. My grandmother died two years ago at the blessed age of seventy-five years old. Like my mother, she was a passionate woman. Too passive, my grandmother allowed Eddie to move in with us after we graduated from high school. I sometimes believe that if we weren't playing house at such a young age maybe Eddie would've married me by now.

I sometimes believe that I also suffer from the same disease that my mother suffered from, the "I can't let go of my baby daddy" syndrome.

My father Bill Edwards and AIDS killed my mother and Eddie and I killed my grandmother.

My father shared a needle with a person who was infected with the HIV virus and contracted HIV. My mother knew that my father had a habit, but she just didn't know the full extent of his habit. She turned a blind eye and acted like she didn't know that he was strung out on drugs. Drug free my mother couldn't understand why he was using. Once my father found out that he had indeed contracted the HIV virus; he just up and disappeared. Shortly, after my father left, he mailed my mother a letter. He told her that he was sick and that she needed to get a check-up. Her check-up confirmed his suspicions. She had contracted HIV.

My mother was doing well until my Aunt Ruthie, my father's sister, told my mother a secret. She knew where my father was. My father was living in Newark, N.J. He had converted from being a Pentecostal and became a Muslim. He met a young lady, in the Masjid, who became his first wife. Heart broken, my mother refused to take her medications complaining she was tired of taking medicine. Her condition quickly changed from the HIV virus to full blown AIDS in a matter of months. A month after my tenth birthday, my mother died in her sleep. She had taken a deadly cocktail of prescription drugs and sleeping pills. She committed suicide.

My grandmother and I were horrified. Suicide, we didn't see it coming. "Baby, your mother just couldn't keep the faith. She placed her faith in man instead of with God." My grandmother cried, as we prayed together.

Baptist, my mother was very spiritual. She kept her baptismal Bible in excellent condition. I wanted to keep it. It made me feel closer to her. When I would feel sad, I would read a psalm or two. A couple of months after my mother died, I was stunned to find a sealed letter placed in the 23rd psalm. Written by my mother, it was addressed to me. It read:

Dear Jasmine,
I'm sorry for hurting you and mama. I know that I've disappointed mama and that I've crushed your spirit. My precious little girl, please forgive your mama

for being weak. I couldn't bare the pain anymore. I've always dreamed of the day that your father and I would get married. I wanted to have a big church wedding. Once my dream had died, I wanted to die. I don't blame your father for getting me sick. I know that it wasn't intentional. He would've never wanted to endanger our family. I do however blame him for killing my dream, my dream of becoming Mrs. Edwards. Precious little one, please find the strength within yourself to handle any obstacle that gets in your way. Don't give up. Learn from mommy's mistakes. Don't let a broken dream end your life. Live to dream another dream. Live to charter a new course. God didn't give up his only son so that you would give up. Don't let my death be in vain. Let my life as well as my death give you the strength to go on, no matter what! Pray for my soul and keep the faith. Mommy loves you and don't you ever forget it.

Love Always,
Mommy

I never told anyone about the letter. At times, I wanted to tell my grandmother but I would stop myself. The letter said, *Dear Jasmine*. That meant that the letter was written for my eyes only. She knew that I would keep her Bible; therefore it was written solely for me.

Fortified by his faith, my father was determined to live. He ate right, took his medications, and exercised daily. Clean for over twenty years, my father now has three wives and a healthy baby boy. A couple of times, he reached out to my grandmother so that he could visit me. Bitterly, my grandmother would tell my father to stay lost and focus on his new family. My grandmother would then pray for forgiveness while telling me that it was for the best.

Unfortunately, my mother and father didn't see the same realities for themselves. My father found something that made him happy and it obviously wasn't my mother. For my mother the beginning of his new life meant the ending of hers. I don't hate my father. How could I? I benefited from his union with my mother, I was born.

They called it suicide but really it was murder. Like father like daughter, I am a murderer now. I killed my grandmother because I didn't have the courage to leave Eddie. Mrs. Winthorp, my grandmother's church sister, told my grandmother that Eddie was seriously dating her God-daughter. She overheard Eddie and her God-daughter discussing their future living arrangements. Upset, my grandmother had a heart attack.

A week before my grandmother's death, I had a premonition. My mother came to me in a dream. She pleaded, "My precious please open your eyes, listen to your heart, and have courage before it's too late."

Maybe if I'd put more stock into my dream my grandmother would still be alive. I killed my grandmother, I AM A MURDERER!

I've tried to convince myself that it was actually that gossiping Mrs. Winthorp's fault, for not minding her own' business. She was always gossiping about everybody with the exception of her late husband Mr. Winthorp. At his funeral, it was discovered that in addition to the eight children that he had with her in Jersey City; he secretly had another six children with some woman who lived in Hoboken. He was taking care of two families! Now, what if I went around talking about the brawl that took place at the funeral? Hmm, I wonder if her heart could've handled that truth.

I never told Eddie that I knew about his affair. I wanted to see if he would have the audacity to leave me, especially after my grandmother just died. She loved him dearly and was there for him when his own mother wasn't. She had hoped to live long enough to see the day that we would've gotten married. I wanted to see if he was indeed like his mother and my father, deadbeats.

I sacrificed my grandmother for him and I wasn't about to let him off the hook so easily. I strategically moved our family to Avenel, New Jersey. I bought my dream house, opened myself a beauty parlor, and funded Eddie's dream of owning his very own detailing shop/garage. Before I moved to Avenel, I asked Terry for some advice and boy did she have a lot to say.

"Jasmine, you need to stop being Eddie's fool. If you want my advice, put the new house and the businesses solely in your name. You need to wise up, if not for yourself then for your children. And for once, can you please refrain from disclosing this information to Eddie? Ignorance is bliss. Eddie will work harder and contribute more to make sure that your home and the business are a success, if he thinks that he truly has some ownership in the properties. Jasmine, he doesn't even want to marry you. Why upgrade him to a home owner and proprietor if he won't even upgrade you to his wife after all these years? Honey, please wake up and smell the coffee! I would never want to suggest breaking up a home. JUST WAKE THE FUCK UP! Look, here is a referral to an attorney in Avenel that can further assist you with any more questions that you may have. You can't afford to hire me and I don't work for free, I suggest that you immediately give him a call." Terry said, as she jotted down the information on a piece of paper.

I instantly started to cry. I knew that if I didn't cry that I was going to scream.

Then Terry hugged me tightly and said, "You're a gem Jasmine and Eddie doesn't even have a clue. He's a fool. You deserve to be treated, a whole lot better. I hope someday, you will realize that."

I cried myself to sleep that night because I knew that Terry was right. Eddie was a fool but my fool. I just asked her for some advice. I thought that was what friends were for. All that extra shit, she could've kept to herself. That's why no one likes to ask her for advice; she always has to be extra. One day she's going to be tested and I want to see if she will have all of the answers. I love Eddie and my children. I'm not letting him go. I love you mommy and I love you nana. If nobody else understands why I stay with Eddie I know you two do and that's all that matters.

I know that everybody thinks that I am stupid for staying with Eddie. I don't care! Everyone is stupid for something or someone. Monica is stupid for money. She would rather trick off for some doe than to go to work and make it the honest way. I never understood that about her. The Freemans gave her just about whatever she wanted and everything that she needed. That's why I make my boys work a couple of hours in the garage with their father every week. I want them to appreciate the life that Eddie and I provide for them.

Charlene is stupid for Derrick. Destiny is about to turn eighteen years old soon and Charlene finally decided to move on with her life. Many men over the years have tried to date Charlene- politicians, businessmen, athletes, and etc. she would just chase them away. I'm so happy that she met and married Godfrey. It gives me hope that someday Eddie will come to his senses and marry me. Godfrey seems to really compliment Charlene. I can't wait until it's my turn.

January is stupid for food. She needs to lose some weight. Monica and I constantly tell her that she's overweight, yet it goes into one ear and right out the other. She could get sugar or worse heart disease. We love her. We just want her to live a long and healthy life.

Terry isn't stupid, she's just power hungry. She has a God complex and is in need of a reality check.

I'm not stupid. I just choose to keep my family together. I'm not hurting anyone. There are far worse things to be caught up on. I chose my poison and I'm willing to die by it but before I do, I guarantee you that I'm not going to die alone. Eddie is going to do right by me one way or another.

Monica, Charlene, January, and Terry are not just my best friends, they're my sisters. We're family. We fuss and fight then we kiss and make-up. January and I were often the referees, the peace keepers. Terry, determined to be the leader of our little clique was always at odds with Monica and Charlene.

I preferred the company of Monica and Charlene because January and Terry were too serious. For fun we would sneak into the movies, play truth or dare, spin the bottle, and crank call people. January and Terry didn't want any part of our fun time. January's pop was a cop and Terry was just Terry. She was always thinking about the consequences. Monica and Charlene use to always tease Terry and call her a herb. A herb was worse than a nerd. It is what happens when you combine a jerk and a nerd.

"I would rather be a herb than a broken down want to be." Terry would respond with a smile.

"Who are you calling a broken down want to be?" Monica and Charlene would angrily respond.

"Who was calling me a herb? Those in glass houses shouldn't be throwing stones."

"Stop, fooling around guys before someone takes it to heart." January would say stepping in between them to prevent a possible fight.

I know that Monica and Charlene could fight but I think I would rather put my money on Terry. Terry is and has always been a certified bitch. Monica and Charlene never tested Terry's chin because they knew January would jump in. January is a big burly bitch. I remember when this guy yoked Monica up by her collar because she dissed him. Out from no were, January cold knocked him out. We ran before the guy came to. We laughed so hard. That jerk didn't even see it coming.

Eddie and I first met in kindergarten. We officially became an item a couple of months after my mother died. He used to make me laugh. He reminded me of my mother. He was always telling jokes and playing pranks, especially on my grandmother.

I lost my virginity to Eddie when I was thirteen years old. I know… we had no business having sex. If it makes you feel any better, it was awful. Thankfully that was something he improved at as time went by. Naïve me never suspected that I wasn't the only one that he was getting his groove on with. I just assumed that he had read a couple of books about the art of love making and/or saw some x rated videos.

Everyone loves a clown especially one as handsome and charming as my Eddie. With his short S curl fade, he was always removing his shirt to flex his massive muscles for everyone to see. Stocky and cocky, Eddie was my sexy chocolate bar. With an even deep dark chocolaty complexion, my Eddie was 5'9" and weighed 230 pounds. Well dressed, girls use to always flock around him. It really got bad when he met his best friend, Derrick Johnson. Together, they were the supreme team. All the girls use to be sweating their jocks. Charlene use to date Derrick and I use to date Eddie. We had to get at some chicks over these dudes, on more than one occasion. My small size caused a lot of girls to sleep on my fighting skills. I even had to give it to a couple of big girls behind my Eddie.

"Did you see those big bitches trying to holla at my Eddie?"

"Did you ever think that it was the other way around? Maybe Eddie likes the big girls?" A sarcastic Terry said, as she smiled at January.

"Hell no, Jasmine is a little cutie! She's more than enough for Eddie." Monica said looking me up and down seductively.

"Thanks Monica," I said, as I started to blush. "Terry, no one asked you for your opinion."

"I thought that it was an open statement, meaning anyone could respond; therefore I could voice my opinion. Hmm… it sounds to me like someone has a little crush on Jasmine. I mean, there was no need to get all excited." Terry responded.

"No one's getting excited. You're just mad that no one is trying to sniff your panties." Monica concluded.

"That's enough folks…must I remind you that we're best friends," Charlene said sarcastically making sure she choked on the word best.

If Terry only knew half the truth, I use to think to myself. She really would go the fuck off.

One cold December night during our sophomore year in high school, Charlene and I slept over Monica's house without Terry and January. Monica confessed that she intentionally didn't invite Terry and January. For once, she just wanted to have some fun without the two goodie two shoes around.

She hosted a private jello shot party for three. A Jello shot is when you add vodka to jello mixture. Accompanied with delicious miniature sandwiches, we had it going on. We played loud music and the game of truth or dare without the truth. All night long we kept daring each other to do crazy things. Then, I guess after too many jello shots, things started to get steamy.

Monica dared me to tongue kiss Charlene, I hesitated but only for a second. Then I did it. I would've never guessed that Charlene was such a passionate kisser, my panties got wet. Monica began stripping down to her underwear.

Shocked, Charlene and I just stared. Monica was built like a comic book heroine. Her small waist made her breast and butt appear to be huge. With her silky smooth mocha complexion, Monica's body was definitely like wow.

"Monica, you're tripping. Put your pajamas back on." Charlene barked.

"You two know that you're curious. I will take it slow," Monica said, as she grabbed me around my waist and pulled me close to her.

Horny and drunk as hell, I just followed Monica's lead. Charlene sat in the corner chair were she played with herself while she watched the show.

As Monica unbuttoned my oversized night shirt, she whispered in my ear, "I've been looking forward to this for a long time." I was wearing a hot pink laced bra with matching panty. Monica's eyes lit up as she took off my bra and saw my bare perky breasts. "Just relax and enjoy yourself… I know I am."

I looked over at Charlene and saw that she was naked. She was rubbing her clit and licking her fingers, "Umm!"

Monica squeezed my breast together and started licking my nipples.

"UMMMM…UMMMM," I moaned, as I enjoyed how Monica manipulated my nipples in her mouth. "AHH, AHH, AHH…" I sighed, as Monica sent surges of pleasure throughout my body. Then Charlene joined in and started tongue kissing me, I guess she enjoyed our little kiss that we had earlier just as much as I did. Monica took that as her cue to quickly take off my panties. As she lovingly stroked my clit with her sharp pointy tongue, I had died and gone to heaven. Unfamiliar flutters of ecstasy were erupting inside of me and I didn't know what to do. Part of me wanted to scream and the other part of me just wanted to moan, as Monica interchangeably licked, sucked, and nibbled on my clit. Gasping for air as the tingly sensations that I feeling was becoming too much, I suddenly roared, "AHHHHHHHHHHHHHHHHHHH!"

I had just experienced my first orgasm from oral sex and I loved it! Eddie has never made me climax from oral sex. I guess that's why ever since that night, I have never let Eddie taste my va-jay-jay again. He frankly doesn't do it for me. So, if I don't ask him to eat me; I know damn well that I'm not going to eat him!

Feeling lifeless, I laid down on Monica's bed. While taking off her bra and panties, Monica instructed Charlene to lie beside me. Opening the top drawer of her night stand, Monica took out a large chocolate dildo. It looked and had the texture of an actual penis. She quickly placed a condom on the dildo and then she gently inserted the dildo inside me. Slowly fucking me with the dildo as she ate Charlene, Monica was turning us out without breaking a sweat. She was a bad bitch. Side by side, Charlene and I just looked at each other as we moaned and groaned in ecstasy. We knew it was wrong but it felt so right.

Once Monica got Charlene off, she then took the dildo out of me, sucked it dry and started fucking Charlene with it. Switching sides Monica then started pussy fucking me. We were grinding and rubbing our wet pussies together. It was intoxicating, all you could hear was all three of us moaning and groaning as the smell of pussy thickly filled the air. It felt so unreal. I love my Eddie... What was I doing? Better yet, what was in those jello-shots? Did Monica slip us a mickey?

"Yeah...yeah...this is some good shit," exclaimed Monica.

We were drunk and extremely horny. To focus on pussy fucking me, Monica stopped fucking Charlene with the dildo. She playfully poked her tongue out to Charlene and as if she was in a trance Charlene started licking Monica's breast.

Monica sighed, "Yes" and started to fuck my pussy whole with her erect clit.

It was a strange and welcomed feeling. Turned on, I started to fuck Monica back.

"Yeah bitch...fuck me...fuck me harder," she exclaimed as she rubbed my nipples with her fingers simultaneously while grinding on me.

"OH! OH! OH! AHHHHHHHH," We both roared, as we simultaneously climaxed.

Exhausted, we all fell back on the bed laughing. Pledging never to tell the others what we did that fateful night. Monica and I slept with each other, on and off, until I got pregnant. Once I became pregnant I had to focus on my family with Eddie. Every now and then when I got drunk, I would call Monica to tell her that I was thinking about her. She would laugh and say ditto.

Monica could lick a mean pussy but Eddie could fuck like a champ. It's nothing like the feel of a pulsating dick inside of you… hitting all your hot spots. There's no toy in the world that can replicate what my Eddie does with his dick. His talented tool strokes me hard and deep as it takes me further and further along the road to ecstasy. I hate to admit it but Eddie has me dick whipped. He picks me up and tosses me around like I'm his rag doll. Lavishing tons of attention on my breasts until I cum over and over again; Eddie would torture me I tell you and I loved every bit of it! Eddie was a monster. Like a gold miner he would go deep into my inner sanctuary as he dug for his buried treasure. He just wouldn't stop until he pleasured every inch of my body. I would moan, groan, and cry in ecstasy as he would reconstruct my insides. Like a true craftsman he wouldn't rush, he would take his time and love me just the way I like it.

Over the years, Eddie and I have had wild and kinky sex. Because I was double jointed, he would twist me into the weirdest positions. No longer was I his children's mother; I became a porno star.

Contrary to what others may believe, I've had only two sex partners in my entire life… my Eddie and Monica. I hear a lot of talk from guys that swear they can put it down better than my Eddie but I'm good. Eddie and my children are my life.

Eddie Jr. looks and acts just like me. 5'3" and weighing 110 pounds, he's interested in music, writing plays, cutting hair, and playing with his pit bull named Scrappy. Eddie often calls him a little faggot and tries to toughen him up by making Eddie III fight him. I hate that side of Eddie. That's why I enrolled the children and myself into kickboxing classes. I'm not going to have anybody make my children feel like a victim. They better fight back.

Eddie III mirrors Eddie. He loves playing video games, working on cars with his dad, and playing sports. Only twelve years old, my baby is 5'11" and weighs a whopping 215 pounds. He has already surpassed his father in height and is still growing. His hot ass has all these little girls from his school ringing my phone off the hook. Luckily, he says that he doesn't have a girlfriend yet. He plays soccer, baseball, basketball, and football. Eddie is determined to make him the next great wonder in football.

Jackie, a natural comedian like her father, is wise beyond her years. It seems as if she had been here before. She reminds me of my grandmother. She loves to read and sit up under her father. Thoughtful, she surprisingly loves to visit Terry and January. Jackie is 4'9" and weighs 125 pounds. Yeah, she is built like her father. She's chunky!

"Eddie, Jackie needs to go on a diet. You may think that I'm being mean but society is meaner. Society views people with weight issues as second class citizens."

"Stop lowering her self- esteem. My baby girl is fine just the way she is. She's only ten years old. She doesn't have to worry about her weight, yet!"

"You don't think calling E.J. a faggot is lowering his self-esteem? You just worry about shaping your boys and leave Jackie to me."

"My baby girl is cute and adorable. She's perfect. Now, as for E.J. he's a little too soft to me. I told you before that you baby that boy far too much. He's definitely your son."

"When you ease up on E.J., I will ease up on Jackie."

Can you believe this fool got drunk one night and insinuated that Eddie Jr. was not his son?

"He acts too much like a little bitch to be my son!" Eddie shouted.

I slapped that fool silly and cursed him the fuck out. Who the fuck he thinks he is with his scary ass? We had to go to the pound to adopt a cat because he almost jumped out of his skin, one day, when he saw a damn field mouse in the house. It was Eddie Jr. who caught the mouse and set him free back into the woods.

I'm looking forward to go to January's premiere party tonight. Besides celebrating her success, it gives me a reason to get dolled up. I think if I remind Eddie that I'm a sexy woman and not just the mother of his three children; he will want to propose to me. It's crazy that January has gotten engaged before me. I've given the best years of my life to Eddie and I deserve to be called Mrs. Montgomery. I refuse to let January beat me to the altar!

CHAPTER 9

IF I RULED THE WORLD-(TERRY)

My favorite song is "If I ruled the world" by Nas. It shouldn't take a rocket scientist to figure out why. I'm at the top of my game and I love it. I was blessed to be born into a strong and loving family. My parents gave me four younger brothers named Floyd Jr., thirty-four, Gilbert, thirty-three, Kenny, thirty-one, Anthony, twenty-nine, and a little sister named Juliet, twenty-five. I have three so, so girlfriends named Charlene, Monica, and Jasmine. And one true friend named January Jackson. I have a successful career, as a partner at a prestigious law firm and a super sexy, super successful and super smart husband named Dexter Delgado. I have it all. What can I say? I got the Midas touch. Everything I touch turns to gold! I know… I know humility isn't my strongest suit. People tend to feel guilty if they're having success and second guess themselves when it comes to life and the pursuit of happiness. I don't.

I tried for years to uplift Charlene, Jasmine, and Monica to no avail. Those simple bitches left their fate in the hands of the men that they dealt with. January was the only one that would listen and take heed to my advice. January and I are captains of our own ships. We chart our own course in life. Throughout my childhood Charlene, Jasmine, and Monica would often call me a herb yet as soon as they got into some trouble or needed some guidance; who did they call? Me. When Charlene wanted to start her own clothing line, who did she call for some advice? Me. When Jasmine's grandmother died, who did she call for some advice? Me. When Monica wanted to invest "her" money, who did she call for some financial advice? Me. These bitches owe me a whole lot of money. Time is money and money is time. If I ruled the world simple bitches like them would be exiled to their very own island. They wouldn't be allowed to associate with the likes of us.

Over the years, I've done a lot for those ungrateful hoes. I've earned the right to speak my mind when it comes to these dizzy broads. I've worked too damn hard to get what I have. I didn't spread my legs and hit the jackpot, like Charlene. I didn't have a grandmother to run into the grave for a hefty insurance policy, like Jasmine. And I refuse to hop from bed to bed in pursuit of a dollar, like that slut ass Monica. January has paid her dues, she deserves the spotlight. I'm not bragging because I'm the first Tucker in my family to become a successful lawyer. I'm bragging because I, Terry, did it on my own.

Growing up in Lincoln Projects has made me ruthless. Average family, my household was one way but once I left my house I was subjected to all types of madness and dysfunction. In one building you would have Chester, Chester the child molester and in another building you would have pretty boy Tyrone who was often visited on the late night tip by the neighborhood thugs. These down- low brothers were not just drug dealers. They were husbands, teachers, policemen, firemen, mechanics, deacons, and even preachers. No one would bother Tyrone because he could easily throw them under a bus. Tyrone knew that I would keep his secrets so he had no problem sharing the sorted details of his latest and greatest conquests. I listened to him because I found it entertaining. Tyrone was my only male friend. The guys in my hood thought that I was either stuck up or gay because I didn't want to give them some play.

"Girl, don't pay those haters any mind. Most of them niggas are gay anyway, trust me. You see I only fucks' with you. Bitches hate on me because they know their men lust for me behind their back. It's not my fault that I'm so fine."

"Tyrone, you're a certified fool but I love how you keep it real. Speaking of real, I hope that you're stacking some of that loot for your future because we're not getting any younger."

Graduating from the school of performing arts, Tyrone invested his money in a recording studio. He would have aspiring rappers and singers from the neighborhood come through to record. "Girl, I'm so grateful that I took your advice to invest into my future. I'm making music, money, and meeting men, hallelujah! Never conform. The world needs more people like you who aren't afraid of the truth and could give a damn who likes them or not."

"Aww… thank you Tyrone. That was sweet."

I took his advice to heart. Who cares if people like me as long as they respect me? I have a very close knit family. With my father being one of ten children and my mom one of five, I have thirty-two 1st and 2nd cousins and more than enough love to go around. I have family in New York, New Jersey, Pennsylvania, Virginia, Georgia, Texas, and etc. Get the picture? I have family on both sides of the law. My family crosses state lines as well as color lines. I'm truly blessed. I was born a proud Tucker and now through my marriage with Dexter, I'm also a proud Delgado.

Having caramel complexion and straight ebony shoulder length hair, I had a 36DD bust line, 28" waist and 36" hips. I was 5'8" and weighed 160 pounds. I was dime piece, if I must say so myself. Focused on my studies, I chose not to seriously date until I went to college. To ensure that my educational endeavors would not be derailed by an unplanned pregnancy, I decided to stay a virgin until I at least attended my first year of college.

If you must know, I was a virgin when I met Dexter. With four very protective brothers, it wasn't like I had any choice in the matter. If a guy looked at me sideways my brothers were ready to set it off. So when I bought Dexter Delgado home to meet my family, I was pleasantly surprised that they immediately took to him.

My family is amazing. We're always joking around and having parties. My mother was always finding a reason to have a get together. She would cook a mini feast every night for dinner, except on Fridays when my siblings and I would give my mother a break. Saturday was always my parents date night. It was her day to be wined and dined by my father. Affectionate, you could always find them snuggling. Married young, my parents moved out of their parents' houses and into Lincoln Projects because it was affordable. Shortly after, my ooh so fertile mom gave birth to me, ten months later my brother Floyd was born.

Having a stay at home mother was a rewarding and a fulfilling treat. That is why I made a vow to myself not to have any children. Children would distract me and make me feel guilty that I would rather have a successful career than to be a stay at home mother. My father was always working to make sure that we had all of our needs and some of our wants taken care of. I'm so grateful to have such giving and devoted parents. They sacrificed their younger years to raise a family.

Like our parents, Dexter and I believe in teamwork. Being chess players, we look at Life as a game of chess. Operating from the position of queen, my king and I are constantly checking our opponents. The goal of course is to win the game and as you can see, we're winning.

Almond in complexion, Dexter was 6'1" and weighed 230 pounds. He wore glasses and sported jet black waves. He had dreamy hazel eyes that could sweep you off your feet. I especially loved his fit body and his deep sexy voice. Of Dominican descent, Dexter was from Brooklyn, New York. I fell in love with his brain as well as with his brawn. Sensitive as well as tough, Dexter had the right touch. He knew how to give me my space to let me be me and at the same time he had the balls to put me in my place when I was getting out of hand and believe me I can get out of hand.

I just love this fucking man. I try not to show him just how much because I don't want him taking me for granted. The only thing that is wrong with him is that he keeps pressuring me to have a baby. We have mad nieces and nephews and he wants us to have a baby. The world is overpopulated as it is, he must be crazy! Dexter told me, when I first met him, that he wanted us to start a family by the time we were thirty-five years old but I just thought, to myself, that I would cross that bridge when I got to it. Well, now I'm at that bridge.

We have a great sex life, travel often, make a lot of money, and truly enjoy each other's company. The times I work into the wee hours of the morning, I find myself missing him. We just don't have any children and I am fine with that. Nowadays I think that he is using this topic as a diversion from his work troubles. A few months ago, shit almost hit the fan over dinner.

"Babe, I've been thinking. I wouldn't mind becoming a stay at home dad, so that you wouldn't have to give up your partnership. I would just have to work part-time from home. I think that I would really enjoy taking care of our little prince or princess."

I wisely responded, in my sexiest voice, "Well, I guess I know what you want for dessert."

I started to undress at the table. Then, we made passionate love all night long. The entire time, I kept asking myself…is he loco or what? I'm honored that he has no problem being the sacrificial lamb but to quit his six figure job to play Mr. Mom, I say…NOT. He would be so pissed if he knew I was on the pill. Until he gets over his I want to have a baby phase that's just the way it's going to be. No way in hell, I'm going to get pregnant at this stage in my career.

Does he know how hard it was for me to become a partner? FOR EIGHT STRAIGHT YEARS, I had to be one of the top three litigators at my firm. I had to be a senior associate for at least four years, surrounded by men, who were on the sidelines betting when I was going to stroll into the office pushing a baby carriage. I had to keep my cool and practically sell my soul to the devil for which I still have a remaining balance. I'm constantly being challenged and dared to maintain my stats. I'm in the big leagues now and I have to sink or swim. I'm not going to stop my momentum with a baby.

Maybe his firm isn't challenging him? I've spoken to him about finding another job but he doesn't seem to be interested. I mean, what's up with this pay cut? Firms lose cases all the time. I believe Dexter left out a couple of details when it comes to the nature of this so called pay cut. I could've understood, the pay cut, if he was the presiding attorney that lost the case but he wasn't, so something about that whole situation doesn't sit right with me. My firm doesn't play those types of games.

Dexter just needs to get another expensive toy to play with. I even suggested to him that after January's premiere party that we go to the Dominican Republic to visit family. Maybe, he needs to be reminded of how fortunate we are and learn to appreciate what we have?

We got married in the Dominican Republic after we graduated from law school. Aligned with tall palm trees, mountains, clean white beaches, clear and clean ocean waters, warm balmy weather, and exotic people, the Dominican Republic was a sight for sore eyes. I felt like I was Julia Roberts in the movie "Pretty Woman." I was swept away by my love for Dexter and the way that his family welcomed me with open arms.

I had no idea how wealthy his family was. His family's resort in the Dominican Republic was the first of many secrets to unfold. We married there in a scene that could only be described as heaven on earth. Thirty acres of tropical paradise, it contained ten Villa styled, single story beachfront homes. The estate had private pools, ponds, landscaped grounds, and stone fire pits that ringed the sand. With tiled floors, high ceilings, central air conditioning, hot tubs, outdoor grills, volleyball courts, basketball courts, and a bar it was an indoor/outdoor haven. Each villa had the minimum of eight bedrooms and eight bathrooms.

The ceremony was held at the family's compound on the resort. It was an outdoor wedding that was held by the pool's clubhouse with approximately a hundred and fifty guests. Dexter's cousin Chad was his best man and my sister Juliet was my maid of honor. Trying to keep it simple I decided not to have bride's maids and the groom's men. I just wanted everyone eyes to be fixed on me.

I wore an antique, ultra feminine, strapless one piece ivory lace wedding dress with scalloped lace detail. I had an ivory scalloped lace shawl and three inch ivory satin and lace shoes. I wore diamond and pearl earrings with a matching diamond and pearl necklace to accent the diamond and pearl tiara, I rocked like royalty. Wearing my hair in a bun, ringlets of soft curls framed my face. I looked heavenly.

My bouquet was a blend of ivory colored roses, lilies, and baby's breath. It was my take on the innocent beauty of matrimony.

My teenage, baby sister wore a simple fitted ivory satin mini dress with spaghetti straps. To jazz up her outfit, she wore dangling pearl earrings and a pearl necklace with three inch stiletto heels and an ivory satin shawl. With her hair in pin curls, she looked adorable.

Dexter and Chad wore matching black three piece tuxedos made from a luxurious blend of fine wool and silk that was complemented nicely by a crisp ivory satin shirt and a black satin straight tie. Dexter was a romantic at heart. He gave me a plain three karat diamond engagement ring to catch me off guard. When the ceremony started, I was amazed that he had purchased the two matching three karat wedding bands that enclosed around the engagement ring. They were gorgeous! I was truly shocked. Dexter's wedding band, on the other hand, was just a simple wide platinum band.

Every member, of the Delgado family, had a role to play in the upkeep of the resort. Every year, the family would have a financial review and equally split up the dividends. I admired how the Delgado family stuck together. It certainly paid off for them. We try to get back there at least twice a year. His parents plan on retiring there.

Mama Delgado worked as a legal secretary and was happy to have a daughter- in- law in the same field. "Terry, you remind me of myself when I was your age. I wished that I continued my education and became an attorney. I should've waited to start a family. I felt that papa rushed me into having Dexter to slow me down. I'm warning you… don't start a family too soon. It will lead you to have to make a choice between your career and my son. I want you and my son to make it. He needs your strength and courage to weather the storms that are sure to come. I fear that papa and I sheltered Dexter too much."

The insight that she shared with me that day has been instrumental in helping me to squash the different problems and beefs that Dexter and I have faced over the years.

Derrick, as his wedding gift to Dexter and I, charted a jet and flew everyone down for the ceremony. Dexter and I took a seven day cruise that included the Dominican Republic as a stop. We wanted to cherish the moment because we knew it was going to be hell getting our careers off the ground. Making the transition from summer to regular associate at two different firms, we knew we'd face challenges in more than just our careers. As Mr. and Mrs. Delgado we were planning a world takeover, hostile if necessary.

To spice things up for our honeymoon, I enforced a no sex rule two months prior to the wedding. After two weeks, we were both horny like a mother fucker. Law school is stressful and sex is an awesome release. Dexter and I had a great sex life. We usually had sex at least twice a week and sometimes as many as four times a week. He was MUY CALIENTE! I especially love how he talks dirty to me when he is about to come…it drives me wild!

Surprisingly, we didn't have sex on our wedding night. We were so tired from all the festivities. We laughed, cried, ate, danced, sang, and drank all night long. We had whole roasted pigs, cows, chickens and goats. We had different variations of traditional rice and beans platters. We had salads galore and any other Spanish and southern dishes you could possibly think of. All the food was made by Dexter's family members. It was all delicious. My girl January even whipped up a couple of dishes. Because we were on a cruise, we only had a one day lay over so after the wedding celebration we had to get back to our ship.

Dexter was so drunk when we got back to our cabin that he slept the night away. I didn't mind as long as we consummated the marriage before we returned to the states. I wanted the first time that we made love as Mr. and Mrs. Delgado to be special. Dexter nasty ass had other plans. He basically said the hell with romance and just ravaged me after he recovered from his hangover. Two months with no sex practically killed him. I never got the chance to wear my sexy lingerie. I spent a lot of money on those sets.

Relaxing, I was just lying in the bed talking on the phone with January when Dexter pounced on me, like a crazed animal in heat.

"Stop baby! I want to put on my sexy lingerie."

"I don't need lingerie. All I need is you," he said in a deep and sexy voice, as he ravaged me.

Kissing and sucking on my neck as he grasped me tightly in his arms, I felt his masculine power and I had no problem submitting to it. His hot breath sent tingles down my spine. All I could do was moan in delight, "UMMMM, UMMMM!"

Growling like a savaged best, Dexter made his way to my breasts. Ferociously licking, sucking, and biting on them, as if he were a man possessed, Dexter sent me on a natural high. "AYE, PAPI CHULO!" I sighed, as his every touch sent my head in a tail spin.

"AYE, AYE," I moaned as he repeatedly muttered, "mi amore."

"Put it in me...please baby... put it in me," I begged as I was caught up in rapture. I needed to feel him inside of me.

With one hand he flipped me over and started fucking me doggy style.

"OOOOH YEAH," he exclaimed, as he thrust in and out of me. "Ahhhhh, Ahhhhh! Your pussy is so hot...so wet...so fucking good." He mumbled, as he went deeper and deeper.

There are times when you just want to take it slow and then there are times when you just want to get fucked silly. This was one of those times. "YEAH, YEAH BABY!" I exclaimed, as I tightened my punany's muscles around his fat head to further add resistance. His mighty dick rammed its' way through my walls of pleasure to swim in my ocean of milky cum.

"Oooooh, Ahhhhh," I moaned, as cum ran all down my legs and all over the sheets.

All you could hear throughout the room was the swishing of Dexter's penis going in and out of my wet pussy and the constant clapping of his balls hitting my ass while he fucked me from behind. Dare I mention the intense sounds of us moaning and groaning? It was the best symphony that I've ever heard in my entire life. He would fuck me in and then out, in and then out, left to right, and then right to left. Waves of pleasure rolled up and down my body leaving me entranced.

"OH, OH, OH DEXTER!"

"EAT THAT DICK...EAT THAT DICK!"

"AHHH, AHHHH, AHHHHHH!" I yelled, as I climaxed.

"UGHHHHHHH, UGHHHHHHH, I'M CUMMING!" Dexter roared.

Smiling, we both collapsed onto the bed. Dexter along the side of me, looked lifeless. Both of us, lying side by side, on our stomachs tenderly gazed into each other's eyes.

"I love you Mrs. Delgado."

"I know."

We both started to laugh.

Suddenly, Dexter got up and went into the closet and returned to the bed with a brown paper bag. "Now let us try this again and see if I hear what I wanted to hear the first time. I love you Mrs. Delgado," he said, as he passed me the brown paper bag.

Puzzled, I opened the brown paper bag. To my surprise, I saw a blue and white box. "IT'S TIFFANY'S!" I opened the box and saw a beautiful diamond and silver hugs & kisses charm bracelet. I started to cry, "It's beautiful!" I then jumped up and showered him with hugs and kisses.

"All I wanted to hear you say was... I love you too, Mr. Delgado."

"Now baby, you know that I love you. I was just being a wise ass earlier. You don't have to give me gifts for me to tell you that I love you."

"I know because I still didn't hear it," he jokingly said.

"I LOVE YOU WITH ALL MY HEART MR. DELGADO," I exclaimed, as I gently kissed his forehead, his nose, his chin, his muscular and hairless chest, his flat and muscular stomach, and then...I yelled "psych!"

"Awe baby, don't tease me like that!" he pitifully said, as I jumped off of him and ran into the bathroom.

"You're welcome to come and join me," I yelled, barely getting the words out before Dexter was next to me.

We gently washed each other as we began round two of our play time.

I grabbed Dexter's dick and started to lick it, Dexter's eyes got big as he said, "Now that is the other response that I wanted."

Smiling, I slowly teased the tip of his dick with my tongue. As I expertly licked around and around his juicy head, I was no longer Terry the lawyer. I became Vanessa Del Rio, international porn star. Licking along the shaft of his cock, I teasing made my way down to his balls.

"YEAH, YEAH, YEAH," Dexter shouted, as I pleasured him.

I moaned with desire because I get turned on when I pleasure my king. He has a beautifully maintained dick. I often shave his dick and ball area bald, for him. Always fresh and scented with oil, I have never caught him off his game. I enjoy the whole eating process. From the beginning, when his dick is small and up until the zenith when his dick is long and erect, I love pleasuring my man.

"OH BABY, I L-O-V-E YOU," Dexter proclaimed in ecstasy, as I sucked his cock harder and deeper.

Literally blowing his mind, his dick now becomes MY cock.

"DAMN BABY… AHHH…AHHHH!" Dexter exclaimed. Amped, Dexter then grabbed me, picked me up, pinned me against the shower wall, and started fucking me.

"OH DEXTER! OH DEXTER!"

"GOOD PUSSY! UMMMM, GOOD PUSSY!"

Dexter worked his throbbing manhood inside of me, as we gazed deeply into each other's eyes. Breathing heavily, we both trembled as he continued to pound my nana. Ripples of ecstasy flooded through me as I felt like I was hallucinating. It was so unreal.

Simultaneously, we clenched each other as we each made a sweet and final cry.

"I love you Mrs. Delgado."

"I love you too Mr. Delgado."

That night was so intense and unforgettable, as we continued to declare our love for each other throughout the night.

———————————

Charlene, Monica, and Jasmine were my childhood girlfriends. January is my BFF, Best Friends Forever. Just because we all grew up together, it didn't mean that we stayed together. Some friends grow closer as time passed and others grow apart. Personally, I out grew those three treacherous bitches.

January is the only one that I not only consider to be my best friend, but to be my equal. She has always stayed true. Good or bad she would always tell me the truth, right or wrong she would always stand in my corner. January has been there for everybody in the clique but can the clique say that they have been there for her. I have my reasons for saying this.

Charlene, Monica, and Jasmine always looked down on me because I came from the projects. They didn't understand that they were the ones with the so called "project mentality". They limited themselves by thinking that life was better to be lived as followers. Their lives were confined to a three block radius. Lincoln Projects prepared me for the world. We had all types of people. Lincoln Projects taught me to realize that there are different types of people: the people that are for you, the people that are against you, the people that are your friends, and the people that are your associates. Some people aren't aware of the different types until it is too late. This world is a jungle; either hunt or get hunted. I'm a hunter…a head hunter.

EVERYTHING THAT GLITTERS ISN'T GOLD.

They always talked about me behind my back but smiled in my face. I only kept the peace because of January. For some foolish reason, she really felt that those bitches were our friends. They were always picking on her with the fat jokes and teasing her because she was the last virgin in the group. Can you believe that? Those bitches were proud to be whores. I wouldn't put it past them, if they had fucked each other.

I use to think that Charlene wasn't that bad until she left me out of the loop when she got pregnant with Destiny. She told everybody except me. January told me but made me promise not to say anything until Charlene did. If Charlene valued my friendship, good or bad, she would've told me the same time that she told the others.

At one time I thought Jasmine was possibly a friend until she told the others that I called her a fool for wanting to keep her family together. I said, NO SUCH THING! I told her to stop being a fool for Eddie and make him accountable for his actions. I wanted her to make him treat her like the queen that she was. There's a difference, a big difference. If you really want my opinion, I think Eddie is a fool and that Jasmine entertains his foolishness. Listen, simple is what simple does. They belong together.

Last but not least, Monica. I knew that bitch was never to be trusted. I was always told by my mother to keep your friends close but your enemies closer. Monica was my frenemy. A frenemy is a friend and an enemy combined together. That crazy bitch is going to get it one day and if she isn't careful it's going to be served cold by me. She thinks that I forgot about her role in getting me jumped. I just don't mention it for the fact that I wouldn't want to wake up sleeping dogs. Especially, now that I'm an attorney and all; the statutes for some crimes are timeless, if you know what I mean?

There was a time when I was equally close to all of them. With age though, you should acquire wisdom. After we graduated from high school, I realized that through it all…January was my only true girlfriend. We allowed one another to be ourselves. Charlene, Jasmine, and Monica clowned and looked down on me because I wouldn't conform and follow them. They would leave me out at their convenience. Friends are to accent your life, not take over your life. That is why I'm proud to say that January is still my BFF. I'm disappointed in Charlene and Jasmine for basically following Monica's crazy ass. I thought they had potential.

I'm glad that Dexter and I are going to January's premiere party tonight. For the past three months Dexter has been acting distant. He wants to start a family and I've been stalling. If the communication between us doesn't change by the end of the party, I guess that I will be forced to suggest that we get a surrogate to carry our baby. I'm not willing to lose Dexter over this baby issue and I'm not willing to halt my career because he wants to start a family. If I have to I will ask my mom or Mama Delgado to babysit our baby while we continue to work full- time.

He's not going to become a Mr. Mom, not on my watch! As of late our relationship has been strained. Perhaps, a night out is just what we need to get back on track.

CHAPTER 10

BREACH OF CONTRACT-(DEXTER)

For me the Ying yang symbol best represents the ideal of matrimony. Ying represents the female which is intuitive while Yang represents the male which is logical. Complementary opposites that interact within a greater whole, men and women come together in an attempt to create perfection, balance. That is why when you accept someone as your mate, you acknowledge and accept their good qualities as well as some of their bad. Basically, you just pick up the slack where your partner lacks.

That being said, the sacrament of matrimony is very important to me. I consider myself to be a thinking man. Introverted by nature I can still be quite outspoken. Generous and understanding to a fault, people perceive me as being somewhat passive but I am not. When disappointed or deceived I become quite aggressive and/or careless. Shit, I become a monster. Once that side of me comes out… I have no mercy. I know my limits, so not to cause any confusion I will always be upfront with my spouse. I give my all and expect the same in return. I would rather be a single man than stay a married fool.

My name is Dexter Delgado and I'm the only son of Victor and Elizabeth Delgado. I grew up in Crown Heights located in Brooklyn, New York. My family owns two adjoining commercial storefront buildings with eight apartments in each building. Growing up my family occupied an apartment on the top floor. My father's logic was that no robber would want to climb over six flights of stairs to rob us. If someone broke into our apartment, it would be personal and not random.

To ensure that my mother wouldn't bitch and moan about doing laundry, my father installed a top of the line washer and dryer inside of our apartment. Trying to silence my mother's bitching and moaning about climbing up all those damn stairs, my father would allow my mother to decorate our three bedroom apartment as often as she wanted, money was no object. What do you think she did? She decorated our apartment as if it was in a home and garden magazine and still complained daily about walking up six flights. That taught me that one should never compromise with the comfort of your woman. Always aim to keep her happy and comfortable. She'll still bitch and moan, just not as often.

My parents were hard workers. After school I would tag along with my father as he performed his various duties around our building while my mother worked long hours as a legal secretary in a prominent law firm. My mother used to come home from work and discuss different cases that the attorneys at her firm were involved in. Intrigued, I would often debate with her on whether or not the client had a legitimate complaint. We would even torture my poor father by having him sit in on a mock trial. My father would be the judge and my mother and I would be opposing attorneys. To keep the peace my father would always let my mother win. I used to laugh and say to myself…poor man.

It was obvious that my father had no interest in hearing my position. He just wanted to score some brownie points with my mother. He would give his ruling with an explanation as if he was actually listening. Those nights he would get lucky! My mother would suggest that I go spend the night at my cousin Chad's house. The next day, my father would be smiling and singing all day long. When my mother came home from work that night, he would hand her a single rose and plant a big kiss on her mouth. If things r-e-a-l-l-y went well, the next night we would all go out for dinner. Again, I would laugh and say to myself…poor man.

I know that my parents loved each other but you could obviously tell that they were complete opposites. My father was 6'1" and weighed about 350 pounds. Having a caramel complexion, he wore a curly afro and was always dressed simple but classy. Drop dead gorgeous, my mother was 5'5" and weighed approximately 145 pounds. With an almond complexion, my mother had long, thick, black, curly hair that she would often blow dry straight. Old fashioned, she never wore pants and believed that a woman should always wear a skirt or a dress. Always dressed professionally, my mother would only put on something sexy if we were having a get together.

My father worked with his hands and my mother worked with her mind. She tended to do all of the reading and writing in the house. My father would seldom read. He was one of those men who would skip reading the instructions when putting something together. He felt that he could wing it and that it would be easy for him to figure out. My mother would volunteer to read the instructions but stubbornly my father would kindly decline. It never failed, shortly afterwards I would see him get his reading glasses and start reading the instructions. Again, I would laugh and say to myself…poor man.

My father loved to drink and was a sports fanatic. My mother frowned when it came to my father's drinking and tolerated us when it came to watching sports. My mother loved to read and was fascinated about anything that had to do with the legal system. Ultimately, their love of music and dancing is what drew them together. They could dance circles around Fred Astaire and Ginger Rogers. Listen, when you hang with the Delgado family you better be able to eat, sing, drink, dance, and be merry.

Being the only child, I often kept to myself. If I wasn't around my parents I was basically over at my cousin Chad's house. Uncle Hector is my father's twin brother. He runs the bodega and barbershop downstairs. Renting an apartment and two commercial storefronts from my father, Uncle Hector always felt that my father was taking advantage of him. They constantly fought over money. Uncle Hector thought that he was being charged too much money for rent and my father felt that my uncle was always trying to get over. So to put some distance between them, my Uncle Hector stopped renting an apartment from my father and just moved around the corner.

Chad and his sister Venus are fraternal twins. My cousins are basically like my siblings. Chad is a jerk and my girl Venus is a sweetheart. I sometimes wish Venus was a dude so that I could hang with her more often. Chad is a show off! He thinks he's slick but he's not. When we hang out he likes to flash a lot of money but he never spends it. I always end up paying the tab. Chad only spends his money on: his clothes, his cars, and his chicks. Now Venus was the opposite, she would give you her last. A hard worker and a genuine person, she would always offer her assistance.

Chad use to call me weak because I would rather study than hang out on the block. That opinion only changed when one day this guy tried to chump him off in front of his girl. I cold knocked dude out. Upset that I didn't let him handle the situation, Chad got mad and didn't speak to me for two weeks. I knew that he could handle the dude, but I just didn't want my cousin to go to jail. One thing that you cannot do is play my cousin out in front of a chick. Dude would've been pistol whipped or worse…killed. Chad was known to carry a gun and wasn't afraid to use it. After that incident, I have never heard him call me weak again. He called me a sucker but never weak. That day, he learned to never sleep on a person's skills, especially mines.

I lost my virginity, freshman year in high school. Chad was dating this girl that had a sister and thought that she was my type. He was right. Teresa had a big booty. I must admit that I'm guilty of being a butt man. You can have a gut with a big butt and I will be in there. You can have zits and no tits but have a big butt…I will be in there. I just love girls with big old butts!

I dated Teresa for two years. I broke up with her because I found out that she had sex with Chad before she slept with me. I told you that he was a jerk. I didn't act out or do anything though. I just told her that it was over. I later found out that Teresa was pregnant supposedly with my child. She decided to have an abortion because I didn't return any of her phone calls and I refused to acknowledge her presence at school. And how did I find this out, you may ask? Chad told me, after the fact.

"Yo, you owe me three hundred dollars. I took your chick to get an abortion and I want my money back."

"Yeah, right mother fucker. You want me to believe that you, mister cheapo, went and paid for Teresa to get an abortion, instead of just telling me. I see that you really think that I am stupid."

"Man, I call myself looking your scary ass out! Now give me my damn money before I have to fuck you up."

"Fuck you!" I said, as I gave him the money that I was saving to buy myself a leather trench coat like Kool Moe Dee.

Chad smiled, as he counted his money. "You're welcome." He replied, as he walked away.

Chad was a certified jerk! Deep down, I knew that it was probably his child. He just wanted to get his money back one way or another. Sometimes…I wonder if he was telling the truth. Is this why Terry and I still to this day don't have any children? Karma is a bitch!

Terry and I met each other in our freshman year at NYU. It was lust at first sight. She had a big, ghetto booty! At first glance you would've thought that she was a snob. Blunt and outspoken, Terry immediately caught my attention. She was fine as hell. Terry had a fat juicy ass, super thick hips, perky big breast, and smooth caramel skin. Once I got her to laugh, I was blessed to see her beautiful smile which immediately drew my attention to her juicy fat lips. And once I finally gazed into her sexy bedroom eyes, I was hooked. Oh, did I forget to mention that she was smart and had a big heart?

Terry played hard to get for about eight months. I wasn't in any rush to have sex because I still couldn't get out of my head that I could've been a father. I tried to calling Teresa a couple of times but she wouldn't answer. I needed to know if it was indeed my baby that she aborted. I needed closure.

When I would bring up the topic to Chad, he would repeatedly say, "Hell yeah!"

You can never tell when dude is telling the truth because he is always lying.

I asked Venus what she thought and she co-signed what Chad said. "What would he gain from lying about that of all things?"

Terry was passionate about law and about life. We made a great couple. We both came from a close family and we had great sex! Her freaky ass never said no. She was as hot blooded as hot blooded could get. From the outside looking in, you wouldn't believe it but she could cook her ass off. My baby was sexy, smart, and loyal.

The ultimate test was to bring her around Chad. Chad felt no woman was off limits if they weren't married. And even then, he would say that he was helping a family stay together. It was obvious that the husband couldn't get the job done.

Chad invited me to a house party that a friend of his was having and I came with Terry. I purposely left Terry alone for twenty minutes and asked Chad to keep an eye on her. When I returned for Terry, she was walking out the door. When I caught up to her, her face looked as if she was crying.

"If you wanted to break up with me, all you had to do was tell me. You didn't have to try to dump me off on your creepy cousin." Terry yelled, at the top of her lungs.

She had passed the test! I knew for a fact that Chad was going to try and test her because that is his STE-LO. He can't help himself…he's a jerk! "Baby, I was on a long distance phone call with my grandmother. I'm sorry. I wanted you to meet Chad because I wanted to set him up with January."

She hugged me tight and said, "When?"

"I will let you know."

Now, I not only lied to my girl but now I had to kiss up to Chad so that he would agree to go out with her best friend. Shocked, it wasn't hard to convince him at all. "Listen, I need you to do me a big favor."

"I'm listening."

"I need you to go on a double date with me. It's with Terry's best friend January. She's pretty but she's a little on the chunky side."

"Cool, I like big girls. Big girls need love too. If she's as pretty as you say and you're footing the bill, I don't mind."

January was a double major in culinary school and had a hectic schedule. She declined our invite. YO! I never heard a chick turn down a date with Chad. Terry even showed her a picture of him and she still didn't budge. I teased him about that for years.

When Terry and I graduated from college I proposed to her. I saved all the money that I made from working at my mother's firm as an assistant and bought a three karat princess cut diamond ring. Two months before graduation I asked her parents for her hand in marriage.

Overjoyed her father offered me some money to go towards the engagement ring. "Dexter, I know your parents are proud of you. They have raised a fine young man. I'm honored that you asked me for my daughter's hand in marriage. You remind me of myself when I was your age. Listen take this money to help you get a ring for my baby. It's not much but it will at least help in eating up some of the taxes." He chuckled.

"No thank you, Mr. Tucker. I'm the one that's honored. Everything has been taken care of, I already brought the ring. I'm just eager to pop the question to Terry before we start law school in the fall. I want everyone to know that she's spoken for."

We celebrated graduating from college by going on a bus trip to Atlantic City.

Terry didn't want a graduation party. "Baby, when we both graduate from law school then we can celebrate with a party. Until then, I'm fine with our little getaway to AC."

We were walking on the boardwalk when I suddenly dropped to one knee and grabbed her hand. "Terry, will you accept my hand in marriage?"

Terry said, in a pleasant voice, "No Thank You," and slowly walked away.

"What the fuck do you mean…NO THANK YOU?"

She started laughing and said, "I got you."

I got so mad that I was about to curse her out.

Sensing that I was mad at her, she in turn got on one knee and asked me. "Dexter Delgado will you please do me the honor of being my lawful wedded husband? Will you marry me?"

Acting like the response that I originally wanted, I started jumping up and down screaming "YES…YES…YES I WILL MARRY YOU!"

We both burst out laughing, hysterically.

When I put the ring on her finger she smiled and said, "I like your style Mr. Delgado. I like your style."

Law school was kicking our butts. Several times I wanted to drop out but Terry wouldn't let me. I already had a decent paying job as an assistant at my mom's job and frankly, I was tired of the long hours of studying. Always having to turn down parties because of my studies, I wanted to have some fun.

"No pain, no gain. Baby, must I remind you how far we've come? We can't turn back now. Just hold on a little longer, we're almost at the finish line. I can taste the nectar of sweet success." Terry would say with an angelic smile.

I know for a fact that I would've never graduated from law school if I didn't have Terry in my corner. I can't believe how much I love her. I can't wait until we have a little Terry. I'm going to spoil the shit out of her.

Once we graduated from law school, we started ironing out what we wanted and expected from each other. Terry wanted us to have a pre-nup. "Baby, I don't want you to think that I was trying to pull a fast one on you. I had no clue about your family's wealth when I met you. Coming from a lawyer's stand point a prenuptial agreement would only be logical."

Upset I responded, "I don't want us to have a pre-nup. Such an agreement makes it appear that we don't have what it takes to make it last…to make it work. I know that we got the makings for a lifelong marriage."

"Are you sure?"

"I'm sure. The only thing that I want you to promise me is that we can start our family no later than thirty-five. I want my little baby girl or boy."

"I promise."

With the wedding set to take place in the Dominican Republic, I had planned a romantic seven day cruise that would make a stop in DR. I loved Terry with all my heart and wanted our love to stand the test of time like our parents.

Chad was in charge of my bachelor's party. He invited Derrick, Eddie, some family and a couple of our childhood friends to a locked door at his boy, Eli's house. I told Chad that I didn't want that type of party but it fell on deaf ears. It was ridiculous, how nasty some women can be. I told Chad that I wanted to keep my promise to Terry of no sex for two months before the wedding. It was exactly a week before my ship was about to sail and damn be damn I'm going to…OH MY! Do I see a BIG PHAT GHETTO BOOOOTY?

I can't believe my eyes. This bitch ass was enormous, her name was Reindeer and she was from the ATL. She was approximately 5'7" and had a smooth caramel complexion. Thick as hell she had 34DD bust, 25" waist, 40" hips, and ass for days. This man was trying to get me killed! Man down, man down, I kept shouting in my head! With the lights dim and strobe light on, the mood was set. Nasty music was thumping loud in the background saying shit like "Put it in your mouth girl" and "swallow it like a champ tramp." She took her thong off and started making her ass cheeks clap. I was getting dizzy, watching her massive round butt cheeks smack each other as they made waves of jiggling sexiness down her thighs. As she made her rounds, all I could see was that booty clapping in rhythm with the music.

I jumped the fuck up and said, at the top of my voice, "Thanks Chad. Thanks fellas. I'm out, PEACE!" Before Chad could pull me back, I was out of there.

The next night Chad asked me to come over to Eli's house suggesting that I forgot something. Once there I was appalled. Last night that jerk was videotaping the entire bachelor party and didn't even tell me? After I watched the tape with the guys, I broke it. "I'M A LAWYER NOW…I CAN'T GET CAUGHT UP IN SHIT LIKE THAT!"

"Yo, you owe me a G note! You destroyed the tape before I could make any copies. I already had some pre-orders. Your duck ass just cost me some easy money."

I wrote Chad a check and told him that I didn't want to see him anymore until my wedding day. The bum is a certified jerk!

Playing matchmaker, I asked Derrick to make sure that January was seated next to Chad on the flight to the Dominican Republic. I was hoping that some sparks would fly between them like how they did when I met Terry. My cousin needs a good woman like January in his life. Maybe with January in his life he will stop being such a jerk off. If I didn't have Terry, I wouldn't be half the man that I am today. That is why I love spoiling my baby… she's the Ying to my yang.

The wedding went off without a hitch. And from what I saw, January was feeling Chad. All I could do was set them up and it was up to Chad to make the love connection. I got so fucking drunk that I couldn't remember anything after the first dance. Thank goodness we have the wedding on video. Unlike most people, Terry and I watch the video at least once every two years. We watch the video to help us stay focused on what is important…us. It was my idea. Sometimes, I feel that I am losing Terry to the corporate world. Especially, since she made partnership at her firm earlier this year all I keep hearing about is how happy she was.

Everything is going right for Terry and my career takes a sharp left turn. My firm lost a costly sexual harassment lawsuit this year. The firm wanted me to represent the accused partner in the firm and I refused. I knew for sure that they were going to fire me but instead they just gave me a smaller office and a big pay cut. They did that to make me want to "voluntarily" resign. They knew that if I had handled the case that they would've probably won. I refused to take it because I knew that the accusations were true. I had spoken to the powers that be a year earlier and told them that I suspected that exact partner was indeed sexually harassing the new male associates. They thanked me for my concern and said that they would look into it.

I knew that I should've minded my own business but I just chose not to. I didn't mention my suspicions to Terry because she would've advised me that I was committing career suicide. She also would've advised me to not only take the case but to win it. She would've smiled and said that they would now be indebted to me.

My conscious wouldn't let me take it. I knew that the only reason that they wanted me to take the case was because the accused was Caucasian and the accuser was Latino. I also realized way too late that they already knew that the accused partner preyed on the new male associates. They have been covering up for this lawyer for years. They were not going to fire me in fear that I might also sue them. I tried to blow the whistle a year prior to the case and because I knew too much they preferred that I resign and went away.

Sometimes I feel that I don't have the heart for this shit anymore. Terry wants me to shop around for a new firm but I know that no one will touch me after I refused to litigate my firm's most important case. I want to discuss my situation with Terry but I'm afraid of the backlash. I'm not stupid. I knew damn well that I should've taken that case. I was just being stubborn and now that I have time to think about it, I was being very stupid. I wouldn't have turned down that case if I had a child. My responsibilities to my child would've held the upmost importance to me. This is actually Terry's fault! She should've given me a child by now. I'm starting to see that we may have a breach of contract, on Terry's part.

We're going to be thirty-five years old this year. Something is telling me that she's not going to keep her promise to slow down and start a family with me. Every time I mention starting a family she wants us to go to the Dominican Republic. That's why we go twice a year because twice a year I bring up the topic. I even suggested that we start going to a fertility doctor because I'm shocked that she hasn't gotten pregnant yet. We have sex like rabbits so where the hell are the little bunnies?

If it walks like a duck and it quacks like a duck then it is a duck. Terry had no intentions on having a baby! She broke her promise to me and that my friend is a breach of contract. I privately contacted a divorce attorney to discuss my options. I told him that I wanted Terry to pay out of her ass for making me waste my time. I even researched and found out that I could make a claim for her to pay me damages for breaking her promise to have a baby. That would set Terry on fire if she thought that I was taking her to court for money or worse spousal support.

I'm hurt. Worst, I'm crushed. I don't want a divorce. I love Terry. I just want her to have our child. If it was the other way around, she would've been taken me to court. I should've listened to her when she wanted us to draw up a pre-nup. Maybe then, she would've given me a baby.

About three or four months ago, I can't remember because I was drunk. I went to Chad's house to speak to him about my dilemma with Terry. I needed someone who would keep it real and raw with me. Recently, Chad has gotten engaged to January after dating her on and off again for the past nine years. I figured that maybe he has changed and could help me with my dilemma.

Chad must've shut off his cellphone because it went straight to his voicemail every time I called it. I rang his doorbell and he didn't answer. His doorman recognized me and allowed me into the building. I heard music playing but many people keep music playing while they're not at home. I really, really needed to use bathroom and I knew it couldn't wait until I got home. Stupidly, I got his spare key from under his floor mat and helped myself into his apartment. The chain was on the door, so Chad must be in there, I thought to myself.

In a drunken state of mind and having to desperately go to the bathroom, I started yelling, "Chad…Chad, open up the door man. I got to go to the bathroom!"

"Hold up!"

Once in, I ran to his bathroom. When I returned to his living room, he shouted. "WHAT THE FUCK IS YOUR PROBLEM? THAT KEY IS FOR ME TO USE IF I FORGET MY KEY, IT'S NOT FOR YOUR CONVENIENCE!"

"Dude, I had to use the bathroom. I tried calling and ringing the bell… you didn't answer. Oh, my bad, is January here with you?"

"Man…What do you want? What is the urgency?"

"I think that I'm about to file for a divorce. I want to have children and I don't foresee Terry slowing down with her career, anytime soon."

"Do you still love her?"

"Of course, I still love her."

While guiding me to the door, he responded. "Well, that's your answer. Don't get divorced. Go home and discuss this with your wife. Tell her if she doesn't make some room in her life for you two to have a baby that she is going to force you to make one elsewhere or worse get a divorce. Goodbye."

"Poor baby," I heard a female voice say as it came from around the corner.

"Monica?" I sighed.

She came forth and gave me a hug while she continued to say, "Poor baby."

"Why are you here? Is January here too? And what do you mean, when you say poor baby?" I asked, as she guided me back to the couch and sat beside me.

In a concerned voice, she said. "I thought that you knew that Terry never wanted to have any children. She's on the pill and she uses a diaphragm."

"What! What! Why didn't you tell me this before? Why are you telling me this now?" I yelled, as I couldn't believe my ears.

"Man, go home and calmly discuss this with your wife. Monica is putting her two cents in where it doesn't belong." Chad said, in a soothing voice.

"I feel the pain in your voice. That is why I'm telling you. I didn't know that she didn't discuss her true feelings about having children before she got married to you. I feel so sorry for you." Monica said.

"Yo, I got some place to be other than here. I'm out. You two can see yourselves out after you two have finished your discussion. Just lock my door behind you and man put my key back under my mat." Chad angrily said, as he made an abrupt exit.

"That cunt, that lying bitch," I cried out in agony.

Obviously familiar with Chad's apartment, Monica went straight to his stash of liquor and poured us shots of Patron. We talked as we killed Chad's bottle of Patron. I was on fire. I was angry as hell that I had to hear from Monica that she didn't want to have any children. It made me think about Teresa. If Chad would've minded his own business I would've had a child. I'm a fool for trusting that bitch! I turned down mad bitches for her. Then the image of the stripper from Atlanta came into my head, REINDEER! I missed out on fucking Reindeer I thought to myself.

"Oh my," Monica exclaimed as she pointed to my hard on.

Thinking about Reindeer's phat ass gave me an instant erection. "Oh, excuse me I need to go to the bathroom."

"What are you about to do?"

"I will be back. I'm going to handle myself."

"The least that I could do is to help you with your problem… that is a waste of a hard dick."

This bitch took off her clothes. Although a little too small for my type, Monica was right. Her little waist made her perky ass look huge. And when I saw that this bitch had her pussy pierced, I almost jumped out of my fuckin skin. Frozen, I just watched the show. This crazy bitch unzipped my pants and with her back faced to me, she sat down on my erect dick!

"AHH, AHH," she moaned as she slowly came down on my rod.

Like I told you before, I'm a butt man and with that being said it was time to get to work. I grabbed her waist and started to pump my rod deep into her hot and oh so wet pussy.

"AHH, AHH, AHH!" She shouted, as I was beating that pussy up with my man of steel.

With my dick still inside of her, I picked her up and bent her over Chad's glass coffee table. If I was going to do wrong, I better do it right. I started slamming my dick into her wet pussy harder and harder. I was straight fucking this bitch.

She kept screaming and yelling, "YEAH, FUCK ME!"

I rammed my dick so far into her that I thought it was going to come out of her mouth. I even started pulling her weave. I wrapped it around my fist while I punished her pussy with my fat dick.

"YEAH, YEAH, FUCK ME DADDY, FUCK ME," she exclaimed, as I tried my best to bring the pain.

"You have been a bad girl," I spouted as I started to get into it.

"Yes daddy! Yes…I've been a bad …AHH…AHH…GIRL!" She passionately shouted as I started to ease up and stroke the pussy.

I have never cheated on Terry and I wanted to savor the moment. "Yeah, yeah…"

"AHHHHH, AHHHHH!" She moaned. Then this freaky bitch did some jiggling thing with her butt cheeks and I was hit.

"UGHHH, UGHHH! I'M ABOUT TO CUM! I shouted, as I tried to pull out and this bitch fell backwards into my nut.

"I want all of it daddy," she said, as she purposely had me nut inside of her.

"I hope that you're on the pill?"

"Nope" she said, with a devilish grin as she then retreated to the bathroom.

I ran to the bathroom to yoke this bitch up but she locked the door. "What the fuck do you mean that you're not on the pill?"

"I'm just kidding Dexter. It's all good in the neighborhood," she said as she remained in the bathroom, giggling.

"It better be," I said as I saw my way out.

Well, as you can see, I'm going to have to back off from harassing Terry to have our baby. Especially, after how I fucked Monica unprotected of all people. How fucking careless? I'm a fool.

For the past couple of months, I basically stayed away from Chad and Monica. I even fell back from sleeping with Terry. I would make up excuses like my stomach was hurting or I was busy working on a project. I mainly used work as my excuse for not having sex. I wanted to wait three months and then get a checkup. You never can be too careful. I even emailed Monica and asked her to send something about her medical history. She actually responded and told me to kick rocks.

Wow, talking about jumping out of the fire and into the frying pan. To clear my mind I just focused on looking for a new job and thinking of a plan B when it came to my life. Tonight I was going to January's premiere party. I decided not to get drunk especially after what I did the last time that I got drunk. Talk about a breach of contract, fucking your wife's girlfriend is THE ULTIMATE BREACH!

CHAPTER 11

BROOKLYN'S IN THE HOUSE-(CHAD)

My father named me Chad but instead he should've named me Brooklyn. I'm representing BK for life. A king amongst kings and a boss amongst bosses, in New York City, there is no other place in the world that I would rather be. There is no other place that can bang with New York. New Jersey tries to but of course they fail to cut the mustard.

My streets are tough but they show a brother much love. You can go anywhere in Brooklyn and my name ring bells. I'm a proud Dominican man who is proud to belong to the Delgado Family. Everything that I've learned, when it has come to business I've learned from my father Hector Delgado and my uncle Victor Delgado. Everything else, I've learned from the cold streets of New York.

Growing up, my fraternal twin sister Venus and I used to help my parents run the family's business, the bodega. My mother spoke very little English therefore my father sent my mother to take English classes. After two years of classes my mother still spoke very little English this used to piss my father off. Why would she always claim not to understand English? Simply to make my father feel needed. My mother perfectly understood and spoke English at her own convenience. Bitches ain't shit, I tell you. My mother taught me that valuable lesson about women a long time ago. So that is why I can't trust them if my life depended on it. I'm not calling my mother a bitch. I'm just trying to stress a point. Bitches are full of shit.

If a woman says that she needs some money, she has money. She just doesn't want to spend her money. She feels your money is her money and her money is her money. If a woman says that she is on the pill, strap up. She practices unprotected sex, need I say more? If a woman says that he is just a friend, then she is fucking him. If a woman says that she is single she has a man, he just doesn't hit it right. And most important, if your woman asks you for your help stating that she doesn't understand something, she's lying. She just wants you to believe that she needs you and only you. In other words she's gassing you up. You can either take it from me or learn it the hard way like I did from the cold streets of Brooklyn.

My father and my uncle taught me well. They taught me that only hard work pays off in the end. Let me put you up on game. I took the principles of hard work and combined them with the idea of getting easy money. Combine the essentials of hard work and easy money together and you will definitely get cheddar…a whole lot of cheddar.

Now realize, I did emphasize on the word…work. You have to put in some work. I am not talking about slaying your girl in bed so that you can get something to eat or get a pack of cigarettes. Oh and let us not forget the common one… to get some minutes on your prepaid cellphone.

It takes money to make money and it takes money to attract money. Money doesn't grow on trees but if you truly handle your business you will see the money that you have… grow. Yes, I have money from my family investments. I also have money because I hustle for it. I own a barbershop and two doobie shops. When times are hard, a reasonably priced new hair-do can do wonders for a person's self- esteem and if that doesn't pick you up, then a little yayo will.

My father and my uncle taught me to always defend myself and my family. I stay with the heat. You can't bring a knife to a gun fight. Taking it a step further, I start shit and I end the shit that I have started. A dog urinates on a spot to show his ownership…his dominance. I start shit so people know that they better come correct or they will get fucked up. People tend to take your kindness for weakness so sometimes you got to stir shit up a little.

Some people think that I'm too arrogant and that I'm too cocky. I am. I can afford to be so because I can back my shit up. If you do dirt you better have a shovel. I do. Why? Because what goes around will definitely come back around and when it does you don't need to get upset. You just use your shovel to dig yourself out of your rut. You just brush your fucking shoulders off and keep it moving.

Game recognizes game and I'm not going out like some lollipop… some sucker. Because if you're a lollipop, you get played like you're sweet. You can either take it from me or learn it the hard way, like I did, from the cold streets of Brooklyn.

Everyone loves the candy man and the candy man wants them to stay in love for as long as they can. The candy man only loves the color of green… money. And that my friend comes and goes, sometimes you have it and sometimes you don't. Don't ever get the game twisted. It's always about the ends. You can either take it from me or learn it the hard way and get yourself killed in the cold streets of Brooklyn. It is entirely up to you.

My cousin Dexter looks at me as being his brother because he's an only child. He's a lollipop. He's always going to be a sucker. Because he's my cousin I try to toughen him up and give him some guidance but he is just a lost cause.

I remember when I hooked him up with his first piece of ass. He didn't have to do any of the work or go through any of the hassles. I was the one that had to do all the hunting just to hand him a guaranteed lay. Her name was Teresa and I was banging her older sister Tonya. I failed to mention to him that I had tested out the goods before I had handed her over to him, all tied up with a big red bow. This soft ass, duck ass, punk ass joker dumps the girl when he finds out through the grape vine that I had fucked her. He should've been happy that I was gracious enough to put him up on some pussy. And most importantly, whoever she slept with before him was her business. Why did he have to trip?

On the rebound tip Teresa wanted to fuck with me again. Feeling responsible for her broken heart I gladly started fucking her again. The condom popped and she got pregnant. I wasn't going to have that whore give birth to my child so I paid for her to have an abortion. I felt that I wouldn't have gotten Teresa pregnant if she had just stayed her ass with Dexter, so Dexter caused her to need comfort from me which caused her to get pregnant. Yeah, that sounds just about right. So, it's only right that I made Dexter give me back my money. Now of course I told a little white lie to get back my money but being a sucker he bought into it hook, line, and sinker. Like I told you before he is a LOLLIPOP.

My sister Venus is harder than that chump. Shit, her temper is worse than mine. Like The Venus Flytrap, she will lure you in and if you're not careful, eat you up alive especially if she thinks that you are playing her. I taught her well or shall I say she takes heed to my advice. A stone cold dyke, my sister knows when to appear hard and when to appear soft...her name fits her oh so well.

I remember when Venus was kicking it with this banging chick named Unique. Thick and bow-legged, she was about 5'5" and had long ebony hair with blonde highlights. Back then, Venus was 5'10", weighed 200 pounds, and had shoulder length curly black hair. Well, honey dip for months was trying to play Venus out. She accepted all the money and gifts that my sister gave her but wasn't trying to give up the goods. Juniors in high school, my sister even paid for her prom dress. Puzzled as to why the girl was still fronting, Venus dumped Unique the night before their junior prom. Dateless, Venus decided to go to the prom with a couple of her friends. Like she suspected,

Unique showed up to the prom with her ex-boyfriend this local drug dealer named Felix.

Not wanting to be a party pooper, Venus waited until the prom was over before she started her havoc. When she saw my man outside, she stretched him out and took all of his dough and jewelry. "Unique, this is what you dissed me for? This bum, wow, I gave you too much credit. I will be expecting you to return all my shit that I gave you by tomorrow. And oh, you can keep the dress. It looks good on you."

That same night, Venus told my parents that she was spending the night at a friend's house. Unique not only gave my sister some ass, that fateful night, she officially became her girlfriend. Unique and Venus continued to date exclusively for about eight years. If that was punk ass Dexter, he would've been without his shit, without his woman, and without getting a piece of that sweet ass. Venus is no joke. Eventually, she dumped Unique because she started hanging with the wrong crowd and got strung out on drugs. Unique didn't realize until it was too late, that her so called friends were jealous of her relationship with my sister. My sister use to spoil the shit out of her. When she finally stopped using drugs, it was too late. My sister had already moved on.

Though we're all different, I know one family trait that all three of us have in common. We like to have and make a lot of money. My sister learned to cook from my mother and decided to take her gift of cooking to the next level. She graduated from cooking school at the top of her class and is currently working as a head chef at January's restaurant. My cousin Dexter, who practically stayed on breast milk until he was eighteen, loved to read and discuss law with my aunt Elizabeth, who was a legal secretary. Dexter lucked up and met Terry in college. Terry not only convinced him to go to law school but she helped him graduate from it too. This sucker always gets the breaks. I can't believe that he actually got Terry to marry him. She's a fly ass chick. Tough as nails, Terry ain't no pushover. She needs a man like me in her corner to take her to the next level. I chose to follow in my father's footsteps and become a businessman. And like as a true businessman, I'm always shopping for the best merger. I just got engaged to January Jackson.

January is hella sexy and is completely down to earth. She has a great sense of humor and enjoys not taking herself too seriously. And she's the only woman that has ever turned me down in my life. She has mad self-esteem, considering she is a bit on the juicy side. Don't get me wrong, I got much love for the big girls. I just never had any woman, let alone a plus size woman reject me before January.

I'm 5'10" and weigh 215 pounds. I've a deep caramel complexion and, from what I've been told, a deep sexy voice. Similar to a Brook, I sport a curly black afro that I maintain by getting weekly shapeups. One of the perks of owning a barbershop is that the barber comes to my loft. Always dressed to impress and smelling good, I'm quite handsome if I must say so myself. January is rare. She has never pressured me to get married or to leave Brooklyn. It was only logical that I proposed to her making the ultimate merger. She has great pussy and has her own money…sold to Brooklyn's finest, Chad Delgado.

At times, I wish that she would get a little jealous. She's too laid back, as if to say that she can take it or leave it when it comes to our relationship. It disturbs me and at the same time it entices me. January is truly a keeper not to mention my family adores her. Venus and January clicked immediately. My sister hopes to learn a lot about the cooking industry by working with her.

January has voluptuous curves. Thick and sexy, she's 5'8" and weighs 245 pounds. Stacked with 42DD's, a 38" waist, and 47" hips my juicy big mama is GOOD. Having ebony shoulder length hair, smooth mocha skin, eyes of an angel, a smile that can illuminate any room, and a heart of gold

At first, I didn't believe Dexter when he laughingly said, "She's not biting dude. January is not interested in meeting you. Terry even showed her a picture of you that I had. The great Chad Delgado has finally been rejected!"

I thought Dexter was just being a hater until I finally got to know her. January wasn't rejecting me. She was just trying to stay focused and on her grind. And baby…baby…baby it finally paid off. My juicy big mama has published two cook books, has her very own restaurant, and now has her very own cooking show. I'm honored to be her fiancé.

On and off again, it hasn't always been peaches and cream. Out the blue, January would often break up with me stating, "We're too young to try and make things permanent. I think we need to slow down and give each other some space to grow. Maybe we need to call it quits for a little while."

Thinking that it was me that wanted to break up, everybody would look at me with the screw face. They would be shocked to know the truth. The truth is that her eyes were always on the prize. The restaurant industry is a competitive industry and she wanted to stay on top her game. January felt romance would just get in her way. Throughout the years, we've always kept phone communication open. One minute we would be talking about politics and the next minute we would be having erotic phone sex. Freaky, we often would role play and meet up at bars. One time an undercover cop, thought that she was a hooker and that I was trying to proposition her. Luckily, January is sentimental and had her wallet filled with pictures of us. We laughed all night long and I dare not mention the awesome sex that we would have when we got to her place.

If we had a nightcap, we normally stayed at January's place in Jersey

City. "Bay, let's just go to my place. Please, I prefer it this way. I can't take any surprises."

"Rocky, it is okay. There won't be any surprises waiting for you at my place. MI CASA ES SU CASA."

She would always decline. Shit, that was great for me. That allowed me to continue to appear to be available. I would often have chicks spend a night or two at my place. Unlike other women, January really meant what she said. If January wanted to come to my crib, she would let me know in advance. We would be chilling on the phone and then she would make a suggestion. "Bay, if you want, I can come over to your place straight after work tomorrow to see you if you don't feel like taking the trip to Jersey? I would rather go home but to keep my baby satisfied, I could come..."

"No mommy, you can go home. I'll see you later. I got a couple of errands to run and I wouldn't want to keep you waiting. You could already be at home unwinding while I do what I got to do, okay?"

"Okay."

Throughout her townhouse, January has pictures of us hanging all over her walls. She has even given me my very own closet and a key. I don't feel threatened at all. I have the best of both worlds. I get to stay in Brooklyn and live a little in Jersey City. January is dear to my heart. She's smart like my father and sneaky like my mother, which leads me to the next question. Do I really know the real January Jackson or is she just running game? I told you before, game recognizes game. I often think to myself this woman is too good to be true...

...I remember when we went to Vegas to witness Charlene and her new beau get married. Trying to be romantic, I privately proposed to January in our suite. That night was the best trip to Vegas that I've ever had. Pleasantly surprised, January freaked me the fuck out. She ordered me to sit stark naked, in an armless chair, keep my eyes closed, and not to move. Happy to oblige, I was delighted when she told me to open my eyes. My sexy big mama came out of the bathroom wearing nothing but a cowgirl hat, in anticipation, my dick instantly got rock hard. Like a pro she slowly straddled me and rode me up and down like a mechanical bull.

"UMMMMM...baby, I just love my ring."

"I'm glad," I replied, as I tried to keep my cool. My baby is hot blooded, she's always on fire. As she repeatedly went up and down on my man, I vigorously licked her succulent black nipples.

"UMMMMM...BABY! Am I your naughty cowgirl?"

"UMM, UMM, UMM, UMM, UMM, you know you are." I replied, as I continued to tease her nipples with my tricky tongue. My baby was riding me like a certain Atlanta stripper, that at this time I can't remember her name. "Yeah baby! Fuck that shit baby!" I grunted, as my juicy big mama was steadily riding my tool.

My baby was doing her thing. I didn't pump back, I just stayed perfectly still. At times, my January tends to be a control freak in the bedroom. Yeah, I got myself a bedroom bully. She refuses to climax until she makes me bust first. She's my juicy super freak and wouldn't have her any other way. She's perfect just the way she is. As January slowed her strokes, I could feel her hot wet pussy pulsating around my shaft. "YEAH, YEAH, IT'S YOURS BABY… TAKE YOUR SHIT!" I exclaimed.

January likes to ride me because she has an extremely fat clit. She loves the stimulation that she gets from her clit rubbing against my shaft while my dick is inside of her pussy. It makes her reach an extreme orgasm. When she reaches that orgasm her pussy tightens up and puts a bear hug on my dick, which causes us to come simultaneously.

"UMMMM… UMMMM! Baby…I love how you do me!" She muttered, as she whined on top of my dick. "OH BABY!"

As her extremely hot and juicy pussy started to get tighter and tighter I knew that she was about to erupt. Trying to get her to bust before me, I would sneak in a couple of pumps as she continued to professionally ride her stallion. Trying to hold on for dear life, I could no longer ignore the grip that January's pussy had on my dick.

"UGHHHH, UGHHHH! I'M CUMMING, UGHHHH!" I exclaimed. Embarrassed that I couldn't show some dick control, I lovingly picked January up and placed her on the bed. I started tongue kissing her while my fingertips manipulated her nipples. As we moaned and groaned, my dick started to get hard again.

"OOOOOH, AHHHHHH, OOOOOOH!" My juicy big mama moaned, as I continued to keep her fire lit until my dick returned to his maximum status.

Then it was time to really get it in, I inserted my hard dick inside her flaming hot pussy. "OH SHIT!" I shouted, as I was afraid that I was about to bust again. January pussy was mega hot and wet. As I started to slowly deep stroke her, I played with her juicy fat clit. Erect, her clit gets as big as my thumb it trips me out every time I play with it.

"UMMMMMMM… AHHHHHHHHH… UMMMMMM!" my juicy big mama moaned, as I steadily deep stroked her pussy in and then out, deeper and deeper, and ever so deep and ever so slow while simultaneously caressing her stiff clit. "UMMMMMMM, OH BABY… OH BABY!"

I was careful not to get too fancy because I didn't want to blow. I was enjoying myself. I wanted to take my time satisfying my baby. "Yeah, you like how that feels… don't ya?" I muttered, as I saw her as eyes roll behind her head. "Yeah, you like that shit!"

I guess she took my comments as a challenge and started to slow wind her hips.

"Stop, January!" I playfully commanded, as I saw the bedroom bully in her start to come out. To deaf ears, January kept slow winding her hips. "YEAH, AHHH, YEAH," I shouted, as I sped up and started to straight fuck her. "You want to start shit?"

"Hell yeah," she shouted, as she then raised her legs up and parted them further apart, to allow me to go deeper. I started hammering her pussy.

"Eat that dick! Eat that dick!" I shouted, as January started to tremble. Deeper and deeper, I would pound her pussy. And then I hit it, her G-spot.

"OH MY, OH MY!" she gasped, as she started to fuck me back harder and stronger.

"YEAH   YEAH…I GOT THIS…THIS IS MY SHIT!" I shouted, as I steadily hit her G-spot.

The vibrations felt awesome. Intense and sharp, the vibrations got stronger and stronger as I kept hitting her spot.

"AHHHHHHH, AHHHHHHH!"

I kept pumping as she started tensing up. "YEAH, YEAH, YEAH, GET YOUR SHIT OFF BABY! YEAH! WHOSE PUSSY IS THIS? WHOSE PUSSY IS THIS?"

"YOURS…YOURS," She stuttered, in between her screaming. January was having an orgasm. She looked sexy as hell.

Showing dick control, I continued to fuck the shit out of her and then she did it. She wrapped her legs around my waist and pulled me close to her torso as she fucked me back from the bottom. "AHHHHHHHHH, AHHHHHHH, AHHHHHH! I…I…I'M CUMMING! I shouted, as I let lose a big one. "Why you just couldn't enjoy yourself for a change? You just couldn't help yourself. You just couldn't lie there and eat that dick."

Laughing she responded, in a fake Jamaican accent, "Because rude boy, me is a bedroom bully, you know."

I started dying laughing. January is a certified freak! You know I had to beat it up again, later on that night. I can't let her get that shit off. A man must maintain dick control at all times. A man, who doesn't maintain dick control, will be controlled by the pussy if he doesn't watch himself. I refuse to be controlled by the pussy. That's why I continue to sleep with other bitches. I'm not going to get so caught up on one bitch. Bitches ain't shit! They're sneaky and can't be trusted. I would rather place my trust in my Smith and Wesson before I ever place it with a bitch.

Now, I'm not calling January a bitch, I'm just trying to stress a point.

January is cool but that's the problem. She's too cool. She gives me space, awesome sex, and sometimes money. I know that I'm missing something. I just can't put my finger on it. Every chick except January sweats me and becomes my stalker. I have had short ones, tall ones, slim ones, thick ones, dark ones, light ones, and all of them sweat me except January. I just can't figure her out. I was actually surprised when she accepted my proposal. I mean really, we've been seeing each other on and off for almost a decade. Most bitches would've trapped a brotha with a baby by now.

I learned after the Teresa incident to always be careful and to always use your OWN condoms. That is why I have a condom tree in my bedroom. I personally refill and inspect each condom before I use it. I've had bitches talk about how they're on the pill or how they take a shot. Fuck that... besides pregnancy, I can catch something that I just can't get rid of! People are going around with that shit just passing it around like it's cool.

I sleep around but I'm selective. If it looks too good to be true I retreat. Some of those fly bitches got that shit and refuse to use condoms. That shit is foul as hell now that person is just wrong. I guess that is why I dig January so much. Every single time we got back together, we would get a complete physical and exchange medical results. To me, that just cleared the air and made everything comfortable as if we never parted ways. The last time we were separated it lasted for two years. That was the longest we stayed not claiming each other. The longest we stayed together was four years. We just got back together a little before we went on that Vegas trip.

I proposed to January because I didn't want some new jack to slip into my spot and sweep her up off her feet. She was about to become big time and I didn't want all my years of hard labor to be in vain. As a true business man, I knew January's worth and I wanted to complete the ultimate merger. Everything has been going smooth between us. This time around I have no doubt about my feelings for her. I want to marry her. If I'm hesitant, it's because I don't want to leave Brooklyn to move to Jersey City. Her townhouse is way bigger than my loft, so it would only be natural that she would want me to move in with her. It would be too good to be true if she would consider moving to Brooklyn. I would be gassed the fuck up if she gave up her precious townhouse, for me.

January loves her townhouse! If she was willing to move to Brooklyn that would mean that she was really feeling me. In that case, I would settle down and give up fucking around. I would just have one side piece. I got to keep one in the hole, just in case she doesn't act right. Bitches will act one way to trap you and once they got you they will switch the fuck up. Bitches ain't shit I tell you!

I have a couple of childhood friends that I hang around with. We play pool, play cards, bowl, and go clubbing. We often go to Vegas and to the Dominican Republic. One year we went to Brazil. I had thought I had died and gone to heaven! Everything that happened in Brazil stayed in Brazil! That is all that I can say when it came to our trip. Against my better judgment, I even invited Dexter to go.

"Terry will only let me go if she can come with me."

"Man, are you stupid? If you bring Terry, January will naturally want to go. What the fuck were you thinking about when you asked Terry could you go? Mutha fucka, I told January that I was going on a trip with my boys and that was it! Nothing more and nothing less, as long as I wasn't hitting her up for money she didn't give a damn!"

I waited a couple of days and then I told him that the trip was cancelled and that I would hit him up when I got the new date. What a fucking lollipop! Why would dummy tell Terry of all people that he was planning a trip to Brazil with me? She knows that I would influence him to sample the sweet nectar of Brazil. Wow, what a duck ass!

I hang with my friends but I don't allow them to hang with me. Meaning, when I want to hang with them, I chill with them. It's not a two way street. Frankly, I have trust issues. I don't trust people like that to let them be around my home, my family and/or my woman like that. It is better that way and a whole lot safer to keep the two worlds separate.

Loosely, I use the word friends because all of my so called friends work for me in some capacity. So are they actually my friends? NO! Do I need to keep a close eye on them? YES! I'm a business man. I always have to balance my professional and personal ties that I have with people, especially the ties that could affect my business.

Last year someone robbed my barbershop and pistol whipped one of my barbers. They only got me for a G note because I unexpectedly picked up my daily proceeds. I didn't tell anybody that I was going to drop by early. About two hours after I left, the shop got robbed. Everyone knows how I get down so why would somebody choose to rob my barbershop over another barbershop? I know that shops get robbed daily in Crown Heights, but mine? Something sounds fishy, doesn't it?

Maybe I didn't make myself clear. I normally collect $5,000 to $8,000 per day from my barbershop. Why would someone choose to rob my shop and just pistol whip the barber and not shoot him? Someone wants me to believe that someone would randomly or knowingly rob my barbershop in broad daylight and leave an eye witness? Let's just say that barber is no longer working for me and I gave him his severance. Keeping a close eye on my business and friends allowed my third eye to tell me, that I needed to start doing business differently. Now, everyone has to get buzzed in to enter the barbershop. I even slightly tinted the window panes to the shop. If you want to know what's going on inside the shop…you have to first get into the shop. I messed up. I normally make it my business to know the intimate dealings of my barbers. Homeboy was seeing an unfamiliar and was running his mouth. You gotta be careful not to pillow talk the wrong shit with bitches that can get you killed. That's also why I love my January so much she doesn't ask too many questions. I know she knows what time it is. Her father is a cop and she lives in Jersey City, need I say more? As long as I keep things discreet and don't put my business out on front-street, she'll continue to ride with me.

I've been fucking January's friend Monica, since she moved back to Jersey from Atlanta. Yeah, I got some big balls. She actually stepped to me. Basically, she was looking to cop without paying for it. I hooked her up and in return she offered to show me her heartfelt appreciation. A little cutie, I let her sample my goods. Truth to be told, January skills are actually tighter than hers in more ways than one. Monica is overrated. Don't get me wrong, she's okay. Let's just say, she packages herself well. Having a tight little body and her willingness to do anything, I can see how someone would fall for her. I just think January is sexier. It's just a personal preference. It's my opinion, like an asshole everyone has one.

I don't know who Monica is fooling but I personally think she's a lesbian. I know her type. She sleeps with men because she's a slut muffin. Slut muffins just got to have it. As long as it feels good and there's something in it for them, they are with it. She's definitely the type of bitch that carries a shovel. She does so much dirt that she can't afford not to. And man, does she have a habit? For a little person, she can drink and get high with the best. I don't use drugs. It's bad business to use the product that you sell. I have people that I use to taste and verify quality. I recently bought this little gadget that is more accurate and is safer to test for quality. A machine can't talk therefore they can't testify.

Occasionally, I smoke some weed but I prefer to drink. Not to disturb the mood, I allowed Monica to get high. Once she was high, I just straight fuck the shit out of her asshole. January doesn't do anal. I figured for now that I'll leave it alone, especially since I have others who love it. Monica thinks she's so slippery and slick. I get a kick out of her because she reminds me of me. I could never take a chick that acts like me serious. That's why I stopped fucking with her. I continued to let her cop from me because she's cool to hang with. She doesn't act stuck up. She actually acts like she's one of the guys when you take the sex factor out of it. I ended it because I knew sooner or later that it would put my ultimate merger at risk…to marry January. She wasn't worth the risk.

I could've killed Monica's ass about three months ago, though. Dexter simple ass used my spare key to let himself into my loft. Monica was there to cop and had just finished giving me a mean blow job when this knuckle head used my spare key. Luckily, I had the chain on the door or he would've seen a lot more than he actually saw.

"YO, stay in my room until I get rid of dude. This joker has a big mouth and will blow shit all out of proportion. It will be quick. He probably wants to blow off some steam about his job or something. Just stay in my room."

"Cool, no problem."

Well, I let Dexter in and he immediately ran into my bathroom. "Mutha fucka, you came all the way to Brooklyn to use my bathroom!"

"No! I got to talk to you about something important."

"It better be for you to use my spare key."

"Chad, I think that I'm ready to divorce Terry. She doesn't want to stop her career to start a family. And I…"

"Man, you're crazy! Terry is banging and she's making mad doe. I sometimes think that your mom must've stepped out on my Uncle Victor! I don't think that you're a Delgado."

"Mother fucker, you better watch your mouth when you talk about my mother! I knew it was a mistake to come over here to talk to you. Nothing changed, you're still a jerk!"

Trying to get rid of Dexter, I quickly apologized about the comment that I had made about my Aunt Elizabeth. "Just calm down and listen. Go home and talk it over with your wife…"

I stopped in mid- sentence, when I suddenly saw this BITCH come out to join our conversation. I told you before that bitches ain't shit! He came to speak to me and not to the slut, I thought to myself. I didn't want him to know that I was cool like that with Monica. Under pressure he might tell Terry and worse…tell January that he saw Monica at my crib.

Now, this is when I really wanted to choke the shit out of that bitch, she then told Dexter that Terry never intended to give him any children. Whether it was true or not…why did she snitch on Terry? What kind of friend is she? This was family business and none of hers. Before I could smack the shit out of her, this big pussy started to cry and she started consoling him.

Disgusted, I just left. I don't fuck with snitches. I don't care what somebody tells me about January. I'm first going to take heed to who is the source? And then most importantly, I'm going to discuss it over with January. Terry is his wife! She's a Delgado; therefore she's my family. This chump is holding onto every word that is coming out of Monica's mouth, as if it was the gospel. Terry is family. Yo, show some loyalty! I told you he's a duck ass! Terry and Dexter have been together for seventeen years and he wants to discuss his marital problems with the towns whore. I saw and heard enough. I just bounced before he started to wonder why Monica was there in the first place.

When I returned to my loft, the next day, Monica was there. She was passed out. At first, I thought that she was dead then I saw my empty Patron bottle. I threw a glass of water on her ass and then proceeded to curse her ass the fuck out. "Bitch you really did it this time! You're lucky that I didn't slap the taste out of your mouth! Didn't I tell you to stay the fuck in my room and that I would handle my cousin? This was Delgado family business and none of yours!" Scared as shit, Monica didn't even try to interrupt me in fear that I would slap the shit out of her. "Bitch, from this day on, you can't come to my loft anymore! This is my fault because I allowed you to get too fuckin comfortable. You better pick up your package from my barbershop or not at all. I don't care how long you fuckin knew Terry… she's currently in my mutha fuckin family. She's a Delgado and dammit you're going learn to shut your fuckin mouth when it comes to my family! Bitch, you're lucky that I don't run up in your mouth, right now! Now, get the fuck out of my home before I change my mind."

Gathering her belongings in haste she tried to make a quick dash towards the door. Shaking her head in disbelief Monica cried. "Chad I am so, so sorry for disrespecting your house. You've shown me much love and I thank you. You're right I should've on the strength of you, minded my business. I couldn't help myself. I will respect all your wishes and I just want you to know that we are still cool in my eyes. Hopefully, when you calm down you will feel the same."

To top things off, Dexter punk ass even left me a message on my answering machine. "Hey Chad, forget everything that I said to you last night. I decided to take your advice and work on my marriage. Thanks for everything. Oh yeah, don't ever mention anything about me ever visiting your loft last night to Venus, January, and especially to Terry."

Hmm, I wonder what happened after I left. He's thanking me, taking my advice, and keeping secrets from Terry…hmm indeed.

Later that week Monica went to the barbershop to cop and bumped into Venus. Venus was getting her usual shape-up. Excited to see Venus, Monica forgot to cop and tried to make a love connection with my sister instead. When my sister told me that shit I wanted to shoot that bitch. That crazy bitch better tread carefully.

Venus can take care of herself so I didn't tell her anything about me fucking Monica. I didn't want to complicate things. Venus loves and adores January, not to mention she works for her. I wouldn't want to mess up a good thing for her. If I would've told her about Monica, she would've become conflicted. Loyal, she would rather quit her job than work around January knowing that I fucked one of her best friends. Monica has met her match with my sister. Always being a captain save a Ho, Venus tends to attract whores.

She gives them chances to redeem themselves and once they do...she dumps them. The reason she dumps them you ask? It's the obvious answer, she can't trust them.

Once Monica started talking to my sister, she instantly stopped copping. She even had the nerve to call me. "Thanks for everything but I will no longer need your services. I'm changing my ways and I would hope that you wouldn't intrude when it comes to Venus and me."

"You want me to mind my own business you say, especially now that the shoe is on your foot? How ironic? I'm cool. I'm not going to interfere. Unlike others I know how to mind my own business. You're going to learn little hare that you're not as slick as the fox."

Monica was so happy that I wasn't going to make any problems for her, she gleefully sighed "Thanks."

Like I said before, Venus can take care of herself. I'm just curious about Monica's sudden change of heart. That bitch doesn't wing shit. Monica is the type of chick that makes a move because she planned it. It will always be to her benefit in one way or another. What's that bitch up too? She snitched on one friend, fucked her other friend's fiancé and now is trying to rope my sister, that trick is always scheming. Well, she's no longer my headache.

In preparing for this premiere January went all out. For the past two months she has been working out with a trainer. She even started to ease up on eating her favorite desserts. I'm proud of her. My juicy big mama sure has come a long way. After the party tonight, I'm planning to take her for a surprise getaway to the Dominican Republic.

Terry called me, out of the blue, "Dexter and I are planning to go to the Dominican Republic, shortly after the premiere. I want to know if you were down to surprise January with a romantic get-away."

Normally, I would've said no because her lollipop of a husband was going but I said, "Cool."

CHAPTER 12

I CAN ONLY BE ME. I'M JUST JANUARY-(JANUARY)

What's up! Where are all my party people at…jump, jump! To know me is to love me. From the outside looking in, people tend to get the wrong impression of me. Silly at times, one might have the impression that I'm immature or stupid. Outspoken at times, one may think that I'm pompous. Political at times, one may draw to the conclusion that I would like to run for office. Charismatic at times, I can be so magnetic that people tend to flock around me. Assertive at times, one may think that I'm too bossy. I choose to overlook the negative and try to shine light onto the positive when it comes to life. For this, I'm looked upon as being a fool but I'm not. To sum it up, it's like that Frank Sinatra song that said, "I DID IT MYYYYY WAYYYYY!"

I try to live life to the fullest. You won't hear me complain about what I should've done. If I did it, I made the decision to do it and that's it. I just have to live with the consequences. Life is for the living. You win some and you lose some. You can't make everyone happy. That's why I try to practice self- love, self-acceptance. If you're not comfortable within your own skin, how in the hell are you going to fight off the haters? Don't be delusional, everyone has haters. Sometimes you know who they are and sometimes you don't. They can be your family and/or your friends. It's okay though because like there is hate, there is also love. In the end, I believe that love will outweigh the hate and that in time love will turn some of your haters into your biggest fans.

I love my family. If you're in my clique then you're my family. If you're my lover then you're my family. If you're my family then I will kill or die for you. In other words, if I hold you dear to my heart I will do whatever it takes to protect you.

I am private when it comes to my most intimate feelings. I can be hurting inside and like a clown I will not let you see a frown. But if you ask me for my honest opinion, I will keep it real. Sometimes too real but believe me, it will be real. I'm like a rose. I'm pretty to look at but be careful, not to get nicked because I have thorns. I am outgoing yet I can be humble. I can be generous and warm hearted but if wronged, I can be cold as ice. I work hard therefore I play hard. I love to save money but I am far from being cheap. One minute, I could be refusing to buy a cup of coffee because the cost went up by a dollar and the next minute, I could be buying a designer bag. I am fickle like that. You just got to love me or leave me alone. I can only be me.

I know that I'm a big girl. How can I forget? I'm constantly reminded by society that I am. Magazines, movies, and television shows reinforce certain stereotypes and images that constantly make a person re-evaluate themselves. I admit, for a minute I fell for the propaganda. Throughout the years, I have tried the wheat toast diet, the grapefruit diet, the green tea diet, the sunflower seed diet, the holding your breath upside down diet, and etc. I would lose some weight and then gain back twice as much. Do you know that once I stopped dieting that I stopped gaining weight?

I have found that there is no simple explanation to why a person is overweight. Only a fool would say that over eating is the sole cause. I know a lot of thin people that can eat three times as much as I can. Why haven't they gained any weight? Easy, everyone's metabolism is different. There is an old saying, "Beauty is in the eye of the beholder." People often tell me that I have such a pretty face. Would you like it if I walked up to you and said, "You have such a fit and banging body but your face is fucked up?" You didn't like those apples, did ya? If you can't fix your lips to tell me that I look pretty period then please don't say anything at all.

What I'm trying to say is treat others like you want to be treated. Stop trying to fix me when you need a tune-up yourself. Variety is the spice of life. If everyone was the same then what would make anyone unique or special? Let's take making a movie for an example. It takes different looks and different personalities to make a movie. If everyone looked and acted the same…the movie would be whack. Well, that is how I feel about being a big girl. I am the star of my movie and no one can tell me otherwise.

Tending to expect little from others, I often give in the hope that by living by example others will follow. I found out the hard way that I was wrong. If you let them, people will continue to take until they have sucked you dry and you don't have anything left for yourself. If you don't believe me, watch for yourself. Say "no" to someone; whom you helped in the past. They will act like you called their momma a bitch. I found out the hard way that everyone loves a "yes" person.

That's why I love my clique. They don't hold back any punches and will let me know if I need some straightening out. Monica and Jasmine would always share their views about me being overweight. I never took their opinions personally. If you ever went to an all you can eat buffet with those two then you would understand why. Those two bitches could eat! We even got banned from a restaurant because Monica's greedy ass tried to smuggle out a slab of beef ribs. LOL! If you could have seen that greedy bitch in action, it was hysterical. Like I was saying, always take heed to the messenger when reading the message. Monica and Jasmine used to get on me because of their insecurities. It had nothing to do with me. Terry use to get mad at them but I just took it with a grain of salt. Nobody is perfect and that includes me.

Back in the day, growing up as a cop's daughter in Jersey City was rough. People couldn't seem to separate real life from the movies. Everyone assumed that I was a cop or worst a snitch, an informant for the cops. They assumed that if I saw or heard anything illegal that I would run and tell my father. Listen, I was a child. I was a civilian just like them. I didn't take the civil service test to become a cop. I was just blessed to have the best daddy in the world, whose chosen profession so happened to be a cop. People are crazy. If anything, people use to harass my father with issues and useless information that was none of his business. He was a cop; not a lawyer, not a judge, and especially not a doctor. When my father was off duty he used to get pissed and tell people to call 911 or Judge Judy. This, my people is a clear case of how people talk from both sides of their mouth. On one hand they hate the cops and on the other hand they can't live without the cops. It's like that old saying, "You're damned if you do and you're damned if you don't."

When my father wasn't at work, you would often find me sitting on his lap. He would talk to me about his childhood. We would watch boxing, basketball, and especially football. We use to drive my mother crazy with all the yelling and screaming. I was a New York Giants fan and he was a Dallas Cowboys fan. If you know anything about football, you know that they are arch enemies. We use to really get excited. One time, my father threw a beer bottle at the television screen and cracked it. I had never heard my mother curse at my father until that fateful day. I laughed myself to sleep that night. Affectionate, my father used to pick me up and give me a hug and a kiss every day until I graduated from grammar school. I know that I must have put a hurting on his lower back. What can I say? I was daddy's little girl.

My mother was an awesome cook. She taught me everything that I know about properly seasoning food. If food is properly seasoned it's flavorful; therefore you don't have to add additional seasoning salt or worse, ketchup. As a chef, I get highly insulted when I see people add salt or ketchup to something that I had personally prepared. It masks the intended flavor of the dish. You will never eat food in my restaurant that is so bland that you have to add salt, unless otherwise requested. My mother cooked all types of dishes and was always willing to experiment with new recipes. She believed the way to a man's heart was through his stomach so she made sure that I not only knew how to cook but that I was good at it too. As you can see with such emphasis on being a good cook, I was destined to have a career in cooking.

My mother was also a talented seamstress. Having an eye for fashion, she would dress me in cute little outfits that she created for me. With me being plus sized, did she really have any choice? Growing up, she didn't have a large variety of plus sized stores to choose from like we have today. I was blessed that my mother had such a gift. I was a "little" princess with my very own tailor. I loved it!

During my high school years, I was scared to date. I feared that I would get pregnant. My father would repeatedly tell me that boys only had sex on the brain. So, I decided not to attract any unwanted attention by dressing conservative which didn't help much because rolling with a clique like mines meant that I would always be caught up in the lime light. Luckily, for twelve years of my life I went to Catholic School. Those nuns would enforce the dress code to a tee. If they thought your skirt was too short they would send you home with a note or give you detention after school. Charlene, Monica, and Jasmine always walked the tight rope when it came to the length of their skirts. It wasn't too, too short and it definitely wasn't long. I didn't get seriously interested in fashion and boys until I went to college. I guess you can say that I was a late bloomer.

I attended Saint Mary's Grammar School/High School. My best friends since kindergarten were Charlene, Monica, Jasmine, and Terry. I love them. They're my sisters for life. We always had some drama and excitement. We would often fuss, fight and make up. Flirtatious and self-indulgent Monica was uncontrollable. Free spirited, Monica didn't like it when Terry would give her advice. She felt Terry was too preachy.

Charlene was idealistic, patient, honest, and very attractive. She got the majority of stares from the boys. We would often get invited to all the house parties because Charlene was our girlfriend. Monica and Charlene at times would hang together without the rest of us. I didn't mind because Terry and I would do the same. And as for Jasmine, she didn't mind because that meant that she could spend more time with Eddie.

Jasmine was extremely emotional. Nurturing, and protective, Jasmine was always willing to give someone a sympathetic ear. She would even cry with you and the whole nine yards. Obsessed with Eddie, all you would hear come out of her mouth was Eddie said this and Eddie said that. Concerned about her obsession with Eddie, we tried to reason with her but it only made her want him even more. If anyone talked negative about Eddie, they would become public enemy number one.

Terry was intellectual, philosophical, and straight forward. She would always keep it 500 whether you wanted to hear it or not. She felt Monica was trifling and always trying to get something for nothing. And I was just trying to get in where I fit in. Tired of all the constant arguing and bickering, I just wanted us to get along. I tended to hang with Terry more than the others because I basically didn't fit into their "I'm little and sexy" mold. I was big and sexy while Terry was thick and sexy, neither of us where little. I never took it personal because I can only be me.

I really started to feel myself when I did my internship at one of the top resorts located in Freeport, Bahamas during my summer break. It was heavenly. I fell in love with the clear blue skies, the clear aqua blue waters, the clean white beaches, the awesome tropical weather, and most of all the warmhearted people. I could get used to this, I thought to myself. I worked my ass off at that resort but when I was off duty it was all fun in the sun. They love big girls in the Bahamas! I felt like I was a goddess. I've never felt so comfortable wearing my one piece swimsuit without shorts or a sarong wrap before even with its' built in girdle. Expensive, my black swimsuit made sure that I kept everything together but I was still reluctant to wear it alone until I went to Bahamas.

All I would hear, with a heavy Bahamian accent, were men shouting. "Pretty American girl…stop…stop! Me want to get to know you better. Me want to get to know your name."

Short ones, tall ones, thick ones, slim ones, light ones, and dark ones, they all wanted to get to know me better. I went swimming, deep sea diving, dancing, bar hopping, and anywhere else that Bahamas had to offer me. I was in big girl heaven and I loved it! It worked wonders for my self-esteem! Dedicated to the very special Bahamian people that I met in Bahamas, I sing to you, "You make me feel, you make me feel, you make me feel like a…n-a-t-u-r-a-l… woman."

While finishing my last year in college, Terry tried to set me up with her fiancé's cousin. "Girl, he is cute if I must say so myself."

"Girl, I'm trying to stay focused on my studies. Another time maybe but for now, I'm going to have to turn down your invite. Not dating has gotten me this far so it won't kill me to wait a few more months. The Bahamas taught me a lot about the restaurant industry and a lot more about myself. I got the right to be selective and to do things at my own pace. I want to stay focused. Terry, now you know that Chad looks like a gigolo in this picture. What good is a gigolo going to do for me at this stage of the game, but to distract me? I'm sure he has others that he can play with. He'll be alright."

"I'm so proud of you." Terry said, as she gave me a big hug and a kiss. "Now that is what I am talking about girlfriend. Growth, it's beautiful! I want you to know that I love you and that I believe in you."

"Wow… a compliment coming from Terry Tucker, this must be my lucky day." I exclaimed, as my eyes got watery.

Once I graduated with my degrees in business and in the culinary arts. I went back to the Bahamas for four years. The resort that I did my internship with offered me employment, as one of their lead chefs. I jumped at the opportunity. I was honored that they would want to extend such an offer to me. Impressed with my work, the resort offered me a four year contract. As an incentive, I was also offered a $5,000 signing bonus if I started immediately. There was nothing to think about, I was on the next flight to Bahamas. Watch out Bahamas here I come!

While in the Bahamas, I wrote and published two award winning cookbooks. Working long hours, I would save a majority of my earnings so that I could one day open up a restaurant in the states. After four long years, I was able to save a pretty penny. Having excellent credit and some financial support from my parents, who refinanced their home, my dream became my reality. I opened up a Caribbean-Soul food Restaurant & Lounge named JANUARY'S, located in downtown Brooklyn, New York.

I was gassed up. That same year, Terry and Dexter decided to tie the knot in the Dominican Republic. Playing match maker, Dexter arranged for me to sit next to his cousin Chad on the flight to the wedding. The wedding was beautiful. Terry looked like a princess straight from out of a fairytale. I was overjoyed. You could feel their love in the air. I have never seen Terry so happy. I just hope that she doesn't sabotage her marriage.

Terry and I are extremely close. For some reason, she doesn't like to share her most intimate secrets with the others. When you first meet Terry, you tend to think that she's stuck up and mean but she's not. She just guards her heart with her cold stares and sharp remarks. And that my friend is what I'm afraid of. I am afraid that she's going to shut Dexter out. Men don't like rejection. When rejected they just go to the next one. Women are stronger than men. We can get rejected over and over again and still wait for that so called man of our dreams, to come to his senses. Charlene loves the hell out of Derrick and she is still waiting for him. I believe that they still kick it from time to time. She's just ashamed to admit that she can't let him go. She doesn't want to appear to be like Jasmine. No matter what Eddie does, she refuses to let him go. Yeah, yeah, yeah, I know that Jasmine has children with Eddie but does that give him the right to take her for granted?

Terry has a good man. Together, they uplifted each other to the next level. Can Eddie say that he uplifted Jasmine? At least with Derrick, he never lost sight of the fact that Charlene was the mother of his child and as such took excellent care of her and Destiny. Man, the more that I keep thinking about it…they must be still fucking! Men are selfish creatures. If the situation doesn't benefit them in some way, willingly they're not going to give up the loot. All I know is that Terry better recognize what she has and don't take Dexter for granted. You can feel their chemistry when you're around them. It's the real thing.

Ever since the wedding, Chad and I have been dating. It has been a little more on the talking side because I'm trying to stay focused on my restaurant. See, you are going to notice Chad because everything about him just says damn! He is sexy as hell! I try not to let it show but baby, he got it going on. I know that he has mad bitches. He says that he doesn't but I know that he is lying. Well, one good lie deserves another. I told him that I was still a virgin. Now, you know damn well, that after four long years in the tropical and oh so beautiful Bahamas, that I had to give up the goods to someone.

I had a fabulous, four year, relationship with this chocolate sensation named Sydney. Ironic, he was a policeman like my father. Ten years my senior, my baby looked as if he was in his early twenties. Covered with muscles, Sydney had smooth coco skin and would often go sun tanning to get a hint darker. He was 6'2" and weighed 230 pounds. Sydney had women from all nationalities practically throwing themselves at him. Who could blame them? He appealed to all of a woman's senses. He was pleasing to the eyes, smelled good, had a deep and sultry voice, and tasted delicious. Now, if you're on some gold digger type shit he also had two jobs, owned his own home and vehicle, has never been married, and had no children. Bahamian born, Sydney knew and accepted that our relationship would end when I returned to the states. Passionate about life, his daily routine consisted of jogging, going to work, visiting his family members, going to the beach, barbecuing, and of course dating me.

Sydney was the man around Freeport and he knew it. I first met Sydney at the resort when I did my summer internship. Cocky, he approached me shaking his head. "You're just a baby. If you were my daughter, I wouldn't have allowed you leave the states let alone go to the Bahamas by your lonesome."

"First of all, I'm a full grown woman, as you can see. Secondly, I'm not your daughter and thirdly, I'm not alone…I have you."

Innocent enough, we instantly became friends and kept in touch by writing letters. So when I returned to the Bahamas to work at the resort, he met me at the airport. "You know that you're welcomed to stay at my house. Bahamas will eat a girl like you alive. I will charge you a lot less than those greedy bastards at the resort and most of all I will protect you."

"Why Sydney Sinclair, shame on you. Are you making an indecent proposal? And if so, I gladly accept." I said, as we both smiled at each other.

Initially, I started to care for him because he reminded me of my father. Over protective, they were always under estimating my ability to take care of myself. Feeling like Whitney Houston from the movie "Bodyguard" Sydney became my knight in shiny armor. As time went by the woman inside of me was awakened and she oh so wanted to fuck him. Sydney had a sexy body. The phrase tall, dark, and handsome wouldn't do him any justice. He had broad shoulders, an iron board stomach, muscular thighs, and a juicy bubble butt. I would instantly become entranced by his sexiness, especially when I stared into his dreamy hazel eyes. I became his Louis Lane and he became my superman. Using his x-ray vision to scan my naked body and telepathy to read my deepest thoughts, Sydney knew he had me under his spell. Then as if that wasn't enough to seal the deal, he would use his big and oh so soft lips to adorn kisses all over my body. A patient lover, Sydney would slowly tend to every inch of my body. Heavily endowed, I didn't think that I could handle Sydney's dick. It had length as well as girth. Always a considerate lover, Sydney would take his time with me and always a perfect gentleman, he would treat me with respect.

Sydney had no desire to move to the states and I, on the other hand, was wet behind my ears and wanted to return home to make my mark by opening up my very own restaurant.

The day I left Bahamas to go back home, Sydney handed me an envelope. "Promise me you won't open it until you get home."

"I promise."

When I opened the envelope, there was a check for $10,000 inside. In the memo section he wrote "Good luck on your restaurant!" Sydney and I shared a deep connection. Like my father, he made me feel loved and cherished. I knew that if I didn't force myself to return to states that Sydney and I would've gotten married and started a family. My dream of opening up a restaurant, in New York, would've gone up in smoke.

In my eyes, since my only sexual relationship happened outside of the states, technically I was still a virgin. Chad felt honored that he was going to be my first. He wanted our first time to be very special and it was. It was a brisk fall day when Chad and I arrived at the Pocono's. He had reserved a rental house for the weekend. It was a lakefront house with a private beach and dock. I was blown away. This 1800 sq. ft. house was romantic. It had two bedrooms, a kitchen, a living room with a fire place and two bathrooms. The master bedroom had a king size bed with sliding doors that opened to a small private deck area. With great views of the lake, the deck was cozy and relaxing. Enjoying the good conversations and the surroundings, I started to see Chad in a different light. There was definitely more to him than meets the eye. Just when I thought it couldn't get any better… he lit the grill and started to BBQ. It was a little too chilly out but I didn't care. I love a man that can work a grill. He reminded me of my father and lord knows he can grill his ass off. Chad even brought along four bottles of my favorite wine. We drank and danced to music all night long. The first day was filled with romance that did not entail sex. I was actually having fun. We played Uno and Pity Pat. He really made me feel special…very special.

Lying on a pile of pillows on the floor in front of the fireplace, I started to feel the effects of the wine. Chad got up and put on a cd. I felt myself smiling as "Scandalous" by Prince drifted to my ears. I thought that I was going to melt away, as Chad lay down beside me and started to passionately tongue kiss me. His fat tongue bossed my tongue around as I tried to get ahold of myself.

"Oh Chad," I sighed, in ecstasy, as his hands started to go underneath my nightgown. It was becoming scandalous alright as he slowly unsnapped my bra. As we kissed, I felt his fingertips gently stroking my stiff nipples. "Ooh! Ooh! Ooh!" I exclaimed, as I parted my legs as to invite him to explore my Garden of Eden. "UMMMM, UMMMM!" I moaned. I felt light headed as I was engulfed in the flames of desire.

"Yeah, yeah," he muttered, as he lifted my gown above and over my head.

Removing my bra, Chad started sucking on my hard nipples. Slowly and tenderly, becoming more rough and aggressive as I moaned, Chad sucked my nipples as if he was my baby and I was breast feeding him.

Adorning my body with kisses as he paved his way towards my nana, Chad ever so gently pulled down my panties. Fittingly "Insatiable" by Prince was now on. This brother had skills, I love Prince's music. With the lit fire place, the great wine, the delicious BBQ food, and the music from Prince, the mood was set for some boots to be knocking. With a strong and forceful grip, Chad pulled me towards him with one arm wrapped around each leg. He then parted my thighs and started to devour my throbbing clit. His big fat serpent tongue slowly licked my outer lips and gently made its way towards my swollen tip. His mouth was so pleasurable. As his mighty tongue entranced me, Chad held complete control of me. I was under his spell and he knew it.

"UMMMM, UMMMM," he moaned, as he slowly licked my juicy clit and tasted some of my hot lava juice for the first time. Chad steadily licked on the tip of my clit as I uncontrollably squirted in his mouth. "YEAH, UMMMM, YEAH," he grunted as he was having fun playing with his new toy, my clit.

As Chad switched between gently nibbling on my clit with his teeth and thrashing his big fat tongue across my clit, he was determined to show me what I've been missing.

"OOOH, OOOH, OOOH!" I exclaimed, as he sent shivers through me. The multiple vibrations were sending shockwaves throughout my body. "OH MY, OH MY," I sighed, as he stuck his finger into my nana while he ate me. "AHHHHH, AHHHH!" I moaned, as he slipped three fingers into my wetness. "AHHHHHHHHHHHHH, AHHHHHHHHHHH!"

"Yeah, baby! Let it out, cum all over my face! " He muttered as he licked the full length of my clit. Around the sides, between my inner lips, and on my tip, Chad ate me until I couldn't take any more.

"FUCK ME! FUCK ME! PLEASE FUCK ME!"

Chad quickly stepped out of his basketball shorts, grabbed a condom and put it on. He then slowly inserted his fat head into my tight, hot, and oh so wet nana. Trembling, I squeezed his biceps as he stroked me only with his swollen head.

As I clammed up he would softly say, in a deep voice, "Just relax baby... just relax."

As I loosened up a little, he gently slid his entire dick inside of me.

"Ooooh, Ooooh!" I moaned as my man stroked me. Chad was 5'10" and weighed 215 pounds of pure sexiness. Having broad shoulders and muscular arms, Chad was more than enough man for me. I would alternate grasping between his arms and shoulders for I felt every fucking inch of his fat dick inside of me.

"AHH, YEAH, YEAH," He moaned, as he slayed me. "AHHH SHIT, YOUR PUSSY IS SO FUCKIN HOT!" He bellowed, as he stroked my wet kitty. "GOOD PUSSY! UMMMMM! GOOD PUSSY!"

"AHHH, AHHH, AHHHHHHH!" I yelled, at the top of my lungs as I started to go into convulsions. I was having an orgasm, as my nana clenched for dear life to Chad's pulsating dick. All she wanted to feel was his manhood inside of her. Chad began to slow down his thrusts.

I in turn started to fuck him back, from the bottom, as I yelled, "Give me my shit! Give me my shit!"

"STOP, STOP! AHHH! AHHH, STOP!" He pleaded.

I wrapped my legs around him and deep fucked him back. "YEAH, YEAH, FUCK YOUR SHIT!" I yelled, as we savagely fucked. I would fuck him and then he would fuck me. "YEAH, YEAH, RIGHT THERE!" I exclaimed, as he hit my G-Spot. The sharp vibrations sent flutters throughout me.

Speeding up Chad started fucking me harder and harder. "UGHHH,

UGHHH! I'M CUMMING!" Chad exclaimed, as I kept pumping him as he came.

"AHHHHH, AHHHH!" I shouted, as I started to cum again.

We sexed all night long and had to force ourselves to catch some Z's because we faced a long ride back home. Scheduled to leave at noon, unfortunately our three day weekend had come to an end. I just love being me.

Over the years, I would purposely put space between Chad and I. I tried to be like Jasmine and ignore the signs of my cheating mate but I couldn't. When it got to be too much, I would tell Chad that I needed us to fall back so that I could focus more on my career. This way I didn't burn any bridges. I know Chad was and is a player and I know that I'm not beat to put up with his shit. Each time Chad and I split, I would attempt to date other people. It would be futile and in vain because we would end up still having sex with each other. It became apparent to me that Chad wasn't going to let me move on and that I suffered from the "She's Gotta Have It" syndrome.

The closest I came to permanently leaving Chad was when I decided to rekindle my relationship with Sydney. I decided to spend my 32nd birthday in the Bahamas with him. As soon as I stepped off the plane, onto Bahamian soil, I locked eyes with Sydney. He was breath taking as usual. Father time had done him some justice for he looked as if he hadn't aged a bit. The only thing changed was that he now had a goatee. What a sexy combination! He has juicy lips and now a goatee, I said to myself as I anticipated kissing him. My kitty got wet as I felt his rock hard dick press against my leg while we kissed. I was on cloud nine for it was in that moment I knew then that he still wanted me and I him. We just picked up our relationship from where it left off.

We tried the long distance thing for about two years. I would go to the Bahamas for a week and then a couple of months would go by and then he would visit the states for a week. We cared for each other deeply. The sex was great, we were attracted to each other, and intellectually we were compatible. Ultimately, we realized that for the relationship to work, one of us would have to make a big sacrifice. One of us would have to move.

"January, I'm not getting any younger. I know that you are the one for me. I would move heaven and earth for my wife. I would leave my career, family, friends, and homeland for my wife." Sydney tenderly grabbed and kissed the back of my hand. He then pulled out of his pocket a 2 karat diamond ring and said, "January, are you that wife? Would you do me the honor of becoming my wife?"

Shocked, I gazed into Sydney's eyes and started to cry. Trying to gather my thoughts, I then responded, "Now Sydney, you know that you aren't ready for marriage. I know that you love me and I love you too. That is why I can't let you give up your life that you built for yourself in the Bahamas to move to Jersey City. The gamble is too costly. Suppose you don't like it here? You would become angry and resentful towards me. I love you too much to let that happen."

Turning ten shades darker, Sydney angrily replied. "Don't turn this around on me! I am a grown man and I know what I want. Hmm, you love me you say. Yeah, you love me so much that you would leave me but not enough to choose me. Ten years ago you chose your career and today you chose to be a coward. I'm not asking you to give up your career, family, and friends. I'm just asking you to have a little faith in me and in our love. For once in your life January, I'm asking you to choose me."

I stood their frozen and in silence as he quickly gathered his belongings and left my townhouse. I knew that he was right and that I was wrong. I also knew that I couldn't stand by and let him do something that I couldn't and wouldn't do for him, which was give up my career for him. I worked too hard to make my restaurant a success.

Always, the one to initiate us to get back together, Chad would call me. "Damn, baby you don't miss me not even a little bit? You don't love me? I'm not ashamed to admit that I miss and love you."

On the rebound from Sydney, I just gave in and started dating Chad again. Emotionally, I didn't have the strength to fight off Chad's advances. I was hurt and confused. I know that Chad doesn't miss me. He is a whoremonger and he will always be a whoremonger! Whoremongers just miss pussy and I'm sure that he had plenty of that when we were broken up. I keep taking Chad back because I'm a shallow and greedy person. Shallow meaning, he looks good as hell on my arm. His body is fit and it's legit. I know that of all people that I shouldn't be shallow but shit this is my life and I want what I want. Then comes the greedy part, I'm insatiable. I like to fuck. Shit, I love to fuck. Chad is a great fuck, plain and simple. As long as he keeps getting the green light from the doctor we're good to go!

What sent my head spinning was when he proposed to me. Why would he play with the holy sacrament of matrimony? He knows that he can't be faithful. Personally, if it wasn't for the direction that my career was heading in, I don't believe that he would've even proposed to me. We never discussed getting married or having any children. Sydney and I did and as you can see, we're not together anymore. I can only trust that men will be men. They will always let you down…in one way or another. To keep it real, we are all fallible and have short comings. I realized too late that I might have made a mistake. I should've accepted Sydney's proposal. To my knowledge, he has never cheated on me but then again, I have never actually caught Chad cheating on me either. Oh boy, when it comes to the affairs of the heart, I don't know whether I'm coming or going.

Well, it's too late to cry over spilled milk. I had already turn down one proposal and it didn't make any sense to turn down the other. At least with Chad, I will never have to choose between having my career and having him. He loves Brooklyn and will be a New Yorker until the day he dies. With Sydney it was an entirely different story. I knew how much Sydney loved living in the Bahamas. I would forever feel guilty for taking that away from him. I guess I made the right choice, only time will tell. I intend on being engaged until I'm sure that I indeed made the right choice. I'm not going to let society rush me into something that I'm not ready for. Chad is a loving man. He has never made any promises to me that he did not keep. I always push Chad away when I feel like I'm getting caught up. I need to just chill and let things flow naturally. I just love how it sounds when I tell people that I'm engaged. When I show them a picture of my fiancé, they get j-e-a-l-o-u-s. I know that I'm wrong for bragging but I just can't help myself. Everything seems to be going right for me now and I'm so happy.

Chad spent the night at my house last night. The alarm woke us up and it's 8:00 am on a glorious summer's day. Chad and I are going to my parent's house for a big breakfast since they declined to go to the premiere with me. My parents felt that I would have more fun with my friends and wanted me to fully enjoy my special night. They're so happy for me, first with my engagement and secondly for acquiring the cooking show. Growing up in my house meant that every occasion was celebrated with some sort of feast, so I chose breakfast because it would start my day off with a bang.

Jasmine and her family were spending the weekend at Charlene's house. Being the oldest, Destiny will watch the children while Jasmine and Eddie accompany Charlene and Godfrey to the premiere. Derrick's stretch limo will be taking them to the premiere and as for Chad and I my publicist reserved a limo to pick us up at around 8:00pm. They wanted to leave earlier, at around 7:00pm so that they would have enough time to pick up Terry and Dexter. Traffic can be brutal and they didn't want to be late. The premiere doors opened at 8:00pm while the premiere itself started at 9:00pm. At noon, Jasmine is coming over to my house to do my hair and my nails. I'm so excited. I spent a lot of money on my outfit and I paid a pretty penny for my girdle too. I didn't want anything to shake, rattle and roll.

Tonight, I wanted to party like a rock star. People ready or not, here I come!

CHAPTER 13

JEALOUS: A. UNEASY THROUGH FEAR OF, OR ON ACCOUNT OF, PREFERENCE GIVEN TO ANOTHER; SUSPICIOUS IN LOVE; APPREHENSIVE OF RIVALRY; ANXIOUSLY FEARFUL OF OR CAREFUL.

COULD IT BE THAT JEALOUSY WAS IN THE AIR?

Ever since Charlene eloped and got married, I got engaged to Chad, Terry made partnership at her law firm, and Jasmine found that distance was the remedy to Eddie's cheating ways, I've noticed a great change in our friendships and how we all related to each other. We made a pact seventeen years ago to stay friends and become successful by the age of thirty-five. Did we really fulfill our pact? None of us have seen or heard from Monica in two months. What does that say about our so called friendships? Were we ever friends? I'm really confused? The last person Monica contacted was Derrick of all people and that was on his birthday, two months ago. Now, what was I missing here? Monica has spoken to Charlene's ex-boyfriend/baby daddy but not to her own parents or any of her childhood best friends.

Why not call Charlene? I mean, for years, she used to stay with Charlene whenever she came to Jersey. They use to party and travel together all the time. There were even talks about Monica possibly moving in with Charlene.

Why not call Jasmine? Since Monica moved back to Jersey City, Jasmine has been doing her hair for free at her beauty parlor.

A couple of days ago, Jasmine confided to me, "Monica played me. Why hasn't she called me to let me know that she's alright? When she needed her hair done she didn't have any problem contacting me."

Yet, Monica took the time to call Derrick?

Last night, I called Terry because I was upset about Monica and I couldn't go to sleep. Disgusted, Terry barked, "January, you're overreacting. Monica has always been flighty and selfish. No news is good news in my opinion. Go to sleep, I can guarantee she isn't losing any sleep over you."

"I know. It's just that this isn't normal for…"

"…this is normal for Monica. That is what I'm trying to tell you. The bitch is selfish! Close your eyes and dream about your premiere. For once in your life take a page from Monica's book and put yourself first. Okay baby girl."

"Okay, thanks Terry for listening."

"No problem, that's what friends are for? Goodnight love."

"Goodnight."

Please forgive me Lord, if I'm wrong. Could it be that jealousy was in the air? There's a strong possibility that Monica is jealous that everybody has a significant other except her. That has to be it! That's the only logical explanation that I can come up with to explain her sudden behavior.

I always knew that Monica was jealous of Charlene because of her natural beauty and relationship with Derrick. Charlene was naturally friendly and attractive while Monica, who was always flirtatious and sociable, had to work harder at it. Similar in traits and strengths, Charlene just seemed to always land on top. To me, what put Charlene on top was that she was honest. Monica was constantly lying through her teeth. I think that trait in her is the reason why, Terry can't stand her. Even Charlene started to put some distance between Monica and her in our senior year in high school.

Jasmine and I used to admire Monica for her ability to be free-spirited and bold. Monica had the gift of gab and could sell a pot of honey to a bumble bee. I always knew that Monica was jealous of Terry because of her intelligence. In school, Terry used to be the one that we would all go to when we didn't understand something. Terry took pride in her studies and made it her business to get all A's. Monica had already been left back a year and always needed help with her studies but would rather go through all of us instead of going straight to Terry. Monica hated the fact that she needed Terry.

Terry would confide, "Monica is too promiscuous and shallow. January, I could do without a so called friend like her. With friends like Monica, who needs enemies?"

I use to try to convince Terry otherwise but now, I don't know.

Tonight is going to be one of my life's highlights and I haven't seen or heard from Monica in months. I'm mad at her but I'm concerned more. I would hate to think that she is throwing me shade because she could possibly be jealous of me. I'm truly hurt.

She could've spoken to one of us by now!

What did I do to deserve this? I've always been there for her and now when I need her support, she ups and disappears. I was the first one to meet her when the Freemans adopted her and it was my mother that encouraged me to include her when Jasmine would come over to my house. It was I, who convinced everybody to give her a chance. When the Freeman's first adopted her, she had issues. She would often start fights with the other kids on the block. It was my mother, who offered to keep her at our house to help her adjust to her new life with the Freemans. If it wasn't for the intervention of my mother, the Freemans probably would've tried to give her back or something.

I have never said anything to Monica to protect her feelings and now she's throwing me shade. I cried one good cry and then said to myself fuck her. If she's not in any danger and does not show up tonight, I'm just going to be down one girlfriend. As a show of good faith, I left her ticket at the front desk of the hotel. I left a message with her mother, on her cellphone, on twitter and on face book; stating where I left her ticket. I hope with all my heart that she not only shows up tonight but that she has a damn good explanation to why she hasn't called me of all people? I just can't stand it when Monica does her disappearing act!

CHAPTER 14

JULY 5, 2009-THE PREMIERE

In the center of New York City, on a clear and enchanting night; my dream finally came true. It was gorgeous, larger than life. From a distance, all you could see were the enormous flashing lights. Rows and rows of lit trees decorated with white lights. There where blue illuminated lights reflecting off all the enormous tinted windows and massive glass doors, to The J Decor Hotel. Moving closer and closer, you see the huge J in the center above the entrance that consisted of two sets of huge revolving doors. The stairs had a luxurious red carpet with floor lights beaming left to right as if it was a Hollywood event. Carefully walking, I had butterflies in my stomach. Who would've thought that my decision to go to culinary school, would've led me to this glorious night. The J Décor Hotel was hosting the party for the premiere of the new fall season line-up of cable network shows and I was a part of it.

I now have my very own cooking show!

I got out of the limo and walked through the glass doors into a dream, a lavish dream. The extreme lighting set the magical mood, bright blue and yellow lights that contrasted with the dim recessed lighting of the lobby. There were floor to ceiling windows reaching upwards everywhere, as if they could touch the sky. Walking through the lobby, I saw a lovely, huge, intricately designed Persian rug that reeked of money. To my right there were plush chocolate brown leather sofas and loveseats with big chocolate furry pillows. To my left there were colorful paintings and tall tree plants that made me feel like I was in an enchanted forest. Straight ahead was the welcome desk that had flameless vanilla scented candles spread across. AHHHHH! The aroma of vanilla in the air added to the ambience. Accented with brown and gold;

the wall behind the welcome desk just made everything seem so royal. As I proceeded to follow the crowd of elegantly dressed people that were ahead of me, I was greeted by a hostess who asked to see my invitation. Once confirmed via radio by the hostess, I was directed to the entrance to the ballroom.

The entrance to the ballroom had draping white sheets that were illuminated by blue and lavender lights. Walking through the ballroom doors; my breath was taken away as I saw an enormous "J" ice sculpture surrounded by flashing lights. To my right I saw white long stretch tables with servers standing behind burners. Each burner had a different type of dish. For seafood they had lobster, shrimp, caviar, tilapia, and salmon. There was also steak, veal, lamb, tacos, miniature egg rolls, mini burgers, salads, string beans, corn, and etc. I started to get dizzy looking at the abundance of food they were serving.

As my eyes travelled around the room, I could see enormous signs with pictures of the new fall line-up. I saw my sign and it had a picture of me with my hands on my hips.

Smiling from ear to ear, I turned to Chad and said, "Baby I'm so happy."

Lovingly looking into my eyes Chad responded, "You should be because you deserve every bit of this baby, you busted your ass for this."

Then he leaned over to me and gave me a tender kiss on my forehead so as not to mess up my make-up, of course. As I continued to look around the room, I could see the extremely large dance floor, with tables set up on both sides of it. If I'm not mistaken, it appeared to be twenty-five tables, evenly distributed, on both sides of the dance floor. The large round tables had settings for ten; each table had an oversized martini glass with fresh white lilies, roses, mini carnations, green buttons, POMs and topped with straws and big red faux apples. It was creative for I've never seen anything like that before. There were tall flute wine glasses on top of cream silken table clothes with red rose petals sparingly spread across the tables.

To the far left of the room, I saw the DJ booth constructed of reinforced glass that was illuminated from underneath. It was made to appear as if it was floating above the dance floor. I was so excited and then I saw them…my friends, everyone except for Monica. We all started to scream with joy.

I was wearing a gorgeous, zippered back, black strapless gown of black satin /taffeta fabric with embroidered lace and crystal gems. With iridescent silver sequins embroidered throughout the bottom of the dress, I wore 2 inch black satin jewel studded dress pumps with matching black jeweled clutch purse. My hair was in a bun with ringlets of curls sparingly hanging out. With dangling crystal earrings and a simple crystal necklace, I looked stunning if I must say so myself. Chad wore a modern style black 2 piece tuxedo with a crisp black satin shirt. With a black satin straight tie, my baby looked so handsome.

Jasmine was wearing a gorgeous yellow pleated one shoulder strap satin dress with gold 4 inch stilettos. Jasmine had her infamous Pocahontas hair do and wore her dazzling gold rain drop earrings and had a gold sequin clutch purse. Jasmine looked like she belonged on the Holly wood red carpet. She looked glamorous all she was missing was an extravagantly large pair of shades. Eddie wore a black 2 piece Armani tux with a crisp yellow tuxedo shirt with a black satin bowtie. All I kept asking myself was why did this man come here looking like a damn bumble bee? LOL!

Terry was wearing a metallic silver sequin low cut mini dress with spaghetti straps. Form flattering, her dress showed her delicious curves that would make any person take a triple take. Extremely tight at the top so that her breasts looked like delicious raindrops; Terry's dress looked super sexy on her and she knew it. With her hair in big luscious curls that she pinned to one side with a big diamond studded comb, Terry wore her real 3 karat diamond earrings and matching bracelet set. To add another touch of sexiness, she wore silver 4 inch stilettos and matching silver clutch purse. Terry went all out, she looked hot as hell. Dexter wore a modern style black 2 piece tuxedo with a crisp black satin shirt and silver satin straight tie. Dexter looked like the distinguished gentlemen.

Charlene wore a red mini satin vertical and horizontal pleated dress that enhanced her curves. The hugging silhouette of the lustrous sheath dress topped with spaghetti straps made Charlene look scrumptious. Wearing dangling pearl earrings and a pearl necklace, Charlene wore these fabulous 4 inch red satin stilettos that had a big blossom red rose. With a matching red satin clutch purse adorned with little satin red roses and her hair in large Shirley temple curls, Charlene looked like an X-rated little red riding hood that was all grown up. She looked awesome! I think that she wanted to get the attention of a certain retired basketball player that we all knew and from what I saw…she got it! Godfrey wore a sharp military influenced black suit with a crisp white satin shirt and black satin straight tie with matching pocket square. I see why Charlene married him, he looked sharp.

Derrick wore a luxurious BOSS black 3 piece tuxedo. With satin highlights on the notched lapel and with fabric wrapped buttons, it looked expensive as hell! The 4 button vest was cut from the matching satin from his lapel. Wearing a crisp white tuxedo shirt and black satin tie, he was smooth like butter. Looking as if he was a damn king, Derrick was blinged out. He wore these huge 5 karat diamond stud earrings, one on each ear, one of his three championship rings, and a diamond studded watch with matching cuff links. Looking good enough to eat, Charlene looked at him as if he was her next meal.

If I must say so my-self, we were the best dressed table in the house.

It was 9:00pm, on the dot, the MC was standing beside the DJ booth he introduced himself and welcomed everyone to the ultimate premiere party. A projector was pointed towards the white wall centered behind him. As he announced each new show, an image of the announced show would appear larger than life behind him. To accompany each image, the MC would give a description of the show and what each show would entail. After each show was featured everyone would briefly clap.

After my show was called and featured on the screen; everyone at my table started to hoot, bark, and shout my name. I was so embarrassed yet humbled. All I could do was smile and say thank you to my friends. I was so happy.

The presentation ended at 10:15pm. Immediately, the MC announced dinner was now served and we were welcome to start dancing, the event ended at 1:00am. "Again, thank you all for coming and please enjoy the night," the MC graciously said as he exited the dance floor.

Everyone started clapping and immediately started to head for the delicious array of food. Hungry as hell, we all went to grab some grub. All of the food was so delicious! Our greedy behinds tried our best to taste every dish that they had to offer. We were all stuffed like Thanksgiving turkeys.

We started to reminiscence about our high school years. I almost wet myself when Terry mentioned the time we were in the school's talent show, during our freshman year. YO! I don't know what made us think that we could actually win. Other than singing in Charlene's Aunt Bird church choir, we have never performed in a talent show. We attempted to sing New Edition's song "Is this the End." We were horrible. We should've picked an easier song to sing. I would rock and lip-synch while Jasmine sounded like the screech of a Path train coming to a sudden halt. Monica forgot the words to the song and made up her own. Terry's silly behind lost focus and started laughing at me when I missed a step and almost fell off the stage. The only person that sounded like something was Charlene. We were a hot mess and we knew it. Would you believe that we won second place? The people actually thought that we were doing a comedy sketch. We almost lost our minds when they announced it.

"Also during that fateful freshman year in high school while we were all on a bus trip to watch the boys' basketball team play an away game, a certain someone let loose a goose egg in the back of the bus. The smell was so strong that the bus driver had to pull the bus over because everybody was choking. Everybody assumed that it was some stank behind boy. Well I know that it was someone sitting at this table and that person is a female, who do you think did it?" Terry said, as she started giggling.

We all started giggling, except Jasmine.

Upset that Terry retold the story, Jasmine pouted and said, "I didn't do it on purpose. I ate too much of my grandmother's cabbage."

Eddie playfully said, "ILLLLLLK!"

We all started cracking up laughing, including Jasmine because Eddie, playfully, started moving his seat away from her. We were just acting like pure tee fools. We were laughing so hard and so loud that I was afraid that someone was going to ask us to leave.

Charlene started to reminiscence about Girl Scouts.

I said, "oh boy" because I had an idea of what she was going to reflect about.

"You guessed it buddy," Charlene said, as she started giggling. "I remember the time when we went camping for the first time and we had to sleep in a tent. I think we were twelve years old. We were told not to bring any food or snacks. Our bags were even inspected to insure that we didn't bring any food to the camp grounds. Well, well, well we were all sleeping when all of a sudden we heard Samantha Clark scream BEAR! BEAR! We all jumped up and start running for the fifteen passenger van. Our troop leader, as she loaded us onto the van radioed for help. Who do I see crying? Saying I'm sorry! I'm sorry! I was hungry! No other than; January's crazy ass!"

Everybody started dying laughing. Chad laughed the loudest because he knows how I can get when it comes to food because we've had a couple of arguments about him eating someone's snacks without telling them. I don't play that. Listen, it is only right that you tell someone when you eat the last of something, I don't think that is an unreasonable request.

"Okay, people... I was only twelve years old," I said, as I tried to hold back my laughter. "There really was no bear so I really didn't endanger anyone."

"Yeah, but Samantha told me that she really saw a big looming shadow and heard some rattling as if the shadow was eating something." Charlene responded.

Trying to keep a straight face, I said. "It was all Samantha's fault that everybody got so excited over nothing. What Samantha saw was me trying to hold a flashlight in one hand while I tried to un-wrap my sandwich with my other. If anything, she actually scared the shit out of me when I heard her scream bear. That's why I jumped up and started screaming bear too."

Charlene looked at me while I was still trying to keep a straight face, and said, in a cool and calm voice, "We were specifically told NOT to bring ANY FOOD."

"I know," I said. "I also know that you are just mad that I didn't share my sandwich with you, admit it."

Laughing Charlene blurted. "You're damn RIGHT! I was hungry like a Mother Fucker. I was mad as hell that you didn't share it with me."

YO! The whole table just started laughing even harder. We all had tears coming out of our eyes. Charlene's face even started to turn as red as her dress. We were laughing so hard that I thought that I was going to bust out of my girdle. Looking back, I guess it wasn't so bad. We had good days and we had bad days but in the end, I can honestly say that the good days outweighed the bad ones. We have been friends for over thirty years and we are all still here to be able to laugh about it. Wow! I can't believe how time flies.

We all looked marvelous and were having a great time. And we all were happy that it was an open bar event. We were getting toasted. All night long, we were all laughing, eating, dancing, and drinking champagne.

I have never been so proud in my life. Just how my internship in the Bahamas changed my life forever, so will this; I was truly humbled tonight. To be surrounded by such loving friends, I was deeply moved. It's times like this that I can't help but to cry tears of joy. I even started to have a change of heart when it came to how I wanted to relate to Chad. I do love him and more and more I want to marry him. Tonight, he reminded me of the Chad that took me to the Poconos nine years ago. He made me feel special, like I was the only one that mattered. I think that I'm going to have to have a heart to heart talk with him when we get back to my townhouse. I think I fooled myself in believing that I didn't want more. Tonight made me see how happy Chad could make me. He made me feel loved. Besides being a great lover and an awesome companion, he was an excellent dancer. We danced until I had to jump out of my shoes. I don't want to brag but I can tear it up on a dance floor, especially house music...what?

I even caught Derrick staring at Charlene a couple of times. I know that look. He wants to give her something that she can feel! Terry and Dexter were acting like newlyweds. They were bumping and grinding as if they were at home and not here amongst five hundred people. Jasmine was a little upset because Eddie switched from champagne to Hennessy. He was druuunk and he tends to get a little out of hand when he's drunk. Poor Godfrey on the sly would throw rocks at Derrick because he must've seen what I saw. Derrick wants an episode with Charlene and it's definitely not PG-13. Besides Godfrey, I can honestly say that we were all having a good time.

It was 12:00am and Chad was about to lead another toast when all of a sudden all our jaws dropped, in shock. Monica walks up to our table and she is obviously PREGNANT! Rocking her hair in a long exaggerated platinum blonde Mo-hawk, Monica, a true fashionista, was wearing a silver halter top mini dress that exposed her very much pregnant belly. Accessorized with daggling silver earrings, silver bracelets, a silver jewel studded clutch purse, and silver 4 inch stilettos with diamond like embellishments, she was definitely the show stopper of the night. Monica's belly was so big that she had to be three or four months pregnant, at the most.

"Oh look, what the cat dragged in," Terry said in a nasty voice.

A glowing Monica ignored her comment and said, "Greetings everybody. I'm sorry that I'm late. I hope that I didn't miss much."

Everyone, still with their jaws dropped, one by one said, "Hey."

"Am I too late to get something to eat," Monica asked, looking around.

"No, you're good," I said, as I hugged her and proceeded to walk her over to get something to eat, before it was too late. As we went to get some food I thought to myself, who in the hell knocked up Monica and why didn't she just stay her pregnant ass at home tonight? I mean really, the focus is supposed to be on me.

"I'm sorry for not calling you. I was out of the country. As you can see, I had a lot on my mind and I wasn't ready to face everybody."

"Monica I'm just glad that you're alright. I was worried that something might have happened to you. It was not like you to not call anyone to let them know that you were okay."

"I'm back now and I'm not going anywhere anytime soon."

"I see"

Walking back to our table, I could see the mood shifting as we got closer. Everyone was laughing and smiling and now they weren't. For a moment, it made me feel like we were in high school again. Always at each other's throat and everyone competing for the spotlight. I finally realized; who was the catalyst for all the drama...Monica. She didn't have to go into hiding because she was pregnant and keep it a secret. I mean, really what is up with that? She's not the first and she will not be the last woman to have a baby without being in a relationship. She created all the drama by making it such a secret and then by revealing this so called secret at my premiere party. What could I have possibly done to her for her to treat me like this?

As Monica was seated, Jasmine blurted out what everyone wanted to say, "Who knocked you up?"

Laughing Monica responded, "No one."

In unison, everybody exclaimed, "WHAT!"

"You have to be kidding me. It's actually none of your business but I will play along for now. I went to a fertility clinic and got artificially inseminated."

Everybody busted out laughing, except Godfrey and Dexter.

"Bitch please! I know damn well, you really don't expect us to believe that your cheap ass paid for some damn cum," Terry said, as she continued to laugh.

"TERRY!" I shouted, as I felt that she spoke a little too harshly. She didn't have to call her a bitch. Everything else could've stayed the same. Monica just continued to eat as she shook her head, left to right.

In a concerned voice Charlene asked. "Monica, why did you do this? Raising a child isn't all fun and games. It takes a lot of dedication, self-discipline, and entails a lot of work. Life is no longer just about you. It's all about your child. It's selfish of you to purposely get pregnant knowing that you don't have a significant other."

"Oh so let me get this straight. It was alright for you to raise a baby without a husband but it isn't alright for me? I am about to turn thirty-six years old unlike a certain someone who was only eighteen years old. As I see it before you can point a finger at me, about being selfish, you need to first look in the mirror."

"BITCH," Charlene shouted, as Godfrey pulled her close to him, gesturing to her to calm down.

"Monica was that really necessary? Charlene was only trying to tell you the truth about motherhood." Jasmine said, as she looked at Charlene giving her a comforting look of support.

"Jasmine was it really necessary for you to not only have had one child but you went and had three children. The last time I checked, you're not married either or has that changed recently. If so…I guess I missed my invite?" Monica said, as she sucked her teeth.

"Okay Monica that's enough!" I exclaimed. "Must I remind everybody that we're at a function, in my honor? We're not in high school and let us not say something that we can't take back. We are all g-r-o-w-n ass women now. Don't ruin this night for me."

There was finally silence at the table. Looking around, I noticed that only the women were fussing. The men were just taking it all in, just listening. Then Eddie asked Jasmine to dance which was a great idea that we all followed, with the exception of Derrick and Monica. They appeared to be having an intense conversation and I wanted to go back to the table to be nosey but Chad wouldn't let me.

Charlene and Jasmine are good, I thought to myself. If Monica would've said that slick shit to me, I would've asked her to go with me to the ladies room. Not wanting any witnesses, just in case I had to slap the taste out of her mouth, I would've blacked out on her. Being mothers, Charlene and Jasmine were just trying to show some concern. I thought that was what friends were for. I already saw how this night was going to end.

It was now 12:30am. Some people started calling cabs because they were too drunk to drive home. I overheard some people say that they were going to try and get a room for the night. And as for my group of misfits…they were still drinking and dancing the night away.

Dexter escorted Terry back to the table and then to everyone's surprise, turned to Monica and asked, "Would you like to dance?"

Monica accepted and Dexter escorted her to the dance floor. Monica must've had the cooties because everyone from our table, that was dancing, immediately returned to their seat. As I tried not to stare, I saw that Monica and Dexter appeared to be having a heated conversation, so much so that Terry walked over to them and made Dexter sit down. She exchanged a couple of words with Monica and then returned to the table.

In a pleasant voice Terry asked Derrick, "I don't mean to rush you but are you ready to go yet?"

Derrick looked at his watch and said, "Wow, it is 12:45am already. Time flies when you're having fun. I'm ready."

Everyone hugged and kissed me goodbye as they again congratulated me for getting my own cooking show. Having been dropped off by a friend, Monica asked if she could bum a ride home with Chad and I.

Before I could tell her to call her friend to pick her up, Chad muttered, "Sure."

I left the two of them at the welcome desk while I went to the bathroom. When they saw me returning, they suddenly stopped talking. My day started off with a blast and ended with a bang, in more ways than one. We dropped Monica off at her parent's house and then retreated back to my townhouse. It had been a long, long night.

By the time I got home, it was 1:45am. Chad and I showered together. We were proceeding to go to bed when I heard my house phone ringing. I got worried because everyone normally called my cellphone. It could be a family emergency so I answered the phone. It was Terry. She was cursing, yelling, and screaming at the top of her lungs. I couldn't understand a word she was saying. Besides, I was so tired that everything sounded like "blah… blah… blah…blah…blah," until I heard Dexter's, Chad's, and Monica's name all in the same sentence. "Okay, slowly start all over again from the beginning," I said, as I was all ears.

"Dexter admitted to me that he fucked that slut Monica about three or four months ago, at Chad's loft."

"WHAT, AT CHAD'S LOFT? ARE YOU SURE THAT HE SAID THAT IT HAPPENED AT CHAD'S LOFT?" I screamed, as I tried to calm down to get all of the information, then it got worse.

"Dexter thinks that Monica is pregnant with his baby."

"Oh my GOD, oh my fucking GOD," I screamed, at the top of my lungs. "Are you sure..."

"...January, what do you mean am I sure? Why would I make this shit up?"

"I'm just saying..."

Trying to compose herself, Terry took a deep breath and said, "The fool says that he wants to be in his child's life and if that meant losing me, then so be it. The sorry sack of shit had the nerve to say that he loved me and never cheated on me before this incident. Monica told him that I was using birth control because I said that I didn't want to have his baby! Feeling like a fool, as if the joke was on him and everybody knew the truth except him, he acted out of anger. The bum said that he knew that he was wrong and that all he could think about, at the time, was how hurt he was. Then the asshole started crying like a little bitch. January, I wanted to fuck him up!"

"You should've." I said as I still couldn't believe my ears.

"No girlfriend, you didn't hear the best part. Dexter said he felt vindicated for sleeping with Monica because I betrayed him first. He only stopped pressuring me to have a baby because he realized that had done the unspeakable. HE HAD SLEPT WITH MY ARCH NEMESIS! Girlfriend, Monica fed him that bullshit and he ran with it. Girl, I tried my best to beat the shit out of him! All, he could do was try to block my punches."

"Did he use a condom?"

"HELL NO! That nasty bitch, not only didn't use a condom with him; she happily let him cum inside of her!"

"WHAT!" I exclaimed. "Where the fuck was Chad when all this shit was happening?"

In a sarcastic voice Terry said, "The DONKEY claims that Chad doesn't know anything about what happened between them. Chad had bounced and left them alone. January that cunt slept with my Dexter. If I didn't know it before, I sure as hell know it now. Monica hates me and the feelings are mutual. That bitch should've kept the beef just between us but oh no, now she had to include my husband. I'm going for that bitch's jugular vein. When I'm finish with her, she's going to want to join the convent to repent for all her sins. This is my fault because I should've gotten that bitch popped a long time ago. January that bitch doesn't realize what she did. She thinks she knows me but she don't. I will not rest until I get that ass back for fucking with what's mine! "

"Did he tell you why Monica was at Chad's loft in the first place?" I asked, feeling sick to my stomach.

"Donkey didn't even bother to ask. He said Monica acted like she was familiar with his place... as if it wasn't her first time being there. Monica went straight to where Chad stored his expensive liquor and bought out his bottle of Patron. The combination of his anger and him being liquored up is what made him lose touch with reality. He says everything was a big blur."

I just didn't want to believe that Monica would stoop so low. If Dexter is telling the truth, Monica has crossed the line of no return.

"Dexter and I are coming to Jersey City tomorrow, I mean later on today, to confront that bitch!"

I didn't want the Freemans to have to hear all this "hear say" about their daughter so I suggested that I call a beehive at my house, to be held at noon. We created the beehive after Terry got jumped in Mahogany Projects. A beehive was our code for calling a sit down. When bees get together in a beehive; they work together to make honey. Bees don't play, they get down to business. Mess around with a bee if you want and I bet that your ass get stung. Someone is going to get stung today at noon the question is who?

Terry said, "I'm cool with that, peace."

"Peace."

Knowing that we were going to get wasted, everyone took today off from work to recoup. After talking to Terry, I knew that notion went out the window. Today, the very foundation of our friendships would be tested. It's now 4:30am and I'm wide awake. Not feeling Chad at the moment, I decided to retreat to my guest room and watch some television until I fall sleep. I set my alarm clock for 8:00am so that I could call the beehive in time before Jasmine left for Avenel. Not to mention, I also wanted to get up early to get into Chad's shit. I had a lot of questions and no answers. Having mixed feelings, I was hurt for Terry, troubled by Dexter, and confused about Chad. Most of all I'm devastated for the clique. For three decades we have been friends, sisters. It can't end like this! I hope after the beehive that all this shit just turns out to be a big misunderstanding?

CHAPTER 15

THE AFTERMATH

My alarm sounded at 8:00am. I called Charlene first because she's a morning person, like me. "Good morning sweetie, I enjoyed your company last night."

"Good morning, same here. What's up?"

"I'm calling a beehive at noon, at my house," I said, feeling like I was in high school.

"Cool! I will tell Jasmine when she wakes up, see you later."

"Alright, see you later."

I forgot to mention, when a beehive is called you ask when and where and that's it. I then called Monica, who was so not a morning person. Surprisingly, she answered on the first ring. "Good morning drama mama, I'm calling a beehive, at noon, at my house."

"Whatever, January," she said, abruptly hanging up the phone before I could say anything else.

She's got some nerve. I'm trying to save her ass from being embarrassed in front of her parents by Terry. Hell has no fury like a Terry scorned. I must give it to Monica though, she's a tough cookie. I just hope that her cookie doesn't get crumbled, by the cookie monster because she messed around and tampered with its' cookie jar.

It's 8:25am. I started cooking some breakfast. The aroma of my homemade biscuits in the oven could be smelled throughout my house. It's 8:55am. I heard Chad in the shower. I knew once he smelled my homemade biscuits that he would get up. Typically when we take time off from work, I would get up early and prepare a big breakfast. Today, along with my biscuits, I prepared: corn beef hash, beef sausages, grits, cheese omelets, and blueberry cheese blintzes. I made a pitcher of freshly squeezed orange juice and combined it with a can of frozen pineapple juice. It's so delicious, you should try it yourself. And then last but not least, I prepared a pot of black coffee for Chad and made myself a cup of raspberry flavored herbal tea.

This morning, I decided that we were going to eat in the kitchen. Normally, we would eat on my balcony, especially, on a beautiful summer day like today. I knew that it was going to get pretty loud in here in about thirty minutes. So, I felt that it was better for us to dine in this morning. It was now 9:25am.

"Good morning baby, everything smells delicious." Chad greeted me, as he planted a big kiss on my lips and sat down at the table.

"Thanks, good morning." I said, as I made his plate, poured his coffee, and handed him the newspaper. I have no appetite for breakfast today. I just wanted to drink my raspberry tea. When Chad saw that I wasn't eating with him, he got concerned.

"Baby, are you alright? What's bothering you? You know you can talk to me?"

"Do you really want to know?"

"Yes."

"Why has Monica been seeing you at your loft?"

"Monica hasn't been seeing me at my loft," Chad said, as cool as a cucumber.

After about five minutes of silence, I finally responded. "That isn't what she said."

In a frightening voice Chad said, "January, it's too early to start shit. You know that I ain't with the he said she said shit. I never was and never will be. After we eat our breakfast, we can take a little trip over to Monica's house. In front of my face, I want to hear that bitch tell you that I let her come to my loft. Because if that bitch tells you that bold face lie; I will give her the cheapest abortion that she has ever had. I would…"

"…calm down, just calm down. There will be no need for all of that. Let me start this all over again. Last night, Dexter told Terry that he fucked Monica at your loft… three or four months ago."

"What! January what the fuck are you talking about!" Chad yelled, at the top of his lungs while pushing his plate of food away from him, as if he instantly lost his appetite. "I don't know what the fuck Dexter is talking about. All I know is that bitch ass better keep my name out of his fuckin mouth. If he fucked that ho it wasn't in my loft and I ain't know shit about it!"

"He also believes that Monica is pregnant with his baby."

Shocked, Chad started laughing and said, "What! What the fuck is that mutha fucka smoking? He must be on some dip! January, I don't know what that man is capable of doing. All I know is that I don't have anything to do with it." Chad exclaimed, as he reached for my hand and looked me straight into my eyes.

Relieved, I smiled and said, "Okay, I believe you."

Chad then got up from the table and grabbed me out of my seat. Holding me tightly in his arms, Chad professed, "Woman, you just don't know how much I love you."

Hungrily kissing me, as if his life depended on it, Chad knew just what to do to set me on fire. He must've felt my body responding to him for I immediately felt his dick rise and press against my leg. Thinking alike Chad jerked his head to his left, gesturing to me to follow him upstairs to my master bedroom, and I jerked my head right back at him, as we simultaneously started running for the stairs. Once in my bedroom, I saw that the clock on my dresser read 10:15am.

"Baby, this has to be a quickie because we're going to have company at noon."

"Well, I guess you better hurry up and drop those draws before I rip them off of you."

Smiling, I hurried up and did what the man commanded me to do. Acting like teenagers, we jumped into the bed and just rolled around kissing. Moaning and groaning, we were ready to set it off. Make up sex is the best sex in the world! Everything is more intense. Chad started stroking my clit with his fingers as he kissed me. I jumped at first because he caught me off guard.

"UMMMM, UMMMMM!" I moaned, as he vigorously stroked my clit. "AHHHH, AHHH!" I exclaimed, as I flooded the bed with my wetness.

"AHHHH, AHHHH! YEAH! YEAH," he muttered as he climbed on top of me and slid his masterful rod inside of me.

"OH! OH!" I sighed.

He slowly stroked me as I swirled my hips to meet his every pump. "UMMM, UMMMMM," he grunted, as he dug deep into my honey pot.

OH! OH BABY! I yelled, as I started swirling faster and faster.

Keeping up with the tempo, Chad decided to hold onto my headboard and ram his rod deeper inside of me. "YEAH, YEAH, UMMMM, THROW THAT PUSSY AT ME!"

"Ooh, Ooh!" I purred, as Chad passionately stroked my nana with his hammer.

"YOU THINK THAT YOU CAN GET RID OF ME THAT EASILY. UMMM, YOU'RE MINE!"

Ladies and gentlemen, it has become apparently clear that what started out be a simple fucking match has now turned into a power struggle. We were fucking each other back harder and deeper as if we were fighting for control. As Chad swayed his hips to his right, I would connect to my left. Relentlessly, he stroked my pussy. Yes, I said pussy because nana gave up and was letting Chad have his way. Sweating profusely, Chad was putting in work. All I could do was moan and groan as I attempted to wipe the sweat from his brow, with my hand.

"AHHH, AHHHH! OH MY! OH MY! OH, OH MY," I yelled, as his dick rhythmically kept hitting my G-spot. The intense vibrations kept coming stronger and stronger. "AHH, AHHHH, AHHHHH!" Tremors of ecstasy fluttered through me, as Chad feverishly continued to hammer my pussy. Trying to reverse the charges, I wrapped my legs around his waist.

"UGHHHH, UGHHHHHH! I'M CUMMING!" He said, as he continued pumping. Then Chad collapsed on top of me and said, "You won. I'm spent."

I started laughing. "I guess so Hercules, you didn't stop for a break."

We looked at each other and started laughing.

Then I heard the bell, "Hurry up and get dress Chad… it's them," I said, as I looked at the clock.

It was 11:50am. I ran to the intercom and told them to give me a minute. I threw on some sweat shorts, a bra, a t-shirt, and ran to the door. I know that I should've freshened up but I threw the beehive…I couldn't be late!

As I greeted everyone, Charlene said, "Girl, how are you going to call a beehive and be late?"

"I'm not late, you're ten minutes early."

Charlene and Jasmine started laughing, as they saw that my hair was a mess. "Okay lusty bunny, we know what you just got finished doing." They playfully said in unison, as I started to blush.

"Okay, you guys you got me but back to the business at hand. I'm glad that you two arrived here first." I said, as I put my hair into a ponytail.

Then the bell rang again, it was Dexter and Terry. Everyone greeted each other as they assembled in my living room. It was exactly 12:00pm. We couldn't start the beehive until all the bees were assembled, so as to not prejudice anyone against the other. We were missing one bee.

"Where's the whore of Babylon? It's 12:05pm. If this skank doesn't show up in five minutes, Dexter and I will have to go over to her parents' house."

Then the bell rang, it was Monica. "January, I know that I'm late. Please spare me of your infamous speech about being late."

"You're only five minutes late. It's no skin off my back. You know the rules. Since you were late, you have to speak last. Everyone is in the living room, waiting."

"Hello everyone," Monica greeted as she sat in my favorite arm chair.

"Hello," everyone replied except Terry and Dexter.

Chad fell asleep upstairs, so I figured that I would call him down when the moment was right. "Well, everybody thank you for showing up to my beehive. Unfortunately, I called this beehive to discuss some disturbing news."

Puzzled, Charlene, Jasmine and Monica looked at each other. Being lawyers, Dexter and Terry looked cool, calm, and collected. I got the impression they came on some united front shit.

"Since I called the beehive, I'm going to go first. Terry will go next and then Dexter. After that the forum is open for anybody to speak."

Monica started laughing and said, "We're not in high school. If I want to speak out of turn I will. We are all equals in my eyes. There is nobody here that is above reproach."

"Monica, first of all, you're in my house and you're going to respect me. You're going to wait your turn."

"Whatever January, it's your house."

Terry started smiling and looked at me, as if to tell me good job.

"Okay, Monica have you ever been to Brooklyn, by yourself, to see Chad?" I said, in a stern voice.

Everybody's eyes got big.

Smiling Monica barked, "January what the fuck? I've never seen Chad's place."

"Is that your final answer?"

"Yes, it is...next question?"

"Okay, I'm done. Your turn Terry," I said relieved that for now my man appeared to be telling the truth.

Terry stood up and faced everyone. In a calm voice, Terry started her opening argument. "Everyone here knows that Dexter is my beloved husband. So, it deeply disturbs me to find out, from my husband that he has had unprotected sex with one of my so called best friends. This incident happened approximately three or four months ago. Someone in this room is approximately three or four months pregnant and I want to know if she's carrying my husband's child."

Charlene's and Jasmine's jaws dropped as they turned their heads to face Monica. Monica shrugged her shoulders at them as to say that she didn't know what Terry was talking about. Terry looked around the room and didn't say another word.

"I didn't sleep with Dexter, in Brooklyn, at Chad's loft and I'm not carrying his baby!" Monica said in a defiant voice.

"I didn't say that you fucked my husband at Chad's loft. I know that my husband told me that you did but I didn't say that."

Stuttering Monica responded, "Well, I know you didn't say anything about Chad's loft, but January did…earlier. Dexter's crazy. He's lying to you, so that you would give him a baby. I didn't sleep with him. You're my friend. I would never do that to you."

Dexter, keeping his cool, shook his head left to right in disbelief.

Going in for the kill Terry then smiled and said, "January asked you if you ever went to Brooklyn, by yourself, to see Chad. She didn't ask you if you went to Brooklyn to fuck my husband. It was you that just said that you didn't fuck Dexter in Brooklyn. Most importantly, how could you infer that you know exactly what my husband wants from me, his wife? And when in the world did you become such an expert on my husband? Can anyone explain to me, why would a married man of his own volition tell his wife that he slept with a woman if he didn't do so? In addition, he not only told his wife that he slept with that woman which so happens to be his wife's girlfriend, he swears to have slept "unprotected" with this promiscuous girlfriend? What would this husband possibly gain by telling this to his wife? Oh, I forgot…to make his wife want to give him a baby."

Charlene, red as hell, jumped up and screamed, "How could you Monica!"

Jasmine started crying as she reached for Charlene's hand. Trying to hold back my tears, I realized that Monica slept with Terry's husband. I had no doubt about that. Terry didn't try to ferociously attack Monica because she just wanted to know the truth. Terry wanted Monica to trip on her own lies. She was good. I never saw Terry try a case. When I looked over at Dexter his eyes were filled with tears of pain. It, suddenly, hit him to the extent to which he'd hurt his loving wife and best friend. The air in the room was so thick that you could cut a slice and get full off of it.

Monica speechless and filled with emotion looked at me and asked, "January can you please go get Chad."

"Oh, Chad will be coming down soon. You just handle your handle."

"CHAD! CHAD! CHAD!" Monica started screaming from the top of her lungs.

Chad quickly ran downstairs as if he wasn't sleep at all. That mother fucker was probably listening from the top of the stairs, I thought to myself.

"What's up? You called me January?" Chad said, as he pretended to have been suddenly awakened from his deep slumber.

"No! I didn't call you. Miss Drama Mama over here called you!"

Crying Monica pleaded, "Tell Terry."

"Tell Terry what?"

Smiling Terry said, "Yeah, tell us all…Chad."

"Man, I don't know why you people are here. You'll need to get a fuckin life! I already spoke to the person that I needed to speak too. We're okay therefore I'm okay. Monica don't you ever, in your fuckin life, call for me like that! You don't know me like that! January and my grandmother are the only two women that can call on me like that."

"I'm sorry for calling for you like that but I need you to please tell Terry that I didn't sleep with Dexter."

Dexter then abruptly jumped up, off the couch. "Bitch, don't put my cousin into this mix! He doesn't know that we had sex because I didn't tell him. You and I both know that we slept with each other unprotected. All this here…doesn't erase that. You don't give a fuck about Terry, so cut it the fuck out. Terry and I are trying to be polite by asking you, if you are having my baby? If we petition the court for a DNA test, you won't have a choice in the matter. If you don't comply with the courts then you will be held, in contempt."

Monica looking shook like a mother fucker turned to face Charlene, Jasmine, and I and pleaded, "Help me…please. They're threatening to take me to court. I swear to you guys that this isn't his baby. You're my sisters."

Dexter busted out laughing and turned to Terry and said, "What did I tell you? We're going to have to take this lying bitch to court. This was a waste of time. She's incapable of telling the truth."

"Monica, I knew that you weren't going to admit to anything. I wanted January, Charlene, and Jasmine to see you for what you really are. You're not our friend and you're not our sister. You're a vindictive BITCH! You couldn't wait to tell Dexter that I was using birth control. You deliberately wanted to put a wedge in between me and my husband. You slept with my husband and probably with everybody else's man in this room. Yeah, you guys would like to think that it was just my man, she fucked. If this Bitch could part her legs to fuck my man then what would possibly stop her from fucking yours? January, wake up baby girl. Why was she at your man's loft, without you? You don't even hang out over there. Charlene you know that I'm right about Monica. What if she slept with Godfrey? Better yet, what if she slept with Derrick? How would you feel? Monica is a wolf in sheep's clothing and not to be trusted around our men. Jasmine girlfriend, you better be cautious and cling to your Eddie before she steals him. We have a man eater on the prowl who's expecting a child and in need of a father candidate."

"Terry, leave my Eddie out of this!" Jasmine said, as she caught feelings.

Ignoring Jasmine's remarks, Terry just smiled as she continued her assault on Monica. "Well bitch, I thank you ahead of time for carrying my baby for me. Once the DNA test confirms that the baby is ours, we're going to take the baby from you. You're not fit to raise my little girl or boy. Come on baby, we got to go home and prepare the nursery for our baby," Terry said as she grabbed Dexter's hand.

As Terry and Dexter made their way to the door, Monica started clapping. "Wait a minute, you self-righteous bitch! Who do you think that you are? Oh I forgot, you think that you are God, not. You're just a sadistic monster. It's not my fault that you're such a prude that men don't want to fuck you. You wish in your wildest dreams that you could be half the woman that I am. You think that you're so fucking smart and don't know shit. This isn't your husband's baby and the hell if it's yours. Witch, worry about your husband and let me worry about my child. If your husband is fooling around on you, it's your own damn fault and not mine's. He's probably tired of your bossy ass, you miserable cow. If you wanted lessons on how to please a man darling, all you had to do was ask. I would've gladly taught you about the real world. Maybe, I don't know much about the book world but the hell if I don't know about the real one. You're just an overrated and overpaid trick. I wonder… what does one have to do to become a partner at a firm? Something strange, I bet? Growing up in Lincoln Projects sure did you some good, they taught you well. They taught you how to bark in packs but they forgot to teach you how to bite when you are alone. Just stop interfering in other people's lives and stay focused on yours, okay sweetie? If you would stop pill popping birth control pills and give your chump a mutt, we wouldn't be here…would we?"

"If anything, sweetie, I've been the teacher and you've been the student taking lessons from me. I've taught you everything that you know. Well, let me give you your final free lesson of the day before I go home, to my own home and not to my parents. When I finish with you, you're going to learn a lot about the book world and the real world. Be careful who you start fights with; you might get fucked up or worse killed! Sweetie, you're a wannabe. Always the chameleon, you rotate who you want to be day to day. I am Terry, 7 days a week, 24 hours a day, and 365 days of the year. You wear green contacts because you don't have natural grey colored eyes like Charlene. You envy us because our birth parents wanted and loved us unlike yours. Even your adoptive parents didn't want you after they got you. That's why you were always in one of our houses. You hate January because she doesn't have to spread her legs to get people to like her, unlike you. Not to mention, she has her own man and made her own money! Then there is Jasmine…, you stay friends with her because you probably want to eat her pussy. You tell me to stop interfering in other people's lives…hmm! I will do that the day you stop with your insatiable curiosity to know how our men feel in bed. Monica your reckless behavior has made a lifelong enemy in me. You have crossed me for the last time, trick. You think I forgot your role in getting me jumped? What did you do with all that cocaine, bitch? The Lincoln Projects in me thinks that you snorted it all. Likewise, I must agree with you when you said that Lincoln Projects taught me well. They taught be how to bark and bite when the time is right. You're not going to be pregnant forever BITCH! Remember that…okay sweetie?"

Ladies and gentlemen, immediately after Terry finished giving Monica her final lesson, the Delgado family left the building. Wow! Charlene, Jasmine, and I were left dumbfounded. Chad was smirking, as to not to burst out laughing. Monica rubbing her belly looked stunned and lost for words. Terry made herself quite clear that she not only believed her husband; she was coming for his baby. If Monica really went to a fertility clinic, she could've easily dead-end this issue by voluntarily offering to show Terry her paperwork. Now she turned what could've been a lifelong friend into a lifelong enemy… ouch!

Monica turned to me and rudely demanded, "Can you conclude with this so called beehive, already? I'm not feeling well and I want to get the fuck out of here!"

"Charlene, do you have anything to say?" I asked, as I was in pure awe.

"Yes, I do. Monica, it's obvious that you slept with Dexter. In the end, you told on yourself. I give it to you though for a minute I actually believed you. You were good but Terry was better. Your dumb ass responded to shit that wasn't even said or mentioned by Terry in her questioning. Just tell the truth man, you slept with Dexter. Admit it! Is that his baby or is it that you really don't know who your baby daddy is? I bet you that is it in a nutshell, isn't it?"

"Charlene you need to shut the fuck up. You don't even know what the fuck you're talking about. I'm not admitting to anything because there's nothing to admit too, case closed. This isn't Dexter's baby and I went to a fertility clinic, period."

Monica started to look a little pale in the face.

"OH MY GOD," Jasmine exclaimed, as Monica fell back in her chair.

Chad rushed to call an ambulance as Jasmine and I attended to Monica. Charlene opened the front door for better air circulation and then went to get Monica a glass of water.

"I'm okay people." Monica muttered, in a low voice. "I just feel a little light headed."

Charlene and Jasmine went in the ambulance with Monica while I called Monica parents and hesitantly called Terry. This could be Dexter's baby, I said to myself.

The doctor told Mrs. Freeman that Monica's blood pressure was slightly high and that both mommy and baby would be okay. The final diagnosis was that she was a little dehydrated. The doctor suggested that Monica drink plenty of water, get plenty of bed rest, and stay away from as much stress as possible.

I felt guilty for holding the beehive. So concerned about some "he said, she said" shit, I lost focus on what was really important...the baby. To make things right, I decided to call Terry for a possible truce. "Terry, I'm begging you to ease up on Monica. For me, Can you chill and put off filing any court papers on Monica? A loving mother wouldn't put her child in harm's way. If you're serious about wanting to raise this baby, if Dexter is the father, then you must start to conduct yourself like a loving mother. At all cost, you must avoid putting any extra stress on Monica."

"You're right. Dexter and I will back off for the baby's sake."

"Great, I will keep you up to date with Monica's condition."

"Alright, speak to you later."

"Cool."

An hour or two went by and then I heard my phone ring, it was Monica. I wasn't expecting Monica to call me so soon. With all the excitement, I figured she would need some time to rest.

"January, I'm sorry for being snappy at you lately. I think it has something to do with my hormones. They say that pregnant women are moody, you know?"

"That's okay, I understand. I apologize for holding the beehive. Believe me when I say that I wasn't trying to hurt you or the baby."

"Apology accepted. I know your heart was in the right place. That's why I want you to please consider being my baby's godmother?"

"Wow! I would be honored."

"Great!"

I accepted because I felt shitty about holding the beehive. Wanting to make it up to the baby as well as to Monica, I figured that was the least that I could do. Charlene, Jasmine, and I agreed to treat Monica with powder puff hands, no matter how slick Monica got with her mouth. We wanted Monica's pregnancy to be a pleasant experience.

Chad and I are still doing us. I believe him when he said that he didn't know anything about Dexter and Monica, supposedly hooking up.

Chad recently confided, "I believe Dexter's dippy ass fucked Monica. I just don't like how dude put my name into the mix when he confessed to Terry about his affair. Growing up, I always thought that he was a sucker!"

"Baby, that wasn't a nice thing to say about your cousin."

"It wasn't nice for my cousin to put me in the middle of his shit! What really fucks with my head though is that damn Monica. That bitch was faking being sick. She just wanted our sympathy. Her blood pressure was high alright! Terry beat her ass at her own game and she didn't know what the fuck to do or say. January, don't be Monica's sucker. You better turn down that bitch's offer to be her baby's godmother. She's going to use that baby to get all up in your pockets. Bitches fall for that godmother shit every time, especially women that don't have any children of their own. You don't have to play godmother. If you want a baby, we can have our own baby. Just leave Monica alone to tend to her baby."

"Baby, I don't know? I don't think that she was pretending. All I know is that I don't want anything to happen to Monica and the baby. Now, as for the godmother thing, I already told Monica that I would be the baby's godmother and I'm not going to let her down. I appreciate all of your concern but I will be alright. And as for going half on a baby, you know your ass ain't ready to start a family."

"The hell if I'm not. Shit, give me the green light I'll knock your behind up with twins. You know they run in my family."

"No thank you," I exclaimed, as the thought of caring twins almost scared me to practice celibacy, not.

Personally, I'm confused. Dexter swears that he slept with Monica at Chad's loft while Monica repeatedly swears that no such incident ever took place. Someone is clearly lying, the question is who? Charlene, Jasmine, and I met to discuss this situation. After a long and heavy debate, we all agreed that Monica slept with Dexter but couldn't tell whether or not it happened at Chad's loft. We all agreed that Monica didn't go to a fertility clinic but were on the fence when it came to whether or not it was Dexter's baby.

We believed Monica didn't know who the father of her baby was and if that is true, is it really any of our business? Our only responsibility as her girlfriends is to assist her if she needs our assistance. Having a baby is supposed to be an enjoyable experience and we were ruining it for her.

Like a faithful girlfriend I'm just going to stand by her. When it's all said and done... it's her baby and it's her life. Monica can only be Monica and I can only be January Jackson!

Chapter 16

THE CONCLUSION: WHAT TERRY
WANTS TERRY GET'S-(TERRY)

Let me make myself clear I'm not perfect. I just get the job done. This is a man's world and being a woman of color in the corporate environment I have to work three times as hard as man to get the same recognition. The truth hurts but it is what it is. It doesn't bother me because it keeps me on my grind and helps me stay on top of my game. I love and welcome challenges for I'm a winner. I'm always going to flip a negative into a positive. I could be in my darkest hour and I will see the light. I'm Terry Delgado and I'm going to stay that way until the day I die. I refuse to be anybody's victim or anybody's sucker for I'm a winner.

Sometimes you have to lose a little to gain a lot. Let's take the game of chess for example. In the quest to become a Grandmaster you're going to lose quite a few games. The key is to learn from your mistakes and never repeat them. The more you play the more skill you develop. That skill combined with your growing experiences will take you where you need to be.

I knew a long time ago that I should've handled Monica. I didn't because she was useful. She reminded me of what I didn't want to become. She reminded me that you could take the girl out of the ghetto but the ghetto will always be embedded within the girl. I'm always going to be Terry from Lincoln Projects. There is nothing wrong with that. One must never forget where they came from or they will become lost. I've just expanded my horizons. I take Lincoln Projects, my life experiences and my school knowledge with me every time I step into a courtroom. This, my friend, has been the secret to my success. This is how I obtain my victories in court and pulverize my competition. When dealing with any and everything in life, you must bring to the table all of your life experiences.

Monica is a lost cause. Although adopted at an early age, she lives her life like she was raised by wolves. How pathetic? Monica was well taken care of and had the clique to have her back. She was the one who never really accepted the fact that she was now a part of a loving family and community. Monica doesn't have to go around in life acting like she was an abused orphan that was dropped off in the woods. She was adopted by the Freemans and by us.

Monica turned her back on us and drew first blood on me. She made herself a loser. She doesn't want to become a winner in the game of life. She had her chance to become a winner when the Freeman's adopted her and she blew it. Monica would rather use her childhood as an excuse for her behavior like a crutch. That's what people do you know? They make excuses instead of just taking ownership for their decisions. That will never be Terry Delgado.

Every two years, the partners at my firm would meet to discuss which candidate that they wanted to make a partner. They used a three criteria system to determine whether the candidate was partnership material. First, the candidate must be a top litigator. Secondly, the candidate must be a consistent top earner. And thirdly, the candidate must get along with others. The majority ruled. If there was no majority rule met then there was no new partner made for that year. They haven't picked a new partner since I've been working for them. For eight straight years, I met all three of the criteria's. There was also an unspoken fourth rule. The candidate had to be a senior associate who had been working for the firm for at least four years. I told myself this was my year. I've been a senior associate for five years and felt that I was ready for the big leagues.

This year there were three candidates but only one candidate would be offered partnership. The candidates were: Bill Goldenberger, Wilfred Rodgers, and me. Goldenberger was a forty-five year old Caucasian male who was 5'5" and weighed 180 pounds. With a thick full head of salt and pepper hair and the kindest eyes you've ever seen, you'd never guess he was a pit bull in the courtroom. A heavy smoker and a non-drinker, he was married with two children. Goldenberger was the 2nd top earner this year and has been with the firm for ten years.

Rodgers was a forty year old, single Caucasian male who was 5'11" and weighed 165 pounds. A vegetarian who didn't drink or smoke, he had enchanting baby blue eyes and a thick full head of honey blonde hair. His pretty boy demeanor belied the fact that he was as vicious as they come. He was the 3rd top earner this year and has been with the firm for four years.

As for me well, I just happen to be the top earner in the firm this year and you already know the rest.

On paper it would appear that Goldenberger had the lead, my top earner status moot in the face of his white maledom. I was beginning to feel some serious pressure until a little birdie informed me by email that it was definitely between Rodgers and me. We were about even and both had what it took to be the next partner. I knew with that all being said that Rodgers still had one up on me. He was a man and I wasn't. Like I've said before, this is a man's world. I had to figure out a way around that little problem. It was time to play chess.

The main person to impress at the firm was Gary Hoffman, whose father was one of the founders of the firm. Married twenty-five years with no children, Mr. Hoffman was a fifty-five year old, Caucasian male, who looked as if he was forty-five. Physically fit, Mr. Hoffman was 5'8" and weighed 155 pounds. He wore glasses that accentuated his baby blue eyes and had a short curly brown afro with golden highlights. Having a friendly disposition, he would often have lengthy conversations with me.

Last year, Chad and January accompanied Dexter and I to my firm's annual Christmas party. They would keep Dexter occupied while I made my rounds, trying to make a lasting impression with the power players at my firm. I introduced everyone to Mr. Hoffman and when he walked away, I overheard Chad and Dexter, amongst themselves, chuckling about Mr. Hoffman's outfit and mannerisms.

"Yo Dexter, I'm telling you man that dude is obviously gay. He needs to just stop playing and come out of the closet, already."

Upset at Chad's derogatory remarks, I barked, "Mr. Hoffman has been happily married for about twenty-five years. You don't know what you're talking about."

"Terry, if you would pry your lips off that man's ass for a minute you would've seen it for yourself. I'm willing to put money on it and I only bet on sure things."

I closed my eyes for ten seconds and then I reopened them. This time I observed Mr. Hoffman as a person and not as my boss. Wow, I guess for once Chad was right. It was right under my nose and I didn't see it. I instantly knew that I was fucked. Rodgers was straight up handsome and very, very much single. I would often see him and Mr. Hoffman laughing it up at the end of our weekly meetings.

FUCK! FUCK! FUCK! I'm screwed! I decided to call my best male friend Tyrone. "Please tell me that there is something that I can do to possibly tilt things in my favor? I don't want to rely totally on my stats." I begged Tyrone, as I was sure he would know what to do.

"Change the lunch meeting into a dinner date and leave the rest up to me. I got you covered."

"Are you sure?"

"Girl, what did I say? I got you."

It was two weeks before the big meeting that would decide who was going to become the next partner. It was now or never, I said to myself. Mr. Hoffman scheduled a lunch meeting with me to discuss the possible partnership. He had already had one with the other two candidates.

I confidently asked, "Mr. Hoffman, would it be possible to change our scheduled lunch meeting to a dinner meeting. I heard that you liked Caribbean and Soul food. I know the perfect place that we could go. It's called JANUARYS, located in downtown Brooklyn."

"Now, Mrs. Delgado, you're not trying to score brownie points...are you?

"I sure am."

"These types of meetings are normally done over lunch but I wouldn't mind a change of pace. Okay, my driver will pick you up promptly at 7:00pm."

"Thanks, I'm sure you won't be disappointed."

We were having a delightful evening. He seemed to be very impressed by my work and even commented on my most recent victory over the federal government. Having an 80% success rate, it's next to impossible to win a case against the government. I pulled off a miracle.

I couldn't help but to notice that Mr. Hoffman kept looking at the table that Tyrone was sitting at. Yeah, you know what time it was. Pretending that he was a friend that I hadn't seen in years, Tyrone came over to our table. He introduced himself to Mr. Hoffman and brought up some interesting topics. Intrigued, Mr. Hoffman invited Tyrone to join us.

In a state of shock, I completely tuned out of their conversation when I heard someone say something about losing a bet and having to get a Prince Albert piercing. I was disgusted! A Prince Albert piercing is one of the more common male genital piercings.

I knew that Tyrone was smooth but damn! For some reason, Tyrone had Mr. Hoffman hanging onto his every word. Tyrone has the type of style and personality that attracted people from all races and from all personalities. Tyrone was 6'5" and weighed 235 pounds. Physically fit, Tyrone was meticulous in his personal grooming. He had thick lips, thighs, and a juicy butt. Golden brown in complexion, Tyrone could wear just about any color and it would look marvelous on him. Tonight, Tyrone was wearing a grey pinned striped suit with a salmon colored silk shirt underneath. He looked as if he belonged on the cover of a GQ magazine. Smelling and looking tasty, he was on point. At the end of the dinner date, I mean meeting, Mr. Hoffman offered to give Tyrone a ride home with us. Let's just say that they dropped me off first.

Tyrone may have sealed the deal but numbers don't lie. My stats spoke the loudest for me in the end. I was the best choice. Once it became official, I was told that the decision had actually been made over a year ago. I would be their first partner that was a woman of color and was being watched closely to ensure that the right decision was made. When I won that victory over the federal government last month, it basically solidified my position. Filled with pride and joy, I graciously accepted my partnership.

Monica can't make or break me. I will not allow her to have the power to determine my destiny. Personally, I don't care what that whore throws at me. She can't hurt me. I am going to leave her silly ass alone to drown in her own misery. Focusing on my career and on repairing my marriage is all that matters to me. December 15th, I will be turning thirty-five years old and I'm going to party like it was 1999! I've been with Dexter since my freshman year in college. He's my first and only love and I refuse to give up on us. Dexter has made it quite clear what he wants therefore I hold my destiny entirely in my own hands. We will make it. God is my compass and he will continue to guide me in the right direction. At this stage in my life, I've overcome many hurdles and accomplished many of my goals that I had set for myself. You may call me selfish but I'm on cruise control and I'm going to enjoy the ride!

ZONIE FELDER

Former Catholic school girl and Girl Scout bring a unique perspective on the complex relationships shared by women. Her rich experiences in life coupled, with a lifelong love of creative writing has inspired her to actively pursue a career in writing. When she's not creating the intriguingly sexy characters she's soon to be known for, this huge football fan enjoys Zumba classes, dancing and spending time with her family and friends. She currently resides in Jersey City, NJ with her husband and family.